Celebrate **15** years with

HARLEQUIN®
I N T R I G U E®

Because romance is the ultimate mystery...

The thrill of a secret lover and the excitement of an unknown threat have always been trademarks of Harlequin Intrigue. And thanks to you, our faithful readers, we are here to celebrate 15 years of breathtaking romance and heart-stopping suspense—an irresistible combination.

And we've got plenty to keep you on the edge of your seat in the coming months!

✓ more 43 LIGHT STREET stories by Rebecca York, and Caroline Burnes's FEAR FAMILIAR—your favorite ongoing series!

✓ THE LANDRY BROTHERS—a *new* series from Kelsey Roberts

✓ and THE McCORD FAMILY COUNTDOWN, a special promotion from three of your best-loved Intrigue authors

Intensity that leaves you breathless, romance that simmers with sexual tension—and you can only find them at Harlequin Intrigue. We won't let you down!

Thank you,

From the Editors

"Do you hate me so much for that summer we were involved?"

she asked him softly. "Is that what this is about?"

"I can't help you, Gillian. Let it go at that."

But she couldn't let it go. Her eyes followed him as he crossed the room and stood by the window where he watched the storm pound the beach. He'd always been such a loner. Finally she realized it was pointless to go on.

"What are you doing?" Cleve demanded as he watched her get to her feet.

"Walking back to my car while there's still enough light."

"Are you crazy? You can't go out in this storm!"

She didn't argue with him when he caught her by the arm and dragged her to him. Before either of them knew what was happening, she was in his arms, clinging to him as he held her tightly against the wall of his chest.

"You were an eyeful back then," he whispered. "It was a pleasure just looking at you. I'd have sworn there was no room for improvement, but I was wrong. You've ripened into one hell of a woman."

It was then that she fully realized her situation. She was trapped here with him in this tiny cottage until tomorrow morning....

My Lover's Secret
Jean Barrett

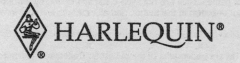

HARLEQUIN®

TORONTO • NEW YORK • LONDON
AMSTERDAM • PARIS • SYDNEY • HAMBURG
STOCKHOLM • ATHENS • TOKYO • MILAN • MADRID
PRAGUE • WARSAW • BUDAPEST • AUCKLAND

To good friends, Barb and Len Pedersen,
for sharing Chicago

ISBN 0-373-22528-8

MY LOVER'S SECRET

Visit us at www.romance.net

Printed in U.S.A.

ABOUT THE AUTHOR

If setting has anything to do with it, Jean Barrett claims she has no reason not to be inspired. She and her husband live on Wisconsin's scenic Door Peninsula in an antique-filled country cottage overlooking Lake Michigan. A teacher for many years, she left the classroom to write full-time. She is the author of a number of romance novels.

Write to Jean at P.O. Box 623, Sister Bay, WI 54234

Books by Jean Barrett

HARLEQUIN INTRIGUE
308—THE SHELTER OF HER ARMS
351—WHITE WEDDING
384—MAN OF THE MIDNIGHT SUN
475—FUGITIVE FATHER

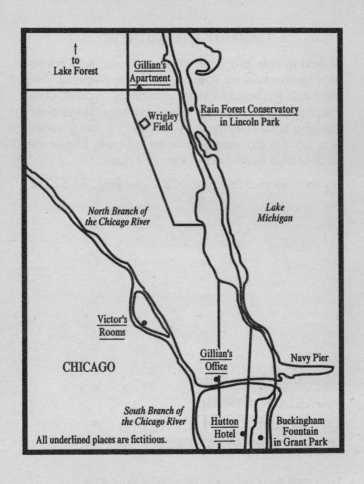

to
Lake Forest

Gillian's
Apartment

◇ Wrigley
Field

● Rain Forest Conservatory
in Lincoln Park

*North Branch of
the Chicago River*

*Lake
Michigan*

Victor's
Rooms

CHICAGO

Gillian's
Office

Navy Pier

*South Branch of
the Chicago River*

Hutton
Hotel

Buckingham
Fountain
in Grant Park

All underlined places are fictitious.

CAST OF CHARACTERS

Gillian Randolph — Her desperate need to survive was far more complicated than it appeared.

Cleveland McBride — The private investigator had never gotten over the woman who had once meant everything to him.

Victor Lassiter — He would go to any lengths to punish Gillian Randolph.

Lieutenant Butch Costello — The homicide detective was convinced that Gillian was guilty of murder.

Charles Reardon — Drunk or sober, he was a nasty individual.

Sarah — She was an innocent instrument of revenge.

Bill Jerome — The prison guard had inside knowledge.

Rudy Martinez — Victor's former cell mate was afraid to tell the truth.

Dan Weinstein — The criminal lawyer was prepared to defend Gillian, but the evidence against her worried him.

Maureen Novak — Did she betray Gillian, or was she merely a pawn in the game?

Prologue

East Moline Correctional Center
Illinois

She was exquisite.

She had the kind of face men worshipped. Framed in red-gold hair, it was an elegant face with delicate features and wide, violet eyes. Her slender body was clad in a long, jade-colored silk gown.

She spoke to him in a falsetto voice, her head tipped to one side in a perfect imitation of her namesake. He hadn't forgotten that particular mannerism.

"Now that I'm here, Victor, what is it you want me to do?"

"Obey me."

"Always. But how?"

"I'm going to star you in my newest production. A unique version of *Sleeping Beauty.*"

She didn't immediately answer him. He watched as she turned and began to pace back and forth along the edge of the table in front of him. He was fascinated by the way her body was able to so believably express her anxiety. She had been carefully weighted and balanced.

She faced him again. "It's a difficult role, Victor. Am I capable of it?"

He chuckled softly. "You were born to play it, Princess. Look, I'll show you."

He demonstrated for her, his deft fingers on the control board above her projecting a subtle magic down through the filaments attached to her puppet limbs. She began to sway as he hummed an appropriate melody, her body dipping and turning in the graceful rhythms of a waltz.

"You see," he encouraged her. "It's exciting, isn't it?"

"It's wonderful!" she agreed in that breathless falsetto. "I feel so alive!"

"You *are* alive."

"When will I meet the prince?"

"Soon," he said evasively.

"I hope he'll be handsome and brave. Will he—"

"You worry too much. Let me do all the worrying for you. Haven't I taken care of you from the beginning?"

"You have, Victor. I owe you everything. But I can't help worrying. *She'll* find out. The real me will find out."

"It won't matter by then," he soothed her. "You'll be asleep. Remember the fairy tale? Sleeping Beauty goes to sleep for a long, long time."

He didn't have the heart to tell her that in his version of the story there would be no prince to kiss her awake. No one would be able to rescue her. She was his finest creation, and he was going to destroy her. It was necessary in order to punish her namesake. He was capable of the sacrifice. He had proved that in another life.

EAST MOLINE was a minimum security facility. There were very few uniformed guards in evidence, and they almost never appeared in the crafts room. Bill Jerome was there because one of the staff had sent for him. They wanted him to share his observations about a young inmate before he went off duty. The guy was giving them trouble.

If you ask me, they got the wrong one, Bill thought as his stocky figure hovered in the doorway of the large room. Now *that's* the one they ought to be worried about, the guard told himself as he eyed a thin, dark figure all alone at a corner table.

Victor Lassiter gave him the creeps as he watched him put that damn marionette he'd constructed through its paces. He could hear him murmuring to the thing. Worse, it answered him in a sweet, girlish voice. Or seemed to. Lassiter was very good at what he did.

He'd been a master puppeteer in civilian life, a virtuoso able to suspend disbelief in his audiences, who had been hypnotised as they watched his marionettes duplicate the same arcs of movement as actual human individuals. Bill suspected it gave Lassiter infinite pleasure to control his small figures, to make them conform to his every wish. Okay when it came to puppets, Bill thought. Not so good when it was people. It's what had landed Lassiter in prison.

The staff here didn't share Bill's opinion about Victor Lassiter. They considered him reformed. He had been transferred from maximum security at Joliet with a clean record. He had served a ten-year sentence. He was getting out soon.

Bill wouldn't have let him go anywhere. Maybe the experts didn't see it, but he did. There was something chilling in Lassiter's black eyes. Something in his cunning, narrow face that said he was capable of anything.

Chapter One

The forest was like something out of a fairy tale. A dark fairy tale, Gillian decided. It wouldn't surprise her if, at the end of this narrow track she was pursuing with such urgency, she arrived at the door of a black castle inhabited by an evil sorcerer.

In a way, it was an appropriate analogy. Fairy tales had a lot in common with legends, and the man she was seeking belonged in that category. On the other hand, since this was Michigan's Upper Peninsula, the track was more likely to lead to a log cabin than an enchanted castle.

At this moment, Gillian would have been grateful for an empty clearing. Anything to break the monotony of the woods that seemed to go on forever with its thick, impenetrable growth. How far had she hiked since having to leave her car outside the padlocked gate at the mouth of the track? It felt like miles.

It was the gloom she found so unnerving. That and the absolute silence. The afternoon sun had vanished under a cloud cover shortly after she'd climbed over the gate. Since then, there had been a deepening twilight under the evergreens. The birds must have sensed an unfriendly change in the weather. They were still now.

Gillian paused seconds later, alerted to the likelihood of a storm by a sullen rumble off in the direction of the lake.

There was a hood on her lightweight green jacket. She drew it up over her red-gold hair, thinking it would be some defense against a downpour.

What are you doing? she challenged herself sharply. *You're out here all alone in the middle of nowhere with no protection and a storm brewing. Why aren't you racing back to the car while there's still time?*

It was sensible advice, and not just because of the threat of rain. There was another potential danger for her in the shape of her objective. Logic told her that a man who buried himself in the wilderness, barricading himself from the outside world behind a locked gate, wasn't going to welcome her arrival.

Fool's errand or not, however, she wasn't going to give up now. Not when she had come all this distance from Chicago, sacrificing precious time away from her practice.

Gillian needed him, and if it was at all possible, she was going to get him.

"You want a private investigator to find your Aunt Tillie, look one up in any phone book. You want results because you're in serious trouble, then you hire Cleveland McBride."

It was years ago when her late father had said that. Considering how he had felt about McBride personally, it was a reliable recommendation, one she had never forgotten. She was facing her own trouble now, and the P.I. was her solution. Maybe. He had always been as independent as the devil, and now...

He had dropped out of sight months ago, closed his office and abruptly left Chicago. No one knew why. No one had been able to offer her an explanation for the mystery. That being the case, what miracle would it take to secure his services?

There was another obstacle. A much tougher one. She and Cleveland McBride had once been something more

than acquaintances to each other. There was no way to
overlook the explosive, and ultimately disastrous, result of
their brief relationship. But that had been long ago. They'd
been two different people then. Surely, after all this time,
he no longer cared. She wasn't sure how much he had cared
even then. And as for her...yes, she was worried about
seeing him.

She tried not to anticipate their meeting, tried to be in
no way emotional at the prospect of seeing him again after
all these years. But the truth was, if she weren't so desperate for his help, she wouldn't have trusted herself to go
to him.

It was with relief that Gillian rounded a bend and caught
the gleam of water through the trees. The woods thinned,
revealing the vastness of Lake Superior. Its surface was the
color of dark pewter in the eerie light of the advancing
summer storm.

And here at last was the clearing she had been expecting.
The hideaway that crouched on its edge, close to the shore,
was neither a castle nor a log cabin. It was a wood-shingled
cottage with a sagging porch and windows that looked like
they hadn't seen paint in decades.

She crossed the weedy yard and mounted the porch with
a sudden sense of misgiving. The place looked deserted.
Maybe he wasn't here. Maybe her errand was a big mistake, after all.

Lifting her hand, she rapped on the front door. There
was no answer to her knock. She tried again with the same
result. What now?

There was a detached garage off to the side of the cottage. It was a dilapidated affair, but tire tracks in the gravel
in front of its lowered door indicated the structure was in
regular use. If his car was gone, she would know he wasn't
around.

Leaving the porch, Gillian approached the garage, when a shrill cry startled her.

Even as she whipped around, she knew it was nothing more than the piercing call of a gull overhead. Nothing to be alarmed about. And she wasn't alarmed—until she saw what was just behind her. A large black dog. A Lab, she thought. He had appeared out of nowhere, suddenly and without any sound of arrival.

She would have been less worried if he had barked at her, even growled a warning. Instead, he stood there rigidly, regarding her out of a pair of alert eyes that looked none too friendly.

Gillian remained there against the wall of the garage, fearing he would attack if she tried to move away. They went on measuring each other in silence.

A second later, out of the corner of her eye, she spotted a tall figure rounding the building from the back. He stopped when he discovered her pinned there against the wall.

"Mike, back off," he called sharply.

With the dog still confronting her, she didn't dare to turn her head to determine the identity of its owner. She didn't have to. The husky timbre of that voice was still familiar. Still had the power to stir her senses.

You can do this, she commanded herself. You're not a teenager now. You're an experienced career woman. You can deal with him calmly and rationally. You *have* to.

"Mike, come here," he ordered.

The animal obeyed him this time, trotting to his side and settling on its haunches with a little whimper of apology for her. His master offered her no apology. He merely scowled at Gillian as she finally found the courage to turn and directly face him. He was carrying a fishing rod. He and the dog must have been off along the shore trying their luck.

He didn't immediately recognize her, probably because the hood still covered her head. Otherwise, her red-gold hair would have betrayed her. Right now she was nothing more than a trespasser to him.

"Hello, Cleve," she greeted him softly before he could challenge her intrusion.

The only sign of his astonishment was a widening of his eyes, those remarkable tawny eyes that never missed a detail. They didn't now as they burned a path down her slender figure.

"You've grown up," he observed, and she wasn't sure whether she read approval or cynical amusement in his tone. He had always been capable of both.

He had changed, too. That rich, bronze-colored hair, like a lion's mane, was flecked with silver. The face was as appealingly craggy as ever with its wide mouth and square jaw, but the crinkles at the outside corners of his eyes had deepened. It had been—what?—almost fourteen years. He must be nearly forty-two by now.

His body was still compact, solid. He still carried himself with that enviable military erectness. But there were signs of what she could only define as an indifference to an appearance that had once been immaculate. His thick hair was shaggy around his ears and over his collar. There was a stain on his shirt, a tear in his jeans. Why had he stopped caring?

"How did you track me here, Gillian?"

"I'm an attorney."

"Yeah, I heard that."

"A *good* one. I don't give up until I learn the answers."

"Meaning," he guessed, "that you got the forwarding address out of my former landlord in Chicago."

"Something like that. I also stopped in the village here to get directions to your place and to phone you I was coming, but your number is unlisted."

"I like my privacy."

She expected him to follow this up by demanding to know why she had violated that privacy. Instead, he looked off toward the lake where the sky was like an angry bruise. The late afternoon light was fading rapidly with the imminent storm.

"Better get inside before this breaks," he said reluctantly.

He led the way toward the house, the dog trailing after him. Leaving the fishing rod on the porch, he preceded her into the cottage. The living room was small and sparsely furnished. It had the shabby look of another era. Its only redeeming features were a fieldstone fireplace and a bank of windows that overlooked the lake where waves folded against the rocky shoreline.

"How did you find this place?" she asked.

"I didn't. It found me. It belonged to a bachelor uncle who died a couple of years ago and left it to me."

He didn't bother to explain why he had isolated himself here, living the existence of a hermit, and she didn't feel she had the right to ask.

"You want a beer? I'm afraid it's all I've got to offer."

She shook her head.

He indicated a wicker easy chair, and she settled on it. The dog, Mike, deciding to be friends with her, flopped at her feet and licked one of her tennis shoes.

Cleve didn't bother to sit. He leaned against the fireplace mantel and watched her as she lowered the hood on her jacket. "What's the matter?" he asked. "Didn't he like it?"

What was he talking about?

"Your hair. You cut it. I always thought your hair and your violet eyes were a dynamite combination. But maybe, if he let you go, your ex didn't appreciate it."

Alan. He was referring to Alan. He knew about their

divorce three years ago. What else did he know about her, and why had he bothered to stay informed? She was afraid to wonder. "It was a friendly parting, and it had nothing to do with externals."

"A conflict of careers maybe. A lawyer, huh? Well, Daddy always wanted you to follow in his footsteps, didn't he?"

Had he always been this caustic? She didn't think so. What had happened to change him? Not daring to ask, needing to keep this meeting as impersonal as possible so he wouldn't guess the feelings churning inside her, she spoke to him briskly. "Look, if we're through playing catch-up, maybe you'll let me explain my business with you."

"Business?" One of his heavy eyebrows elevated sardonically. "Hell, Gillian, I was hoping you came because you missed me. Decided to look me up to see if any of the old magic could be revived."

After all this time, did he still resent her for vanishing from his life without a word of explanation? Even hate her? Was that why he sounded so bitter?

The painful effect of his sarcasm must have been evident on her face, because he muttered a regretful, "Forget it. I was never very good when it came to polite manners, and I guess living in isolation doesn't help. See, ol' Mike there is immune to my rudeness."

He sat down on the edge of the raised hearth and leaned toward her, his big hands planted on his spread knees. "All right," he said brusquely, "I'll listen to you. But I warn you, if this has anything to do with private investigation, you're wasting your time. I'm out of the business. *Permanently*."

She hoped he would change his mind after he heard what she had to say. Years of experience in front of judges and juries had taught her confidence and how to focus on her arguments. That was why she tried to ignore the storm outside as she marshaled her thoughts. It wasn't easy. There were whitecaps on the lake by now, lightning forking on the horizon, and rain already spitting against the windows, driven by a rising wind. It was a dramatic display. But what she had to tell him was more powerful.

"Victor Lassiter," she said abruptly. "Do you recognize the name?"

He shook his head. "Could be it sounds faintly familiar. Something in the news long ago maybe."

"Ten years ago. Victor was a gifted puppeteer."

"Say again?"

"You know, puppets on strings. Marionettes. He and his wife, Molly, operated their own small theater at Navy Pier before the pier became so trendy after all those renovations."

"Sounds cozy."

"It wasn't. Victor was obsessively jealous of Molly. He couldn't stand to share her with anyone else. He controlled her, just like he controlled his marionettes. He made her life absolutely miserable."

Cleve nodded. "I get the picture. Hell, I've had enough cases like it. This Molly…a client of yours?"

"It wasn't that straightforward. She was my cousin."

One of his eyebrows lifted again, a sign that he hadn't missed her use of the past tense in connection with Molly, but he said nothing.

She went on. "I tried to get her to end it legally, to move in with me. I promised her that, if it proved necessary, we could arrange for a restraining order."

"And she wouldn't budge," he guessed.

"No, she…" Gillian hesitated. She had to be careful at this point not to betray an old promise. But Cleve was shrewd. He was watching her suspiciously. She pretended to be distracted by the storm. She could hear the thunder overhead and the rain beating on the roof.

"Molly didn't trust any of that," she managed to continue. "I helped her to do what she wanted. She relocated to another city under a new identity."

"Victor?"

"He was furious. He tried everything to find her."

"Did he?"

"Not then. That came later, after a few years. Molly met someone she wanted to marry. And that was when she made a terrible mistake. Victor seemed to be no longer making efforts to locate her, so she decided he'd stopped caring, that it was safe to contact him. He agreed to meet with her in a neutral, public place to discuss the divorce she so desperately wanted. I didn't know what she was doing. No one knew—until it was too late."

"You telling me that he…"

Cleve left the rest unsaid. The expression on her face must have told him that, loving Molly as she had, she found the episode unbearable, even after all these years.

"Victor determined that, if he couldn't have Molly for himself, then no one else was going to possess her. He killed her in a blind rage."

"Did he run?"

"I wish he had tried that. Then maybe he would have received the life sentence he deserved, instead of what he did get."

"Meaning he turned himself in."

"Victor is vile, but he's also clever. He knew the value of giving himself up with a plea of temporary insanity. That, along with some crafty bargaining from his defense, reduced his sentence to a minimum." She paused to draw a slow, steadying breath. "He served that time. He gets out in less than two weeks."

''And you're worried about that,'' he said perceptively. ''Why?''

''Because he wants revenge. That sick mind of his is convinced I was responsible for his wife's desertion, that if it hadn't been for my interference, he wouldn't have killed her. He swore to see me suffer as he's suffered.''

''When did he make this threat?''

''Before he went to prison.''

Cleve sat back on the hearth, spreading the fingers of his hands in a gesture of dismissal. ''Ten years ago, Gillian. You really think the guy has been nursing some murderous grudge all this time? That he intends coming after you when he's released?''

''Yes.''

''Why?''

''Because of this.'' She opened her shoulder bag and withdrew from one of its pockets a large snapshot. Getting to her feet, she stepped over the sleeping dog and crossed to the fireplace, placing the photo in Cleve's hand. ''This photo came in my mail a couple of days ago.''

He looked down at the picture, issuing a long whistle of surprise. ''It's *you*. It's a damn puppet, but it's you. He's captured all the essentials.''

''I told you he was gifted.'' Leaving the photo with him, she returned to the chair and sat down again. ''There's a message on the back,'' she said calmly.

She was feeling anything but calm as she watched him turn the picture over, listened to him read the scrawled words aloud.

'''Hope you won't be offended by the likeness. She's a beauty, isn't she? I'm planning to put her to work for me when I'm released. Blessings on you.'''

Cleve looked up from the snapshot. ''How can you define this as anything but an innocent compliment?''

''On the surface I can't, but underneath I know better.

This is his sly, safe way of letting me know he hasn't forgotten me. Or forgiven me."

"You can't be sure of that."

"Yes, I can. He created a replica of Molly, too. It was just before he killed her."

There was silence except for the sound of the rain stinging the windows and the roll of thunder somewhere over the lake. She watched Cleve as he stared for a long moment at the photo in his hand. Then he looked up again, his gaze probing hers.

"Is that everything?"

"Yes," she lied.

"You sure?"

She hesitated only for a moment.

"I'm sure."

His thumb stroked the glossy edge of the photo. "Okay, let's suppose you're right. That this is Lassiter's way of tormenting you before he strikes. Maybe even the first step in a campaign of terror. The cops—"

"You know the police can't do anything."

He did know. Until a stalker actually tried something, and by then it was often too late, the police were powerless to act. "So you came to me instead," he muttered. "Sorry, Gillian, but you can see I'm in no shape these days to play bodyguard."

"If that's all I needed, I would have hired a protection service back in the city."

"Then what is it you do want?"

It was hard for her to press him like this. She had always been able to take care of herself, was proud of that. But she couldn't risk her life. It was vital that she remain alive and well. "I need someone who'll watch Victor's every move and, if possible, collect enough evidence to send him back to prison."

"Chicago is full of private detectives, Gillian."

"None of them with the abilities this situation demands."

He laid the snapshot aside on the hearth. "I'm not interested. This is where I belong now. Hey, I love it here. Life is good."

He refused to meet her gaze. "Do you hate me so much for that summer we were involved?" she asked him softly. "Is that what this is all about?"

He startled her when he surged to his feet, angry. "I can't help you, Gillian. Let it go at that."

But she couldn't let it go. Her eyes followed him as he crossed the room and stood by the windows where he watched the storm pound the beach, his hands shoved into the pockets of his jeans. He had always been a loner. But never a brooding one, a man battling inner demons.

Forgetting her earlier resolve, she leaned forward in her chair and asked earnestly, "Cleve, what happened? Why have you lost yourself in this place? You used to be..."

"Less tarnished?" There was a hard edge to his laugh. "Well, things happen," he said evasively. "People change."

Before she could pursue the subject, he swung away from the windows. "Gillian, be smart. Take a long vacation. Somewhere far away from Chicago where he can't reach you. Once he's out and had a chance to realize that—"

She stopped him, emphatically stating, "I can't do that, even if I would choose to run away. I have an obligation to a client who's counting on me. I'm in the middle of preparing litigation on her behalf, a case that involves a large sum."

"Money," he growled. "I should have guessed that's what's important here. What is it they say about the apple not falling far from the tree?"

It was her turn to be angry. He didn't want to listen.

Didn't want to understand the woman she really was and why her work was essential and had to be safeguarded. It was pointless to go on with this.

"What are you doing?" he demanded as he watched her get to her feet, fasten her jacket, draw the hood over her hair.

"Walking back to my car while there's still enough light."

"Are you crazy? You can't go out in this storm."

"I've got a killer coming after me. Do you think I'm worried about a little rain?"

"Gillian—"

But she was already at the door, and before he could stop her, she had plunged into the storm. She could hear him behind her, shouting something from the porch. She refused to pause or look back. All she could think about in her race across the clearing was getting away from him and reaching the shelter of the woods where she would be protected from the worst of the rain that slashed at her here in the open.

She was near the place where the path entered the forest when lightning split the twilight with a brilliance that blinded her. In the next second there was the sound of rending wood and then the crash of a massive pine toppling directly across the mouth of the track in front of her. Just a few short yards from death.

The deeply scored tree was steaming, the air acrid when Cleve reached her side. "Are you all right?"

Still dazed, she managed to croak a brief, "Yes, fine."

"Then where's your brain?" he railed at her. "Don't you know enough not to go near trees in a thunderstorm?"

Dear Lord, he was right! Even a small child understood the hazard of not sheltering under a tree in weather like this, and she had been about to hike through a whole forest of them in her stubborn flight from the cottage.

She didn't argue with him when he caught her by the arm and dragged her back to the house. As they entered the living room, their clothes soggy with rain, Mike lifted his head and gazed at them solemnly, letting them know that he had enough sense to stay inside and keep dry even if they didn't.

Cleve left her standing inside the door, her slacks and jacket dripping on the mat as he moved around the room, turning on the lamps. He continued to lecture her.

"If you'd waited five damn seconds, I would have taken you back to the gate in my car. Now neither one of us is going anywhere, not with that tree blocking the drive. And you can forget about my clearing it away with the chain saw until tomorrow morning when it's light, and if it's still raining by then—"

"Would you please not yell at me anymore?" she appealed to him in a low voice that was suddenly as weak and wobbly as her legs.

He came back to the door where she continued to stand. "Look at you. Why aren't you peeling out of that wet jacket?"

She started to undo the jacket, but she was still shaken by her narrow escape in the driveway. Her trembling fingers refused to obey her.

"Here, I'll do it," he said impatiently.

He unzipped the jacket, began to remove it. But something happened when his hands came in contact with her shoulders. Something tantalizing and treacherous. Before either of them knew what he was doing, she was in his arms, clinging to him as he held her tightly against the hard wall of his chest.

"You were an eyeful back then," he whispered, his eager hands gripping her, his lowered cheek stroking hers as he referred to that long-ago summer when she had been eighteen. "It was a pleasure just looking at you. I'd have sworn there was no room for improvement, but I was wrong. You've ripened into one hell of a woman.''

It was still powerfully there, the attraction that had sizzled between them fourteen years ago. She'd worked in her father's firm before going off to college, typing and filing all those tedious briefs. That was where she had met Cleveland McBride. He had handled difficult investigations for her father and one of the other attorneys.

Gillian hadn't forgotten his forceful sexual energy and how it had impacted her the afternoon he'd stridden into the front office where she was filling in for the vacationing receptionist. All rugged charm, he'd leaned over her desk, noticing her existence with a wicked grin. The subsequent passion that had flared between them had been wonderful and intense. It had also been unwise. For one thing, she'd been young and unsure of herself, and Cleve a mature, experienced twenty-eight. Their relationship had been brief, and ultimately painful.

That was what she remembered now as he held her. The wrenching pain of being separated from him. The awful loss. It was something she had promised herself never to repeat.

''No,'' she said, straining away from him.

For a moment he tried to hold the embrace. Then, realizing she meant it, he released her and stepped back. His tawny eyes gazed down at her speculatively.

''We're not going there, Cleve,'' she informed him firmly. ''Not this time.''

His response was wry. ''I'll try to remember that, but it's going be a long night.''

And that was when she fully realized her situation. She couldn't go anywhere until tomorrow morning. She was trapped here with him in this tiny cottage.

THE STORM, which cleared off after dark, was followed by another one in the middle of the night. Though there was no lightning and thunder this time, the winds were more severe, the rain hard and steady.

Gillian lay awake on the narrow bed in the spare room next to Cleve's, listening to the wild waters on the lake and the gale battering at the double casement windows a few feet away. They shook restlessly in their frames.

She was nervous. But the storm had less to do with that than the man in the other bedroom. Better not think about him, she told herself.

In spite of her tension, and the wind relentlessly worrying the casements, she drifted off. The cottage was old, the window latches unreliable. Minutes later, the persistent wind finally triumphed.

Gillian came awake with a startled cry when the double windows burst open with a sound like gunfire. Disoriented for a few seconds, her terrified brain conjured up an image of Victor Lassiter with a smoking revolver in his hand.

But it was rain and a cold wind that were attacking her, not a demented killer. Scrambling off the bed, she sped to the windows, which were banging loudly now against the wall. She was only dimly conscious of a shout from the next room followed by the slap of running feet.

Gillian struggled to close and fasten the casements, but she was hindered by the whipping curtains and the driving rain. A pair of stronger hands was suddenly there to help her.

There was a stillness in the room after the windows were shut. When she turned to face Cleve, the breath was stuck in her throat. The night-light from the hallway outside the open door revealed enough of him to convince her she was in trouble.

He wore nothing but a pair of briefs. *Snug* briefs that emphasized his riveting masculinity. There was a potent sexuality in every line of that exposed body. The flesh of

his arms and hair-darkened chest was slick from the rain
that had soaked them, and that, too, was maddeningly pro-
vocative.

Even worse, she could only guess what she looked like.
She wore nothing but her panties under one of his shirts he
had lent her for the night. She could see his silent awareness of her in the way his slow, heavy gaze caressed her
unrestrained breasts beneath the thin fabric of the shirt. She
could actually *feel* that awareness from the heat of his body
which stood close to hers. Much too close.

She was vulnerable, and he was prepared to take advan-
tage of that vulnerability.

"Did I promise you something earlier?" he muttered
thickly. "If I did, the hell with it."

Before she could stop him, or for that matter exercise a
self-control of her own, his arms slid around her and drew
her against him so tightly that she could feel his immediate
response.

When his mouth crashed down on hers, there was such
hunger in his deep, probing kiss that it inflamed her senses.
But only for a moment. Because there was something else
that she detected in his kiss. An underlying anger that
shocked her with its intensity, warning her this was a serious mistake.

There was a wounded look in his eyes that tore at her
when she broke away from him.

"Yeah, I remember," he said, his voice like an accusation. "We're not going there anymore."

"Cleve—"

"Do you know how I felt about you that summer, Gillian? How you tore me apart? I was on top of the world
whenever you were with me and in hell every minute you
weren't. And when you left like that without a word, not
one *damned* word of explanation..."

"I'm sorry," she whispered. She didn't know how to deal with his anger.

"Well, it's all ancient history, isn't it? Forget it."

He turned away from her, started to leave. She couldn't let him go like this. "Cleve, wait."

He stopped at the door, looked back. "What?"

"About that summer...I'd like to explain."

"Why?"

"Because it's obvious you've never forgiven me. And I suppose it's the reason why you refuse to help me, but—"

"I get it," he interrupted her, his tone mocking. "You want to cut a deal. That's what lawyers do, isn't it? You make with the explanations, maybe even offer something sweeter than that, and I agree to go after Lassiter for you."

"I didn't deserve that."

"No? You telling me you're not desperate? That you're not ready to show me just how grateful you'd be if I reconsider my refusal?"

She looked at him sadly. "There must have been a very good reason why I came here. Maybe it's because I remembered what they used to say about you. That you weren't a P.I. because you liked the thrill of danger. That you didn't want to admit it, but what really gave you a rush was helping people who had nowhere else to turn."

Cleve stared at her for a moment, then he shrugged. "I guess whoever *they* were didn't know what they were talking about."

He walked out of the room, closing the door behind him. Gillian stared after him, her nerves raw from their encounter. It had been a shock to her, perhaps for him as well, to discover that after all these years the passion could still flare between them. And, even worse, the emotions that drove that passion.

She hadn't gotten over him. But she would, she promised herself. She *had* to for the sake of her survival. And that made it essential that she leave this place the first thing tomorrow morning. Because now, without Cleve to help her and on her own, she had to prepare herself to withstand the menace of Victor Lassiter.

Chapter Two

This was it!

Cleve had been trying to locate the guy for weeks, but every lead had been a dead end. Not tonight. Tonight he was going to nail the bastard. It gave him satisfaction just picturing the joy on his client's face when he put her daughter back in her arms.

He had to be cautious, though. You never knew what these guys were going to pull. Hell, if they'd kidnap their own kids and then vanish with them just to spite an ex-wife, they were capable of anything.

But Cleve knew his business. He knew how to look bored and disinterested as he followed his target up the stairs at the el station on Addison. The guy was too distracted to be aware of him anyway. Trying to pacify the little girl in his arms. It was long after midnight, and she was fretful. She was less than three years old and should have been in bed hours ago, not out here on a Chicago street.

Some father, Cleve thought angrily. But what could you expect when the guy wasn't much more than a kid himself. A skinny punk who hustled in pool halls. It was one of Cleve's contacts in the pool hall the punk had just left who'd called and given him the tip. Cleve had arrived just in time.

No way was he going to lose him now, but he kept his

distance as they waited for a southbound. There weren't many trains running at this hour. They were the only three people on the platform.

Cleve knew better than to risk snatching the child out here. Heroics like that could end tragically for everybody. His job was to tail the punk to his current address, call the cops, and then wait outside until there were safe results.

A northbound train rumbled along the other tracks. Cleve glanced at it. His attention couldn't have been diverted for more than a few seconds. But when he looked back down the platform on his side, the worst had happened.

He had underestimated his target. The punk had somehow gotten suspicious. Convinced he was trapped on the platform, he'd panicked. He had actually jumped down onto the plank bed between the rails and was sprinting in the direction of Belmont. The little girl was still in his arms.

Cleve didn't hesitate. He leaped down between the tracks and charged after them. He had to recover the child before her father killed her. Stupid punk! Didn't he realize that if he happened to touch the wrong rail, he'd fry both himself and his daughter?

As he ran, he kept listening for the sickening roar that would tell him a train was hurtling down on them from the rear. But all he heard was the rush of the street traffic under the el and the pounding of the blood in his ears. He refused to consider what that pounding signified.

The punk glanced back over his shoulder, discovered that he was being pursued. And that's when he abandoned his load, parking his daughter beside the tracks as if she were no more than a bundle of old clothes before disappearing into the night.

The little girl was screeching with terror when Cleve reached her. He crouched down and scooped her into his arms. It was in that crucial moment the raging in his ears *accelerated into a sudden, stabbing pain deep inside his skull.*

Not again, he prayed as he staggered to his feet with the child. Please, not this of all times.

But his brain was already exploding with the headache that preceded the darkness. He was still protectively clutching the little girl when the loathsome blackness swallowed him. The last sound he heard as he sank to his knees was the thunder of the approaching train....

CLEVE JERKED AWAKE with a startled grunt. For a moment he lay there in the gray light before dawn, collecting his wits while his heartbeat slowed to a crawl.

He hadn't experienced the nightmare since leaving Chicago. Except it wasn't a dream in the true sense, not something invented by his subconscious, but a reliving of an actual scene. In the reality, however, an alert attendant at the Addison station had stopped all el traffic, averting what could have been a disaster.

Everything else matched the nightmare, though. It had happened, and it had been the final episode that brought an end to his career.

He swung his legs to the floor, but he didn't stand. He sat on the edge of the bed and wondered what had triggered the dream. Gillian's visit the other day? Maybe.

He certainly hadn't been able to get her out of his conscious thoughts since she had left here so abruptly. The image of her alluring face and figure haunted him. But there was nothing new about that. She had been haunting him for years on one level or another.

Damn her anyway for coming here like that and spoiling his peaceful solitude. But who was he kidding? There'd been no contentment to destroy, just the illusion of it. He'd built that self-lie to keep himself from hating his barren existence in this place as much as he hated the reason for it.

Raking a hand through his rumpled hair, he got to his feet and dragged on a pair of jeans. He didn't bother with a shirt or shoes. He went into the tiny kitchen where the timer on the coffeemaker had done its job. Pouring himself a mug, he moved toward the front door, the Lab trailing after him.

Cleve needed to do some serious thinking, and there was only one place for that.

Bare-chested and barefoot, he padded down to the shore where he perched on the edge of a flat boulder. He didn't mind the cool air off the lake. He drank his coffee and watched the sun come up. The dog investigated a chunk of driftwood and then settled down in the sand near his feet.

"What do you think, Mike? Should I have explained to her why we're here and just why I had to turn her down?"

Hell, Cleve thought, he's probably smarter than I am. He knows I didn't have the guts to tell her the truth. Pride. I didn't want her feeling sorry for me. I couldn't have taken that. Not from Gillian.

"Know something, Mike? I don't think I was the only one keeping a secret."

It hadn't been just his old private investigator's instinct telling him the night before she left here that she was withholding some part of her story, maybe even the vital part. There was something more solid than that.

"Uh-huh, I know, Mike. If I'd given her half a chance, maybe she would have told me. Only I was too busy being a bastard. Wouldn't even let her explain why she walked away from me that summer without a word."

What had happened, he wondered, to send her off to Europe like that without ever looking back?

"You think it was her old man who broke us up? Naw, not likely."

Gillian had been of legal age and her own boss. Anyway, if her father had disapproved of him, there had been no sign of it. Harmon Randolph had remained friendly, had continued to use Cleve's services long after his daughter departed.

"What am I doing? What am I letting myself in for here?"

The Lab sat up and thrust its snout against his thigh. Cleve fondled the dog's ears and finished his coffee. The sun rose, bathing the lake in a golden glow. The air was spicy with the fragrance of the pines. And Cleve couldn't keep himself from being haunted by what she had said to him the other night.

"There must have been a very good reason why I came here. Maybe it's because I remembered what they used to say about you. That you weren't a P.I. because you liked the thrill of danger. That you didn't want to admit it, but what really gave you a rush was helping people who had nowhere else to turn."

Her words had been a kind of indictment. A *painful* one.

"She doesn't understand, Mike. She thinks I'm here because this is what I want."

A situation removed from all emotional and physical pressures, the professionals had urged. He hadn't listened to them. Not until that last attack had nearly cost him both his life and an innocent child's. After that he had reluctantly recognized the necessity of their advice. The result was this self-imposed exile.

It had worked. There had been no more blinding headaches, no more terrifying blackouts. Just a quiet, simple existence. And this enormous frustration.

"I can't do it anymore," he said, banging the heavy mug down so savagely that it cracked. "I'm not alive. I'm dead in this place."

One more case. If he could handle just one more case,

prove to himself that he was still the man he needed to be. *Her* case.

What were his chances of helping her? Maybe not so bad. There hadn't been a problem in months, not a sign of trouble. Maybe all this idleness had cured him. Could be he was going to be all right, at least long enough to see her through Victor Lassiter.

Was he crazy to try it? He couldn't help it. He had to find out. He had to test himself. See if he could function again.

"I'm gonna do it, Mike. I'm gonna come out of retirement."

The Lab only wanted his breakfast. Cleve gave it to him in the kitchen. Then he went into his bedroom and unlocked the case he kept on a closet shelf, removing his Colt .38 Special. He hadn't touched it since Chicago. He would clean it before he took it out in the yard and set up a practice range for himself. He had less than two weeks to get himself in shape before Victor Lassiter was released.

His license and insurance were still in effect. No difficulty there. There was only one problem. Gillian. He would have to explain to her why he had changed his mind when he turned up in Chicago. He wouldn't mention his condition. He didn't want her refusing him because she thought he might be risking himself.

He'd think of something to tell her, maybe that her case had intrigued him and in the end he'd been unable to resist the challenge. No lie actually. The other subject he needed to make every effort to avoid was his infernal weakness for her.

THE STREET in front of Gillian's office building on North LaSalle was torn up for repair. The taxi bringing her from a long afternoon in court had to drop her at the corner. She walked the half block to her firm.

It felt like ten blocks. Nothing was hotter than a sultry August in Chicago. The concrete of the city stored up heat like a kiln so that even now, with the street in late shadow, it was sweltering.

Her burden didn't help. She was carrying her purse and her attaché case. Both of them were loaded. Nor was she dressed for comfort. She wore a pale yellow summer suit, the high heels she felt she needed when dealing with a difficult judge on his lofty bench, and her red-gold hair pinned up in a French twist that contributed to her image of an earnest attorney. All of it had looked sleek and fresh in an air-conditioned courtroom. But she was convinced that out here she resembled a wilted daffodil.

The heavy glass doors were locked when she reached the front entrance of her building. Gillian wasn't surprised. The business day had ended almost an hour ago. Besides, this was Friday. There would have been a prompt and eager exodus from every office.

The night security guard came from his station in the lobby to admit her. "Been watching for you, Ms. Randolph. Your assistant warned me before she left that you'd be coming back to your office. Delayed again at the court-house?"

"By a very windy politician, Hank." She sighed with relief as she was embraced by the cool air of the building.

"Hot enough to fry out there, isn't it?" the friendly guard observed, carefully locking the doors behind her.

She agreed as he accompanied her across the lobby to the elevators.

"Place is all yours tonight, Ms. Randolph. Guess the rest of them couldn't wait to get home to shorts and cold drinks."

She was entering the elevator when Hank stopped her. "Almost forgot. There was a package delivered for you a while ago."

Gillian nodded. "From one of my clients. She said she'd send it over today."

"Mac put it on your desk when he went on his rounds just before he took off," he said, referring to the other guard who was always on duty with him.

"No partner tonight?"

His round, good-natured face broke into a grin. "Mac's wife went into labor again. They think this time it's for real. Believe me, I can handle the building on my own. With this being the start of the weekend and no cleaning crew until the morning, won't be anyone stirring in the place but you and me. You have a good evening, Ms. Randolph."

Gillian was aware of the total silence as she emerged from the elevator on the sixth floor and walked down the deserted corridor to the suite of offices occupied by her firm. But she'd been alone here too many times to let it bother her. Besides, the security in the building had always been tight and reliable. She'd never appreciated that more than she did now.

The first thing she did when she reached her office was to kick off her heels and remove her suit jacket. Once comfortable, she opened her large thermos and poured out a generous measure of the iced herb tea that she was addicted to both winter and summer.

Sipping the tea, she checked her answering machine. No messages. There were two penciled memos on the blotter from her assistant, Gail. Neither of them demanded her immediate attention.

The package brought to her office by the security guard was sitting at the side of her desk. The carton was somewhat larger than a shoe box and wrapped in brown paper sealed with tape. Gillian knew that it contained materials like family photographs, testimonials, a service medal, and anything else her client had been able to obtain to help establish the character and record of her late husband. Gillian might not use any of it in court, but she was always thorough with her research.

Deciding that the package and its contents could wait, she settled behind her desk, reading glasses in place, and began to study the lengthy depositions provided for her by the firm's paralegals. It was going to be a tough suit, and it demanded her careful attention to every detail.

Gillian was grateful for the challenge. She needed to keep her mind occupied, her thoughts closely focused on her work, even if she couldn't forget underneath it all that what she had been dreading had happened. Victor Lassiter had been released from prison two days ago.

She couldn't deny the nervous tension of knowing he was out there somewhere, maybe even now preparing a surprise for her, but she refused to let that concern cripple her. All she could do was exercise caution. And hope that the private investigator, to whom she'd paid a retainer after Cleveland McBride turned her down, would produce results. But she didn't have a great deal of faith in the man. If only Cleve had agreed to...

But what was the point in dwelling on his refusal and that painful episode in his cottage? It was finished, and she didn't want to remember how he had looked, how he had felt when he held her. Didn't want to remind herself of her shock in discovering that after all these years she still cared about him. Maybe even deeply cared. It was a hopeless situation, had always been hopeless, so why go on punishing herself with it?

The thermos was empty and twilight deepening over the city when Gillian finished with the last deposition. Removing her reading glasses, she slipped back into her shoes and suit jacket. She was tired. Time to go home.

Then she remembered the package. For a moment she thought about leaving it for Monday, dealing with it then.

Well, maybe she'd take just a quick glance now. She was curious to know if any certain item would be particularly useful.

Standing by her desk, she tore away the wrapping and lifted off the lid of the oblong carton. There was tissue paper inside. The contents had been carefully packed. She parted the layers, revealing what was underneath. Then she drew back, her hand flying to her mouth in horror.

Dear God!

The delivery was not from her widowed client. It was not a collection of evidence.

Nestled inside the box on a bed of tissue was a puppet. Victor Lassiter's twisted tribute to her. The violet eyes exactly like her own were wide and staring in an imitation of death.

The marionette had been cruelly savaged. Its silk gown was slashed and bloodied in several places, its limbs severed, and a toy ax buried in its skull. There was a sickening reality about the thing. Gillian felt as if she were gazing at the remains of an actual victim who had been inhumanly tortured before she died.

The message it conveyed was shockingly clear.

Steadying herself with an effort, she examined the package's outer wrapping. Her name and address were there but not those of the sender. No surprise in that. Nor was there a label identifying a legitimate delivery service.

Maybe Hank could tell her more. If not…well, what counted in this moment was her need to hear a familiar and reassuring voice. Picking up the phone, she called down to the security desk in the lobby. For several long, tense seconds she let it ring before realizing that the guard wasn't going to answer.

Snatching up her purse, Gillian headed for the elevator. Though it was well lighted, the long corridor seemed menacing. Why had she been such a fool as to work here on her own after hours? Why had she stayed so late?

She reached the elevator, ordered herself not to surrender to imagination as she descended to the lobby. Her prayer was that Hank would be there at his station, reading his newspaper as he did every evening. But there was no sign of the guard when she emerged from the elevator.

Unless there was an emergency, one of them was always here at the monitor, but since he was alone tonight... And then she saw it! It was there on the control board, a small wet patch, red and unmistakable. Not paint like on the marionette upstairs. This was real blood, and she feared Victor Lassiter was the cause of it.

For a heartrending moment she panicked. Then, struggling for control, she examined her options. She couldn't flee into the street; the thick front doors were locked, and the keys were with the guard. Should she use the phone here to call the police? But it could be too late by the time they arrived. She had to help herself—Hank, too if he wasn't already beyond help. She needed an immediate means of defense and at the same time a channel of communication with the outside. Gillian knew where to get both of them.

Her car was parked in the underground garage. It was equipped with a phone, and locked inside the glove compartment was a gun. She had purchased the compact weapon the day after Cleve refused her offer. But though she'd been rigorously instructed in the use of it on a firing range, she hated the thing. She had ended up tossing the revolver into the glove compartment when she should have been regularly carrying it.

Never mind. It would serve her now—if she could reach her car.

Hurrying into the elevator, she stabbed the *P* button. The doors closed with an agonizing slowness, the car seeming to take forever to sink to the lowest level. But when the doors finally rolled open again, she hesitated.

The underground facility, shared by the much larger office building next door, stretched away in front of her like a vast subterranean cavern. Crossing this gloomy expanse when her enemy could be lurking anywhere in the building, even down here, was going to be an ordeal.

Steeling herself, she left the elevator and moved quickly in the direction of her car. The clicking of her heels on the concrete sounded unnaturally loud in the stillness, probably because the place was so hollow. At this hour there were only a few widely scattered vehicles, making the garage seem bleak and eerie. Her car would, of course, be at the far end.

She was breathing hard in the stale, humid air when she finally reached the familiar green Volvo. Her relief turned to despair as her hand groped inside her purse for the key that would unlock the doors.

She had forgotten! Her keys weren't in her purse. She had shoved them into her attaché case this morning after unlocking one of her desk drawers. And the attaché case was still in her office on the sixth floor where she had left it in her haste.

What now?

She couldn't climb the ramp and exit the garage on foot. The automatic steel door at the top required a coded key card, and the card was with her other keys. She was a prisoner of the building's security.

Did she have the nerve to go back for that attaché case?

Testing her courage, Gillian retraced her route. Her uncertainty was still strong when she reached the elevator. And then her indecision no longer mattered because the doors were closed. Someone had summoned the car to an upper level.

She could hear the hum of the elevator. It was starting

down again, the lighted indicator telling her its destination was the garage. Trapped!

There was nowhere to hide, but Gillian made the effort anyway. Removing her heels, she ran on stockinged feet toward the only vehicle that was within her reach. The sedan had a flat tire, which probably explained why it was still here. Better still, it was parked in a corner against a dividing wall. The narrow space between the car and the wall was dark with shadows. She dived into them just as the elevator doors slid open.

Crouched there, hugging the front wheel of the sedan, Gillian heard his approaching footsteps. If he decided to search for her with any care, there would be no way he could miss her, though she was prepared to squeeze underneath the car if she had to.

The footsteps slowed, came to a stop within a few feet of the back end of the sedan. There was an agonizing silence in which she held her breath and counted on heaven to help her.

"Yo, Gillian! You down here anywhere?"

It was a deep voice. An impatient voice. The most wonderful voice in the world.

Shaken, but her heart pumping again, she rose to her feet and moved out into the light where he could see her. "I'm here," she croaked.

He greeted her with a casual grin. Just as though she'd been expecting him. Just as though there was nothing in the least extraordinary about Cleveland McBride's being here.

"What were you doing down there?" he wondered. "Changing a tire? Hate to tell you, sweetheart, but it's this one back here that needs changing."

She had the depressing conviction that she must look exactly like she *had* been dealing with a jack and a lug wrench. She was hot and perspiring with tendrils of damp hair escaping from her French twist, there was a smudge on her yellow skirt from contact with the wheel, and she was standing here without shoes, her stockinged feet filthy from the floor.

Why her appearance in this situation should matter to her at all was annoying. And puzzling. Maybe it was because Cleve himself had never looked better.

He sported a fresh haircut, and wore crisp summer slacks and a matching shirt. There was even a new energy in the way he carried himself, something that, if she didn't know better, could be defined as cheerful. How had this change happened? *Why* had it happened? And what business did she have in being so exhilarated at the sight of him like this?

"Guess you want to know what I'm doing in Chicago, huh?"

As a matter of fact, she did, but that part could wait. "Let's start with what you're doing in the building. How did you get in?"

He jerked his thumb in the direction of the lobby upstairs. "How else? Guard let me in from the street after I displayed my credentials and explained I was looking for you. He tried to ring your office, but you'd left. Said maybe I could still catch you down here before you drove off."

"Hank is all right?"

"Uh, yeah, if you don't count a finger he sliced on a soda can, which he'd gone and mopped up in the rest room and was still nursing when I arrived. So why are we discussing the health of your security guard? Hey, you okay? You don't look so hot."

"You noticed," she said dryly. "I'm not, and there's a reason for it. I wasn't down there changing a tire, Cleve. I was hiding."

"You want to explain, Gillian?"

"I do." And she did.

Then, before she could object, or even determine if she wanted to, she found herself being dragged into the elevator. The car stopped just long enough in the lobby for Cleve to ask a startled Hank to send for the police before it went on to the sixth floor.

Minutes later the private investigator gazed down at the mutilated marionette on her desk. "The guy is one sick bastard," he said grimly.

"He's playing with me. Just like he must have played with the marionette before he—" She broke off, shuddering.

Cleve put a steadying hand on her arm. "Take it easy, Gillian. Sending you something vicious like this has to be a violation of Lassiter's parole. There's a good chance you can have him put back inside before he tries anything else."

But the uniformed officer who arrived in her office while they were still discussing this possibility had no authority to guarantee such a result. All he could promise after questioning them was that the matter would be promptly investigated. Then, assuring Gillian that the department would contact her as soon as they knew anything, he left with the evidence.

Cleve turned to her when they were alone. "You look like you've had enough for one day."

"I have," she admitted.

"My car is around the corner. I'm taking you home."

"I have my own car in the garage. That's why I was down there, remember?"

"Leave it. You can pick it up on Monday. You won't need it before then, because I'll be around to drive you wherever you want to go."

"Now hold on. Just when did we agree that you were in charge of—"

"You're not going anywhere on your own. Here, give

me that case. I'll carry it. Well, don't just stand there looking at me. Let's go."

Again he gave her no choice, and she was too tired to
argue with him. She was briskly conducted in the direction
of the elevator. He had been nothing like this at his cottage.
What on earth had come over him?

IT WAS SILENT in the underground parking garage. They
were gone now, Gillian and the man who had joined her.
It was safe for Victor to emerge from behind the thick pillar
where he had been concealed in the darkness.

He'd been there the whole time, watching her panicked
flight to the Volvo, then her ridiculous effort to hide along
the side of the other car. He'd enjoyed every second of her
terror, knowing he was the cause of it. Knowing she was
suffering.

He could have killed her. At any second he could have
destroyed her. But that would have been too quick, too
easy. He had other plans for Gillian.

She had stolen from him, and she had to be punished.
She had taken the most important thing in his life. It was
because of Gillian that Molly had run away from him.
Then, when he had found her again, she refused to come
back to him so he'd had to kill her. All Gillian's fault.
She'd turned Molly against him, and for that she must pay.

His gaunt figure moved like a wraith in the direction of
the Volvo. He wore a coverall and carried a toolbox. That's
how he'd gotten in and how he'd get out.

The security was less rigid in the adjoining building that
shared the garage. He had entered from there during the
rush hour. The guards had never noticed him in the crowds
pouring from the offices. No one had challenged him. Why
should they? He was just another building mechanic on his
way to some repair.

When he reached the Volvo, he placed the toolbox he

carried on the floor. Removing a pair of plastic disposable gloves from one of his deep pockets, he put them on and closely examined the doors of the car.

Victor had learned some practical things in prison from his fellow inmates. Among them had been detailed instructions on how to break into a car and leave it without the owner realizing that you'd ever been there.

Useful, he thought with a chuckle, if you wanted to plant a bomb. He didn't. Not his style.

He was inside the Volvo in no time at all, searching it thoroughly. If he didn't find anything worthwhile, he might see about getting into her office upstairs. Turning up something there.

It wasn't necessary. Nothing could be more interesting than what he discovered inside Gillian's glove compartment after mastering its simple lock.

Careful not to disturb her prints that had to be on the grip, he removed the revolver, wrapped it in plastic, and tucked it inside his jacket.

"I think maybe we can have some fun with this, Gillian," he whispered in the dimness. "You're going to love it."

Chapter Three

The car was low and sporty and, like its owner, it had attitude. An impatient beast, it snarled as it forced its way through the downtown traffic. Cleve at the wheel was equally assertive with Gillian beside him.

"From now on you open no more packages, either at work or at home. I don't care who sent them or how much you trust them. You let me do the unwrapping, and that's only after I check them over first. Hell, the next one could be a bomb."

"And just when did I agree that you could— Watch it! The light is changing!"

"I see it."

It didn't seem to matter to him, though. He whipped through the intersection without a pause, ignoring the horns barking furiously behind them. She had forgotten how reckless he could be when he got behind a wheel. His driving had seemed daring and exciting to her when she was eighteen. At thirty-two it simply left her praying she would survive.

"Now that I'm on your case," he continued, "there's a few other things we need to get clear about."

"I hate to spoil all this miraculous self-assurance you seem to have recovered in less than two weeks, but you're not on my case. I've already hired another private investigator."

"Who?"

"Otis Johnson."

His laugh was as brash as his driving. "The guy's a joke. Fire him."

There was another traffic light in front of them. This one was already red. No choice about it. The car slammed to a halt, jerking her against her seat belt.

"Chicago traffic," he grumbled. "I'd forgotten how bad it is."

"Which is exactly why I leave my car in the underground and use taxis when I'm downtown. And I don't see why I should fire Otis Johnson just because—"

Another interruption. This time a cold, wet one at the back of her neck. Gillian gasped in alarm.

"Relax," Cleve said. The light changed. The car leaped forward. "It's just Mike."

She twisted around. In the dark she hadn't noticed the sleeping Lab in the back seat. He was awake and active now, seeking attention as he thrust his nose at her. Gillian gently pushed him away. He tried to lick her hand.

"I don't know who's more persistent here, you or your dog."

"You want results, don't you? Well, you won't get them with a bum like Otis Johnson."

"He came very highly recommended, and I've already paid him a retainer."

"And now you're going to ask for a refund." One of his hands left the wheel to boost the blower on the air conditioner. "Heat in this town is as mean as the traffic. Another thing I don't miss in the north."

"If you love your lakeside wilderness so much," she challenged him, "then why did you leave it?"

"Don't worry, I'm going back there just as soon as

you're safe from Victor Lassiter. Ah, now we can make some time.''

With a burst of speed, the car zoomed onto Lake Shore Drive and headed north on the expressway.

"Which," she said dryly, "still doesn't explain why you changed your mind and decided to take my case."

For a moment he didn't answer her. He was too busy zipping around cars and switching lanes with a casualness that left her breathless.

His reply, when it occurred, was equally blithe. "Had to. Remember those storms that night you were there? Well, now the roof leaks. Have to get a new roof."

"I see. And the fee I pay you for your services..."

"Right. You're going to buy me a new roof."

She didn't believe him, but she suspected it was the only answer she was going to get. At least for now. In any case, what with her tension over his driving and the dog hovering at her shoulder with his hot breath, she was in no condition to demand a better explanation. She wondered if her nerves would last until she got home.

Speaking of which, Cleve had never asked directions to her apartment, although he was traveling with a confidence that indicated he already knew her address. Which he probably did. Cleveland McBride never took a case without checking on the essentials first.

And once he *had* accepted a case... Well, his tenacity produced results. But that was only after his client suffered his high-handed, take-charge attitude. Like now. Gillian suddenly felt overwhelmed. And secretly relieved.

She eyed the man beside her. She could feel the energy and decisiveness that radiated from him. They had once been characteristic of him on almost every level. Including, she remembered against her will, his potent lovemaking. She could feel her face flaming with heat as she recalled the long, exciting sessions when his body had branded hers with an exquisite possessiveness. He had been a tireless, tender lover. And whatever else she had convinced herself of since then, Gillian knew that she'd never really recovered from those interludes with him.

But those old qualities of energy and decisiveness hadn't been there when she'd visited him at his cottage. Again, she wondered what had happened to produce this change in him. As she had observed back in her office building, it was a physical metamorphosis as well. An *appealing* one. And that, she realized, stirring uneasily in her seat, could be a problem. A major one.

Her apartment was located on the North Side a few blocks in from the lake. It was on one of those narrow, quiet streets that are welcome oases in the city. A place where someone always seems to be walking a dog under the locust trees and where you can never find a parking spot.

Cleve did manage to find one just opposite her building. He regarded the structure thoughtfully as they climbed from the car. It was a brick three-flat from a more substantial era, with an English basement and a square bay from street to roof.

"Nice. Any restrictions against pets?"

"Uh, none that I know of, but—"

"Good. Then I won't have to put Mike in a kennel."

"You expect me to keep your dog for you?"

"I don't think you get it, Gillian. I expect you to keep *both* of us."

"You're not serious? You *are* serious."

"I don't have a place anymore in Chicago. I let it go when I moved, remember? Where do you expect me to live?"

"You've heard of hotels, haven't you?"

"No good. With Lassiter on the loose and already threatening you, I need to stick close. Come on, why are you being so squeamish about this? You've got a spare bedroom up there, haven't you?''

''There's a guest room,'' she conceded.

''Well, then there's no problem.''

Oh, but there was a very *definite* problem with such an arrangement. All the way home she had been aware of his disarming nearness. His hard body squeezed beside her in the narrow confines of the car. His husky voice that stirred her senses without any conscious effort. Even his virile scent that made her breath stick in her throat.

She was much too susceptible to him, and after the painful mistakes of the past...

''Cleve, I don't think this is a good idea.''

''What are you worrying about? This is strictly business. Two people sharing an apartment because, like they say in chambers, counselor, it's expedient. Hey, I haven't forgotten what *didn't* happen up north, or why it didn't happen, either. So let's just forget about it and concentrate on getting Lassiter.''

Gillian hesitated, still concerned about the intimacy of such a situation. Wondering if she could trust either him or herself.

''Are we going to stand out here and wilt under this streetlight, or are you inviting me up?''

She didn't remember issuing the invitation he wanted. But she must have agreed to something, because a few minutes later he was following her into her second floor apartment with Mike and a battered suitcase.

While she turned on the lamps and adjusted the air-conditioning, he checked out the surroundings.

The rooms were spacious, with hardwood floors and the generous woodwork of an earlier decade. Her furnishings were a comfortable mix of traditional and contemporary.

''What's this?'' He had paused before her collection of

baseball mementos. "You're still in love with the Cubs, then?"

"Somebody has to be," she said solemnly.

He made a sound of disgust. She hadn't forgotten that, with his South Side blue-collar origins, he was a loyal fan of the White Sox.

"With this Cubs shrine staring me in the face, I don't know why I have an appetite, but I do. You eat yet?"

She shook her head. "I never managed to get around to it."

"Me, either. How about I fix us a late supper?"

She looked at him skeptically. "Let's see if I remember this correctly. The last time you offered to cook for me— a romantic, candlelight dinner in your apartment on Halsted, I think it was—you set the kitchen on fire, and the landlord threatened to evict you."

"I've improved since then. I only burn the food now. Come on, trust me to find my way around your kitchen. You know you're dying for a chance to get out of that legal uniform."

"Fire extinguisher is on the wall next to the stove," she informed him. Then she disappeared into her bedroom before she could change her mind.

When she emerged twenty minutes later, revived from a shower and clad in jeans and a comfortable top, he was whipping eggs for an omelette.

"What can I do?" she offered.

"Sit down and relax." He paused to drink from a can of diet soda. "Your tall, cool one is waiting for you at the table."

Gillian was too tired to argue with him. She settled at the kitchen table, reaching for the glass he'd indicated. He had filled it from the jug she kept in the refrigerator. Iced herb tea. He had remembered her preference for it after all these years.

You're exhausted, Gillian. That's why you've suddenly got a silly lump in your throat. It's nothing more than that.

She distracted herself from risky emotions by concentrating on Mike. He was pacing restlessly from kitchen to living room and back again.

"What's wrong with him?"

"Nothing. He's just getting used to the place, that's all."

"Cleve, he's panting. Did you give him water?"

"He doesn't need any water."

"That's mean. I'm going to put down a bowl of water for him."

"Have it your way, but you're making a mistake."

Gillian found a shallow bowl in the cupboard, filled it at the sink, and placed it on the floor. The Lab lapped at it greedily.

"You see, he was thirsty."

She had seated herself at the table again when the phone rang.

"Stay," Cleve commanded. "I'll get it."

Before she could object, he plucked the receiver from its cradle on the wall. She could tell after listening for a few seconds that he was talking to the police. She watched his face, but his expression revealed nothing. When he hung up, he went back to fixing the omelette.

"Well?" she asked, frustrated by his silence.

"The cops have checked out Lassiter and the package," he told her reluctantly. "Seems he reported the theft of his marionette at the precinct nearest to him sometime around noon today. It's on the record. He was shocked when they told him what had happened to his beloved creation."

Gillian, understanding the significance of the department's message, drooped in discouragement. "Which means there's no proof he ever sent the marionette to me. As far as the police are concerned, anyone could have sent it."

"They're looking into just how it was delivered."

"But they won't learn anything useful, will they? He's too cunning. He's thought of everything to keep himself on the loose out there."

"We'll get him."

She laughed wryly. "Yes, but the question is, will he get me first?"

Not while I'm around, Cleve thought grimly. He tried to concentrate on the omelette bubbling now in the pan, but it wasn't easy. His gaze kept wandering in Gillian's direction.

She was barefoot, and her silky red-gold hair was loose now, the makeup cleaned from her face. She looked much younger like this. Younger and far more vulnerable.

The trouble was, there was more stirring inside him than just an urge to protect her. That damn top she was wearing managed to reveal the lush appeal of her breasts. He couldn't stop himself from remembering, even after all these years, how those soft, sweet breasts had felt when he'd stroked them with his fingertips, how they had tasted in his eager mouth. She had driven him crazy, and if he wasn't careful, she could make him frantic again. It would be so easy to give in, so—

Keep your mind on the stove, McBride, and your hands where they belong. You made her a promise before you moved in, remember?

Yeah, and it was going to cost him his sanity to keep it.

Understandably, Gillian didn't have much of an appetite when he finally served dinner. The omelette and salads he had fixed weren't bad, but she only picked at them. He tried to keep her from dwelling on Lassiter by asking her things he didn't care a hang about.

"So, is your mother still living up in Winnetka in that barn of a house where you grew up?"

She shook her head. "Mother remarried two years after Daddy died. They relocated out east."

"Uh-huh. And what about your ex? Where did ol' Alan wind up?"

"He's practicing corporate law in Indiana. It's all right, Cleve. You don't have to hold my hand. We can talk about the subject that really matters. What are we going to do about Victor?"

He swallowed a mouthful of salad. "Wait. It's about all we can do until he makes a move. In the meantime, I'll learn everything I can about him. Where he's living, working, what he's up to. I'll start on Monday. Not many sources available on a weekend."

She nodded slowly. He could see that her mind had already moved off in another direction.

"What is it?" he asked.

"I was just thinking that… Well, it's going to be difficult enough living and working side by side, but if we keep stumbling over our past…"

"Yeah, I get it. You want to explain to me why you walked away that summer. Didn't we already try this scene at my cottage?"

"Cleve, I owe you—"

"No." He shook his head emphatically. "Let's leave it in the past where it belongs, Gillian. Let's just keep this friendly but professional."

Maybe he's right, she thought. Maybe it's safer not to go back. What could an explanation achieve now except to ease her own guilt? Because if he was no longer interested enough to—

She checked herself. He was gazing at her intently.

"What?" she asked.

"If you're in a mood to confess," he said, "then why not tell me something I can use."

"I have told you all you need to know."

"I don't think so. I sensed up at the cottage you were holding something back, and I still feel it. Oh, you've got a solid enough reason for being worried about Lassiter, but it runs deeper than that."

"You're wrong."

She looked away before he could see the panic in her eyes. She was afraid he would start questioning her in earnest and was grateful when Mike suddenly relieved the tension in the kitchen. The dog had gone to the back door and was whining softly.

"What does he want?" she asked.

"He needs to go out. And after all that water he drank, he'll probably need to go out a couple of other times through the night. That's why I never give him water after seven o'clock."

"You might have told me."

"I tried, but you weren't listening." Cleve grinned at her.

Glaring at him, she tossed her napkin on the table and got to her feet. "You've got a stinker for a master, Mike. Come on, I'll introduce you to a nice fenced-in backyard."

Flipping on the outside light, she unlocked the door and pulled it back, disclosing a landing and a long flight of stairs to the yard. The Lab needed no urging. He bounded ahead of her down the steps. Gillian went only as far as the edge of the landing to make sure he was all right. Then she started back into the kitchen to help Cleve, who was already busy loading the dishwasher. She never reached his side.

"You want to run this tonight," he asked, his back to her as he fitted their plates into the rack, "or wait until we add the breakfast things tomorrow?"

She didn't answer him.

"Hey, Gillian, now or in the morning?"

When her silence persisted, he looked over his shoulder.

She was squeezed back against the wall just inside the doorway. There was a look of such shock and anguish on her face that his heart leaped inside his chest.

She was staring at the lower half of the open door. A message had been spray-painted across its outer surface in sprawling, bloodred letters.

Did you enjoy my surprise today?

When Gillian opened her mouth and tried to speak to him, nothing came out but a long, ragged moan. Cleve threw the pan he was holding into the sink where it clattered against the stainless steel. Crossing the kitchen in three quick strides, he drew her into his arms.

She trembled as he held her, burying her face against his neck. He forced himself to remember she was in his arms for no other reason than a need for comfort. But her softness was a painful temptation. It brought back in a sudden rush all those poignant memories of the long nights they had once spent in his apartment. Nights when he had made love to her repeatedly, when her young body had responded to him so willingly, so eagerly.

Come on, McBride, exercise some self-control before you lose it altogether.

"It's all right," he soothed her.

She pulled back and looked at him. There was anger now in her face. "No, it isn't all right. He invaded my workplace. Now he's managed to invade my home."

It wasn't necessary for them to discuss who was responsible for the graffiti on the door or what it alluded to. They both knew that Victor Lassiter had been here today and that he was taunting her about the mutilated marionette.

Cleve removed one of his hands from her back long enough to reach out and close the door so she wouldn't have to go on seeing it.

She started to object. "Mike is out there. He'll—"

"Don't worry about him. He'll let us know when he

wants back in.'' He went on holding her. "I'll clean off that thing, or paint over it if I have to. First thing in the morning after the cops see it.''

"But it won't really help for them to see it, will it? There's no proof it was Victor who was here and did it, just like there was no proof he sent the marionette.''

She drew away from him. He reluctantly let her go. She had squared her shoulders in an effort to restore her courage, but her voice was still shaky.

"Where will he be next, and what will he try?''

"Whatever it is,'' Cleve promised her fiercely, "you won't have to face it alone. Because this settles it. From now on, where you go, I go. No exceptions. If that bastard wants you, he's going to have to get past me first.''

"You're sure about that?''

There was an expression now in her violet eyes that he didn't like. "What?'' he demanded.

"There's a black-tie fund-raiser at the Hutton Hotel tomorrow night. Come on now, Cleve, it's no good your looking at me like that. I can't skip it, because I'm scheduled to speak. Anyway, I'm not going to let Victor Lassiter turn me into a recluse.''

"Gillian,'' he pleaded.

"I know, I haven't forgotten. You'd rather have a root canal than attend anything more formal than a funeral. But if you mean what you say... Well, we're going to have to rent you a tux tomorrow, because I can't imagine you own one. Cleve, stop groaning. It could be worse. I could be dragging you to the ballet.''

Chapter Four

The fund-raiser at the luxurious Hutton Hotel on Michigan Avenue was underway. And Gillian, standing in front of a mike on a lighted platform in the vast, ornate ballroom, was currently the focus of attention.

"Let me tell you about Chicago," she began in a strong, enthusiastic voice, while on the enormous screen above her appeared an image of the Art Institute. "Chicago, ladies and gentlemen, is more than the world's finest collection of Impressionist art."

Cleve had to admit she had the ability to capture the interest of a bored crowd. From his position at a center table, he could see she had attracted gazes from every side of the room. He didn't appreciate the eager male ones.

"And Chicago is certainly much more than tall buildings that break records," she continued.

There wasn't a man in the room, including him, who even glanced at the Sears Tower now glowing on the monitor. They were all feasting their eyes on Gillian in that clinging sea-green dress which, even if it was floor length and high-necked, managed to be more tantalizing than a string bikini.

A figure like hers should be illegal, Cleve thought, wishing he could smack the grins off the faces of the men around him.

"What Chicago is really all about, ladies and gentlemen, is people. People like these." The screen shifted to a montage of the faces that represented the various ethnic cultures of the city. "People with sons and daughters who are the future of Chicago. I'm convinced the neighborhood youth centers will play a vital role in the direction of that future, but they badly need our support..."

There was spirited applause when she ended her appeal several minutes later and left the platform. Cleve realized that, looks aside, Gillian could be very persuasive.

Well-wishers were gathered around her when he finally managed to squeeze through and reach her side. She looked tired.

"You all right?" he murmured.

"It's nothing that something cold and wet won't fix."

"Want me to snag a glass from one of those trays?" Waiters were circulating through the crowd with trays of hors d'oeuvres and champagne.

She looked at him wistfully. Understanding her silent plea, he rolled his eyes.

"Gillian, they're not going to have iced herb tea in this place. Not already brewed, anyway."

"Just plain iced tea will do. I'd go myself, but—"

"I know, you're tied up here. Okay, just stay and keep selling those youth centers while I see what that bar back there can come up with. Good job, by the way."

Pleased by his casual compliment, she watched him slip away through the crowd, knowing she wasn't imagining what the tux he so hated did for him. There were admiring female glances on all sides as his erect, broad-shouldered figure moved off in the direction of the bar.

She turned her attention back to the individuals waiting to congratulate her. A moment later, she was reemphasizing the need to fund the youth centers when a voice behind her snarled, "Maybe we'd have something left to donate to charity if greedy lawyers weren't robbing us with their law-suits."

The gathering stirred in discomfort. Struggling to pre-serve her pleasant smile, Gillian slowly turned around. The man she confronted, with his thin, badly dyed hair and pompous, coarse-featured face, was no stranger. She and Charles Reardon had clashed before, though never outside of a courtroom. She meant to keep it that way.

"Mr. Reardon, how nice to see you."

"Is it? Then why are you trying to destroy me any way you can?"

The man had a reputation for being overbearing and ver-bally abusive to his enemies. Even so, as the head of a large company, he should have been smarter than to attack her like this in public. Or, considering the suit she had filed against his company on behalf of her client, to approach her at all.

There was a simple explanation. He had been drinking. She could see that by his flushed face. In which case, there was only one way to handle him.

"Excuse me," Gillian murmured.

She started to turn away, but Reardon stopped her. "Hey, don't play this cool act with me. Admit it, Randolph. You're on fire inside because you don't stand a prayer of winning a dime for that bitch. Everybody knows Maureen Novak is wrong and that you only took her case because you hate my guts. No, you won't win this time, but you're gonna cost me an expensive lawyer anyway, aren't you?"

"That lawyer would advise you, Mr. Reardon," she warned him quietly, "that, since you and I are involved in a pending litigation, this exchange is highly inappropriate."

He laughed. "What? I'm not supposed to discuss some-thing with someone who's trying to hurt me?"

The situation, with all these attentive bystanders, was growing increasingly awkward. Gillian wanted to end it.

She tried again to move away, but this time he stepped into her path.

"Just tell me something," he persisted. "What have I ever done to you that you've got this personal thing to get me?"

If Charles Reardon had been sober, or knew her better, he might have recognized the signs of her anger. When she tipped her head to one side and considered him with a tight little smile, as she did now, her courtroom adversaries could have told him she was taking his slow measure, like a fighter squaring off just before he struck.

"Now listen to me," she informed him with a dangerous edge to her voice, "because I'm only going to tell you this once. If you don't stay away from me and my client, I will take action to make certain you don't bother either one of us again."

"What's that supposed to mean?"

"It means—"

He didn't let her finish. "Why, you're threatening me!" he said loudly. "You all heard her! She's threatening me!"

There were embarrassed murmurs in the gathering around them. Gillian didn't hear them. Nor was she paying any further attention to Charles Reardon. She was too stunned by the sight of a face that had suddenly loomed into her line of vision just beyond Reardon's shoulder. The glowing eyes in that face briefly locked onto her gaze, then he melted off into the crowd.

A second later she was vaguely aware of Cleve's arrival. Carrying a tall glass of iced tea, he shouldered his way through the group. The tough expression on his craggy features was a clear indication that he had heard at least the last part of her dialogue with Reardon and was prepared to deal with him. Gillian was too shaken in this moment to be anything but grateful.

"You're being obnoxious, pal," Cleve informed Reardon in a tone that meant business. "I suggest you take a walk."

"Who the hell are you?" Reardon challenged him.

"Somebody you don't want to tangle with. Now are you going to leave voluntarily, or do you want me to escort you away from the lady?"

"You'll regret this," Reardon said, directing his resentment at Gillian before he turned and swaggered off in the direction of the bar.

With his departure, the others around them drifted away, leaving Gillian and Cleve to themselves.

"What was that all about?" he asked.

She didn't answer him. She was still staring off into the crowd. The expression on her face worried him. She had looked just like this last night when she'd discovered the graffiti on her door.

"Gillian, the drunk is gone. It's okay."

She shook her head. "The drunk is Charles Reardon, and I've handled his kind before. That's not why I'm standing here in a daze."

"Then what—"

"Victor Lassiter," she said, gripping him by the sleeve. "Cleve, he's here in the ballroom. He was just a few feet away not more than a minute ago."

"Where is he now?" he demanded, turning to scan the crowd.

"There, on the other side," she said, locating him in his white uniform. "The tall, thin one with the tray."

"A waiter?"

"I don't know how or why, but, yes, he's one of the waiters."

There was the glint of steel in Cleve's tawny, narrowed eyes. "Stay here," he ordered, handing her the glass of iced tea.

"Cleve, what are you going to do?"

"Have a little chat with the bastard."

"Don't! He could—"

No use. Cleve was already striding off across the ballroom, heading purposefully in the direction of Victor, who had moved toward a pair of swinging doors that led to the service areas.

VICTOR DISAPPEARED into the service regions before Cleve could reach him. But he didn't let that stop him. He burst through the swinging doors, almost colliding with a server bearing a load of glassware. The young woman stared at him, startled by his presence in what turned out to be the pantry.

Before she could challenge him, he swiftly demanded, "The waiter who passed through here a second ago—where did he go?"

She pointed toward a passage opposite another set of swinging doors where there came the clamor of a busy kitchen. "Uh, that way, but—"

Cleve didn't wait for her objections. His long legs carried him across the pantry and along the passage. It was silent here, deserted. There was a closed door at the end. He opened it and found himself in what appeared to be a lounge for employees.

The room was unoccupied except for Lassiter, who was standing by a range of lockers where he was just about to unlatch one of the metal doors. He turned at the sound of Cleve's entrance, his voice as smooth as oil.

"This area is off-limits to the guests, sir."

"Not if they have business with one of the hotel staff." He crossed the lounge until he was standing directly in front of the gaunt figure in the white uniform. "Assuming, that is, you are a legitimate member of the staff. Are you, Lassiter?"

The impassive expression on Victor's narrow, pale face didn't change. The only sign of surprise was in his eyes that searched Cleve's face. They were the blackest eyes he had ever seen.

"Who are you?" he asked in that slow monotone.

"Name's McBride. Cleveland McBride."

"I don't know you."

"You will." He thrust his face close to Victor's. "You'll get to know me in a way you won't like, if you don't stay away from my client. I guarantee it."

Lassiter shrugged. "And why is that?"

"Because I'm a licensed private investigator, hired by Gillian Randolph to make sure she stays safe. Now do we understand each other?"

There was no flicker of concern in the black eyes. "I haven't been near your client."

"What do you call being here tonight? Just a little co-incidence?"

"I'm a legitimate waiter on the hotel staff. Why should that be so hard to believe?" Emotion crept into his voice for the first time. Only slight, but it was there. A note of bitterness. "What other kind of work is there for an ex-con?"

"I'll check that out, if you don't mind."

"Maybe I do mind. Maybe I think you've got no business coming in here threatening me like this when all I'm doing is trying to earn a living. Even an ex-con has rights."

"Not when he's sending nasty packages and spray-painting vicious messages."

The black eyes in the white face were livid now. "You'd better go back to your lady lawyer and see what she has to tell you about the seriousness of false accusations."

Cleve backed away from him slowly, maintaining eye contact with each step. "Sure, I'll do that, Lassiter, but you remember our little talk. Stay the hell away from Gillian."

He left the lounge, closing the door behind him.

Victor stared after him for a few seconds. This private investigator presented a problem he hadn't anticipated, though he should have realized Gillian would hire herself a protector. Not that it mattered in the long run. Nothing was going to stop him from punishing her.

He would just have to be careful about McBride. Learn his weakness, maybe. Every man had a weakness that could be used against him. And in the meantime...

Victor turned his attention back to the locker that had been assigned to him. Opening it, he withdrew a manila file that accompanied him everywhere. It contained newspaper clippings he had been collecting since his first month in prison.

The file was thin now, but it had been thick before his release. He had weeded out the material he'd used as a cover, all those unrelated articles that had convinced the prison authorities he was engaged in a harmless hobby. But sandwiched in with the rest had been his real interest—any and every story, no matter how insignificant, that had managed to mention Gillian.

Those clippings had been his salvation. They had helped him to survive the long years of prison, nourishing his hate for Gillian while reminding him of what he owed her. But they had served another purpose, too. Ammunition. An accumulated knowledge of his target that would one day prove useful.

The latest addition to the file had already been valuable. A story in the *Tribune* about tonight's fund-raiser and its speakers, Gillian among them. It was because of the article that Victor had made use of his connection here at the hotel. Waiters were always in demand anyway, and he had to work somewhere to meet the conditions of his parole. He'd been reluctantly hired by that contact with a warning not to breathe a word of their past connection. His impulse to be present at the fund-raiser had paid off.

But it was a slightly earlier clipping in the file that he wanted now. He removed it from the pouch, checking its contents to be certain he was correct about what he had overheard in the ballroom between Gillian and Charles Reardon.

Yes, the story verified it. Maureen Novak, and Gillian was representing her. What a ripe little plum for him. But before he could pluck it, Victor would need to conduct further research on Charles Reardon and the widow Novak. He was confident he could manage it.

GILLIAN EXPRESSED her relief when Cleve rejoined her in the ballroom.

"You had me worried. Victor is dangerous. He has an insane temper."

"But he knows how to disguise it. No emotion in that voice or on his face. The guy's creepy." He briefly explained what had transpired between him and Victor.

"You think it *might* be just a coincidence he's working here?"

"Who knows. Anyway, he's been warned, and for now that's about all we can do."

She watched him as he raked his fingers through his bronze-colored hair flecked with silver. There was a restlessness in the gesture and in the way he gazed around at the sea of figures in the ballroom.

"You have any reason to stay on here?" he asked her suddenly.

"No, we can leave anytime." The place had been buzzing about her since her scene with Reardon. She wouldn't regret getting away from that.

"Good. I need to recharge my batteries." He caught her by the hand, drawing her toward the exit.

"Where are we going?"

"Outside where I can breathe. You have any objection to stretching our legs before we head home?"

"No."

She didn't tell him that her shoes weren't exactly appropriate for hiking. He obviously needed to unwind. She could feel his tension begin to ease when the lavish gilt and marble ballroom was behind them. It wasn't Cleve's kind of setting. He would have been far more comfortable in a ballpark with a cold beer and a hot dog. Truthfully, so would she, though she doubted he'd believe that.

Reaching the street, they crossed Michigan Avenue and began to stroll through Grant Park in the direction of the lake. There was a cooling nighttime breeze off the water that was a welcome contrast to the blistering heat of the day. Even the sounds of the traffic seemed less harsh.

Gillian couldn't deny it. She enjoyed being with him, even in silence. His company tonight recalled for her the simple pleasures they had once so lovingly shared in this city. Window shopping in the Loop, wandering through an open-air art fair in Old Town, feeding each other slices of savory pizza from a street vendor's cart outside Shedd Aquarium. These were the images she wanted to hold on to, not the piercing recollection of how it had all ended abruptly and so cruelly. Because even now the memory of their parting hurt.

And you have to stop punishing yourself like this. It was years ago. Forget it.

"This character who was giving you a hard time just before you spotted Lassiter—"

"Charles Reardon."

"Yeah, Reardon." He hesitated. "He have anything to do with why I'm on your case?"

"No connection." Gillian was amused. She knew that Cleve was eager for the details.

"So, there's no reason for me to hear an explanation."

"Not really."

"Uh-huh." There was silence between them again as they moved on along the sidewalk, and then his impatient, "Are you going to make me beg?"

She laughed softly. "Can't stand it, huh? All right, there's no reason you shouldn't know at least the essentials. Since they're public knowledge now, I wouldn't be betraying a client's confidence."

They paused, looking back across the park to the dramatic skyline of the city they had both known and loved all their lives. Every high-rise was spangled with lights. They admired the scene for a moment. Then Gillian began to share the story with him.

"Reardon and I are old enemies. We've faced each other in court before. I don't consider him a very desirable human being."

"I could tell."

"Yes, I'm sure that was pretty clear."

"What's the case this time?"

"A wrongful death suit I'm bringing on behalf of my client, Maureen Novak. Reardon owns a company that specializes in large-scale excavations around the city. It uses a lot of heavy equipment."

"Somebody get killed on the job?"

Gillian nodded as they walked on in the direction of Buckingham Fountain. "Maureen's husband, who worked for the company. There was an accident involving a gantry crane. Harry Novak was crushed to death. Reardon and his insurance company are claiming that Harry had been drinking and died as a result of his own negligence."

"I assume there's another version to this story," Cleve said.

"Yes, the *true* one, which is all about equipment that wasn't kept properly maintained by a man who valued profit over human welfare. I'll prove that in the end, but in the meantime Harry Novak's widow is being denied the benefits she's entitled to." Gillian's voice sharpened with anger. "Maureen has three young children to raise and a very limited income now. It's infuriating!"

Cleve raised his hands in mock surrender. "Hey, take it easy, counselor. You've convinced me."

"Sorry," she murmured. "I didn't mean to treat you like the jury. Look, isn't it beautiful?"

They were approaching the elaborate, enormous fountain which spewed countless jets of water high into the air. For another silent moment they watched the lighted display. Then Cleve turned to her.

"You told me up north that you refused to run away, that you had a client who was counting on you. Maureen Novak, huh?"

"Yes."

"And this is the secret you've been withholding from me?"

"Yes."

She realized at once that her second yes had come too quickly, too eagerly. She should have hesitated just a little. Would he believe her?

He had stopped, swung around to fully confront her. Gillian held her breath as he searched her face in the glow from the illuminated fountain.

His nearness in this moment was seductive. She was far too aware of the heat of his hard body, of the way he leaned toward her with a yearning that, wise or not, she was prepared to answer.

"You're a remarkable woman, Gillian," he said in a lazy whisper, "one that I like very much."

The colored lights shifted over the fountain, its streams of water arcing into the night like fireworks. It was a dazzling display, and it was matched by their own splendor when he gathered her into his arms and began to kiss her.

Clinging to him, Gillian surrendered to the sweet sensations of his mouth melding with hers, of their breaths mingling as his tongue caressed her with warm, wet strokes.

As their kiss deepened, she savored his male scent in her nostrils, the clean taste of him inside her mouth.

But as rich as these sensations were, in the end they weren't enough. She found herself battling an unwelcome emotion that crept through her haze of pleasure. Frustration. The frustration of wanting to be possessed by him completely. And the fear of what that would involve, all the harsh complications she wasn't prepared to handle. It left her aching inside.

The terrible longing shattered when Cleve abruptly released her. Bewildered, she looked up into his face, seeking an explanation. But his alert gaze had turned away from her.

Swiveling her head, she discovered with a little gasp what he had already sensed with his honed skills. They weren't alone. There was movement off to the left of them. Before she could react, a tall, thin figure rushed toward them out of the darkness.

Cleve gripped her and thrust her behind his protective bulk. His other hand flashed toward the inside of his coat. Gillian knew what he was reaching for. She had felt the hard bulge there during their tight embrace. Had tried to pretend it didn't exist.

He was on the point of withdrawing the gun when another shadow flew toward the first one, calling out in a young woman's voice, "Come on, Quint, don't run off like that. I said I was sorry."

The tall, thin figure stopped and turned. His companion caught up with him. "Why do you have to be so touchy?" she complained.

There was a soft, murmured exchange, a forgiving laugh, and then the two lovers moved away from them. Gillian drooped with relief. There had been no need to panic. Victor Lassiter had not been stalking them. At least not on this occasion.

Cleve cursed savagely as his hand dropped away from his holstered revolver.

"Cleve, it's all right. Nothing happened."

"No, it isn't all right. I had no business bringing you out here like this, and I sure as hell had no business kissing you when I should have been looking for trouble. Come on, let's get back."

He grabbed her by the hand, pulling her in the direction of Michigan Avenue. Gillian, struggling to keep up with his swift stride, could feel his anger.

"This isn't going to happen again," he muttered.

His vehemence jolted her. He regretted their kiss, regarded it as both a weakness and a lesson. And now he was telling her there could be no further tender moments for them. They were dangerous. She knew he was right, but the realization left her with a gnawing ache.

You lost your head, Cleve raged at himself. *First it was that damn jealousy back in the ballroom when any man dared to look at her. Now this. What's wrong with you, anyway? You know the risk of getting involved with a client.* Yeah, but when that client was Gillian...

Forget it. You don't touch her again, even if she is driving you wild.

It's this tension, he tried telling himself. Waiting for Lassiter to strike. Cleve found himself wishing Victor would make a move so he could take care of him and go home to his lake and his woods. He needed to get out of this town before he no longer wanted to leave.

Chapter Five

There was a solemn expression on Gail Sanchez's face when she appeared in Gillian's office early Monday morning.

"Problem?" Gillian asked, looking up from the brief she was composing.

"John spotted this in his newspaper," Gail said, referring to one of the firm's legal secretaries. "I thought you'd better see it before one of the partners discovers it and starts asking questions."

Her petite assistant reluctantly placed a folded copy of the *Examiner* on Gillian's desk, pointing to a circled item in one of the paper's popular gossip columns. She waited quietly while Gillian read the piece.

Chicago's movers and shakers gathered Saturday night at the Hutton for a fund-raiser that proved more entertaining than fund-raisers are supposed to be. Gillian Randolph, our personal candidate for sexiest lawyer of the year, was heard to blast her favorite opponent, Charles Reardon, in a gutsy face-off. No question now of how she feels about this guy. Who said fireworks like that only happen in the courtroom?

Gillian slid the newspaper back across the desk. "It's an exaggeration," she said angrily, "but one I don't need right now."

Not when she had Victor Lassiter to worry about, she thought. And not when the conservative senior partners in her firm were already nervous about her contest with Reardon and his company.

"What is it?" Cleve demanded, immediately sensing the stress in her office when he appeared in the doorway, bearing a cup of coffee he had just fetched for himself from the machine down the hall.

Gail handed him the newspaper before turning back to Gillian. Her loyal assistant was prepared to comfort her, but Cleve stopped the woman after scanning the item.

"Gail, why don't you take me down to the lobby and introduce me to the daytime guards? I haven't had a chance to check out the building's security yet."

Gillian was grateful for his suggestion. He wisely understood that she didn't want to pursue the subject.

Cleve and Gail headed for the elevator, leaving her alone. Ignoring the sound of the jackhammers below her window, where the street was being repaired, she made an effort to return to the brief she was preparing. This whole silly thing about her quarrel with Charles Reardon was better forgotten.

But, as she learned a few moments later, that wasn't going to be possible. Her phone rang. Picking up the receiver, she identified herself with a pleasant, "Gillian Randolph."

"It's me, Gillian," said a woman's voice.

For a second she was unable to recognize the caller, probably because there was such an unfamiliar note of anxiety in her tone. Then she realized who it was. Her client, Maureen Novak.

"What's wrong, Maureen? You sound worried."

"I guess maybe I am a bit." She hesitated, then went on in a halting manner that indicated her discomfort. "I...well, I saw the story in the *Examiner* this morning, and—"

"You're upset about it. Maureen, it doesn't mean anything."

"I know." She paused again. "The thing is, it got me to thinking about the lawsuit. Gillian, I'm not sure anymore that I'm doing the right thing. Maybe I should just forget the suit and accept what they're offering. I mean, this is all getting to be so complicated."

Gillian removed her reading glasses and spoke earnestly into the phone. "Maureen, if you want to drop the suit, that's entirely your decision, and I promise you that I'll respect your choice. But we ought to sit down and talk about this face-to-face before you make up your mind, and I think we should do it right away."

"I guess that would be a good idea, only I can't leave work." Maureen had a job with the park district.

"Come in after work, then. I'll be here in my office for you as late as you need."

"That's no good, either. I'm heading home at noon. I've got this miserable cold, and I just have to take it to bed for a few hours before the kids get back from the sitter."

"No wonder you sound a little raspy."

"Summer colds are the worst. I wouldn't have come in at all today, but we're shorthanded with people on vacation, and the boss really needs this job finished."

"Then why don't I come to you? Would there be any objection to our talking while you work?"

Maureen sounded relieved by her suggestion. "No, that would be great, only I hate to inconvenience you."

"You're not inconveniencing me. This is too important to you not to sort it out immediately. Where are you this morning?"

"At the top of the Lincoln Park rain forest grooming plants."

"I'll find you. Look for me in about a half hour or so."

Gillian was clearing her desk when her assistant returned. "Gail, I have to go up to Lincoln Park to see Maureen Novak. I don't have any appointments here until eleven. I'll be back before then, but if I should get delayed—"

"Whoa," came a gruff interruption from the doorway behind Gail. "You're not going anywhere. Are you forgetting there's a lunatic out there just waiting for a chance to make you his target?"

Gillian fought her exasperation as Cleve strolled back into her office and perched on the edge of her desk.

"Cleve, I have a job, and I can't do it by hiding out in my apartment and my office." She explained about her need to meet with Maureen.

"Fine. *We'll* go together, but only after I make sure that Lassiter is busy elsewhere. Gail, I left my cell phone in my car. Can I use the phone on your desk while you and Gillian finish up in here?"

He was giving her no choice, just as he had given her no choice yesterday. She had spent all of Sunday with the dog in her locked apartment while he had been out most of the day renewing valuable contacts, one of whom was a bellboy at the Hutton Hotel. The bellboy, whose name was Sammy, had been able to verify for him that Victor Lassiter was legitimately employed by the hotel. Sammy had explained to Cleve that the hotel was always in need of waiters and that Lassiter apparently had some experience. Anyway, the director of food services had taken a chance on him, though the grapevine said he was strictly on trial.

Gillian suspected Cleve's Sunday errands had been a convenient reason to avoid her. Of course, whenever he regarded it as necessary, like now, he stayed physically close to her. But since Saturday night and that episode at

Buckingham Fountain, he'd maintained a determined emotional distance.

Gillian knew it was all for the best, except it did hurt. But where Cleveland McBride was concerned, that was nothing new.

She was putting her signature on a letter of opinion when Cleve came striding back into her office.

"My bellboy tells me Lassiter is on duty at the hotel at least through noon, so I guess we don't have a problem there."

She thought he almost sounded disappointed that Victor wouldn't be lurking somewhere up in Lincoln Park just waiting to grab her.

"I'll drive," he insisted.

She'd been afraid of that. It meant another perilous ride in that lethal machine of his. But there was no sense in complaining about any of it. After all, he was only doing what she'd hired him to do. She just wished he would be a little less overbearing about it. And much less attractive.

THE DRIVE to Lincoln Park, which stretched for several miles along the lakefront north of the Loop, was uneventful, unless you chose to count a near miss with a CTA bus. Gillian did. When they arrived in the park, she controlled an urge to kneel down and kiss the pavement of the parking lot. Instead, as they left the car and headed along the sidewalk, she explained to Cleve, "Maureen works as a gardener for the park district."

"So just where is she working today?"

"In there," she said as they emerged from a grove of trees that had screened their destination from view.

Cleve stopped on the walk, staring at the soaring structure she indicated. All glass in a steel framework, it was a massive, multistoried geodesic dome.

"When did *that* get built?"

"It opened just this spring."

"Turn your back on this town for a few months," he grumbled, "and the whole place gets reinvented. And you wonder why I like my wilderness."

Maybe he did, she thought, but Cleve had always had a love-hate relationship with Chicago. She found herself silently hoping that hadn't changed, while at the same time she was afraid to wonder why it should matter to her so much.

"Looks like a damn mountain," he said as they approached the enormous conservatory.

"That's just what it is. It simulates a tropical rain forest from a valley to a peak, with all the levels of growth in between. I know the city already has its share of conservatories, but this is a very popular exhibit."

"In January maybe."

He was right. The area was completely deserted. With Chicago in the grip of a heat wave, a sweltering tropical forest under glass was the last place anyone wanted to visit.

Cleve felt himself wilting in the blast of heavy, humid air that met them as they entered the dome through a pair of glass doors. The temperature outside was bad enough. In here it was almost unbearable.

The lush growth that surrounded them, with its ranks of palms, thick crotons and sprawling liana vines, made him think of a primeval jungle. He wouldn't have been surprised to see a dinosaur emerging from behind a tree fern.

There was a stillness in the place that had him feeling he was violating something sacred when he observed to Gillian, "Nobody here. Where's your client?"

"Up on the summit."

He groaned inwardly at her indication of the wide ramp that ascended in gradual stages through the luxuriant vegetation, twisting toward the faraway top of the dome in a series of switchbacks.

"No elevator, I suppose."

"Afraid not." She smiled at him. "Think of it as a horticultural adventure."

What he actually thought was unmentionable as they mounted the long, winding ramp. The palms and jade vines gave way to ficus, bamboo and swarms of orchids. The air, rich with the odors of moss and damp earth, seemed to sweat. It was hard to breathe.

They must have traveled a third of the distance to the mountain's peak when, without warning, the pain exploded deep inside Cleve's skull. For a stunned moment, struggling against the sudden raging in his ears, he refused to believe it was true.

This wasn't supposed to happen! Not after all this time, not when he had cured himself back at the lake!

But his angry denial was useless. It couldn't stop the war inside his head, which must have been triggered by a combination of the intense heat and the exertion of their climb.

But what difference did it make why it was happening? All that mattered now was the outcome. Because if this attack followed its old pattern, and he knew it would if he tried to go on, it would result in another of his humiliating blackouts.

Coming to a stop, he seized the handrail to steady himself. She spoke to him, her voice seeming to come from a long distance away.

"Are you all right?"

"Yeah," he managed to answer. With an effort, he found a handkerchief in his pocket, using their halt as an excuse to mop at the moisture dripping from his brow.

Silently cursing his weakness, he searched for a reason not to push on to the top of the dome. If he stayed where he was and remained quiet, the warning inside his head would fade and go away. The hammers were already easing.

"The way we came in down there," he said slowly. "That the only entrance?"

"As far as I know."

"Look, you don't need me up on top. I think I'll go back there and cover those doors. Just to make sure the wrong person doesn't wander in here while we're not looking."

He could tell by the way she gazed at him that she was a little surprised by his intention, but she made no objection.

"I won't be long," she told him.

He watched her until she moved out of sight around a leafy bend. Then he sat down on the curb of the ramp, hating his sense of helplessness as he waited for her.

The storm in his head rapidly retreated. It hadn't been a serious attack. *This* time. What worried him was the next time. How would he deal with it? Because he *had* to deal with it. He refused to desert Gillian.

GILLIAN WAS MORE than halfway up the man-made mountain when she was startled by the sudden hum of machinery. It wasn't until fog began to rise through the vegetation that she realized the climate-controlled dome was equipped with an automatic misting apparatus. Its timers must have kicked in.

The place already felt like a giant sauna, but the machines continued to pump out humidity as she moved on. The fog thickened around her until the plants on both sides of the ramp were no more than pale ghosts.

The stuff was blinding by now, and when Gillian blundered into a wet eucalyptus she came to a stop. Except for the hiss of the escaping mist, there was an eerie silence in the vast hothouse. A little nervous about it, she lifted her head and called out toward the upper reaches of the dome.

"Maureen, it's Gillian. Are you there?"

There was a brief pause. And then the widow's voice,

muffled by the fog, floated down to her. "I'm here. Come on up."

"This fog—"

"It'll quit in a few minutes and clear off. Just stick with the walk, and you can't get lost."

Reassured, Gillian went on. But the drifting mist had been drawn upward, collecting at the top of the dome into a choking mass that left her completely disoriented as she neared the end of the ramp.

"Maureen, where are you? I can't see a—"

Something went off in the fog, bursting the silence. An alarming sound. In the next second, a figure that was no more than a phantom shape charged toward her. Dodging to one side in confusion, Gillian slammed up against the trunk of a tree. Then the figure was gone, disappearing into the wall of mist.

Someone was shouting from the lower depths of the dome. Cleve? She didn't answer him. She had lost the ramp. She needed first to regain the familiarity of the ramp. Searching for it, she struggled away from the tree, groping through the fog. Where was the pavement? Which way?

She plunged through the vegetation. And then she gasped as something huge and brilliantly red loomed out of the mist. It was nothing more harmful than a royal poinciana in full bloom. But in her panic it was a scarlet menace. What was happening here? *Why* was it happening?

Gillian backed away. She stumbled over something. A vine? No, it felt more like a log. Whatever it was, it cost her her balance. The next thing she knew she was on her hands and knees. And looking down on something else that was crimson. It was not an exotic flower this time.

The misting machines had shut down. The air was clearing. Gillian found herself staring at blood oozing up from a bullet hole in a man's chest. The thing over which she had stumbled was neither a vine nor a log. It was a body. The very dead body of Charles Reardon.

CLEVE KNEW gunfire when he heard it. Surging to his feet, he yelled for Gillian. But there was no answer from the top of the dome. He didn't hesitate. Drawing his revolver, he sped up the ramp.

He was wild with fear and worry. He should never have let her go on alone. If something had happened to her— *Don't think it. Don't even consider it.* But he found himself praying as he ran.

A second later he heard shrill cries from the summit. A woman's cries. "Hang on, Gillian!" he shouted. "I'm coming!"

His head was throbbing by the time he arrived at the top of the dome. He ignored the signs and by some miracle, or maybe it was pure willpower, he managed to resist a blackout.

Gulping mouthfuls of air to fortify himself, he looked around, searching for Gillian. The fog had cleared, but there was no sign of her. Nor any further cries.

And then, to his great relief, he located her on the other side of a feathery Cook pine. She was huddled down in a bed of some exotic plants. She looked unharmed, but there was a dazed expression on her face that scared the hell out of him. He learned why when he joined her. She was bending over the body of a man he recognized from Saturday night. Her old antagonist, Charles Reardon.

She surfaced from her shock when he crouched beside her, turning her head to gaze at him with an imploring expression in her violet eyes. "I think he must be dead," she whispered. "Cleve, is he dead?"

He didn't have to disturb the body to know that. Reardon's eyes were open, but they were sightless.

"I think it's safe to say that," he muttered.

He watched her look away from Reardon's blank stare, shuddering in horror. But this was no time to comfort her. If he was going to help her to survive this mess, he had to have some answers. Starting with the most urgent one.

"Gillian," he said grimly, "where's the gun that shot him?"

She stared at him, not understanding.

"Gillian, what did you do with the damn gun?"

She got to her feet, disbelief in her eyes. "You think *I* killed him."

He rose and faced her, tucking his revolver back into its belt holster. "Take it easy. I'm not accusing you of—"

"Yes, you are! You're saying I shot him!" She was clutching her purse, which she'd somehow managed to hang on to. Now she opened it and thrust it toward him, her voice angry, almost hysterical. "Why don't you look? Why don't you search inside? Then search me and everything around here to find the gun I must have hidden!"

Her skirt had dirt clinging to it. There was a smudge on her cheek, and her hair was damp with perspiration. She looked alone and defenseless. And he felt like a bastard for even considering the possibility that she had anything to do with Reardon's death. Before she could stop him, he took her into his arms.

"It's all right, sweetheart," he crooned. "Of course, you didn't kill him."

For a moment she resisted. Then she wilted against him, burying her face against his chest. And Cleve could suddenly feel nothing but an overwhelming longing to take care of her.

He went on holding her until she stopped trembling. Then he released her, took her hand, and drew her away from the body. When they were back on the flagged walkway she looked around, the frantic edge still in her voice.

"Maureen. Where's Maureen? She can explain what happened."

"She isn't here, Gillian. No one is here but us. That's why for a minute there I thought— Anyway, you can see that for yourself."

"But she was here a minute ago. She called down to me. You heard her call down." He was silent. "Cleve, you must have heard her."

"I was much farther down. I didn't hear anything until the shot."

Gillian remembered something. "There was someone who ran by me." She quickly explained about the figure in the fog. "You had to have seen whoever it was. They had to have passed you."

He shook his head. "No one passed me. I didn't see anyone."

"This is crazy. There *was* someone, and whoever it was must have killed Reardon."

"Man or woman?"

"I don't know, I couldn't tell."

She ran a hand through her hair, looking so distracted and anxious that he wanted to hold her again.

"We have to search," she said. "If the killer didn't pass you, that means he must have hidden somewhere in all this growth. Cleve, help me find him."

"Gillian, calm down. You're not thinking clearly. If he did hide until I passed him, then he's already slipped out of the place. And if he didn't manage to get away and has a gun—"

He paused, listening to the sound of car doors banging outside the dome. "I think," he continued wryly, "we don't have to bother searching in here. I think it's about to be done for us."

Taking her hand, he drew her over to the curving glass wall of the dome where they could look down on the parking lot below. There was a patrol car there. Two uniformed officers had just emerged from it and were heading toward the entrance to the conservatory.

"Looks like someone else heard that shot and called the cops," he muttered.

"Or," Gillian said, her voice slow and grave now, "the killer himself phoned them so that I would be caught here. Because I have this sudden, awful feeling that I've been set up. I can't prove anyone but me was with Charles Reardon when he was shot, can I? Cleve, I'm going to need a lawyer."

"Sweetheart," he reminded her gently, "you *are* a lawyer."

"I practice civil law. For the kind of trouble I'm about to face, I'll need a criminal lawyer. Our own Dan Weinstein is one of the best in the city. I don't think he'd hesitate to represent me."

It tore him up to see her like this, steeling herself for the worst. "Damn it, Gillian, don't talk like that. You haven't been accused of anything."

She turned her head to look at him, her face solemn. "But you almost accused me, didn't you? So how do you think the police down there are going to react?"

"I don't know, but whatever happens," he promised her fervently, "we'll beat it together."

Chapter Six

He smiled at her from his chair near the window. His name was Butch Costello. He had sandy hair and a freckled face, and he looked as harmless as a puppy. Gillian knew better.

Lieutenant Costello was the homicide detective assigned to handle the investigation of Charles Reardon's murder. She was composed as she faced him from where she sat on the sofa. Inwardly, however, she was badly shaken by the situation.

"I sure appreciate your agreeing to meet with me like this, Ms. Randolph. I'll try not to take any more of your time than absolutely necessary."

It was midafternoon. They were gathered in Dan Weinstein's paneled office down the hall from Gillian's at the firm.

"This is an informal interview, Lieutenant," Dan reminded the detective from behind his desk. "When it begins to sound in any way like an official interrogation, the session is over."

"Wouldn't dream of it being anything else," the plain-clothesman agreed.

The lawyer, dark, good-looking, and impeccably dressed, turned to Gillian. He had heard her story this morning and already advised her, but now he cautioned again, "If there

is any question you don't want to answer, or I tell you not
to answer—"

"I know. It's all right, Dan. I want to cooperate. I want
this all cleared up as soon as possible."

The detective offered her another smile, produced a notebook, and reviewed with them the statement she and Cleve
had earlier given the two uniformed officers on the scene.
Polite almost to the point of exaggeration, Costello kept
thanking her for her assistance as he verified the statement.
And all the while Gillian had a sick feeling at the bottom
of her stomach.

That she was the chief suspect, even though she had been
released from the murder scene, she didn't doubt. The detective's lack of interest in Cleve, who shared the sofa with
her, told her that much. Costello's attention was focused
entirely on her.

As for Cleve, who was squeezed close beside her...
Well, she'd never been more grateful for his nearness. Nor
more worried by his tense silence.

"McBride, unless a question is directed at you," Dan
had instructed Cleve before the homicide detective's arrival, "I want your promise you won't say anything. Not a
word. Let me and Gillian handle it, please."

Gillian understood the reason for the lawyer's request.
Cleve had been seething for hours over his failure to accompany her to the top of the dome, damning himself for
her plight. The lawyer was afraid he was in a mood that
could result in an aggressive outburst.

Because she trusted Dan, Gillian had urged Cleve to
comply. He had, grudgingly, but she could tell by the way
he was squirming now on the sofa that his promise was
costing him a considerable effort. She wondered how long
he could maintain his self-control.

The lieutenant looked up from the notebook. "Is this all
correct, Ms. Randolph?"

"Yes, except I'd like to emphasize that I wasn't alone with Charles Reardon at the top of the dome. Someone else was definitely up there in that fog with me."

Costello nodded thoughtfully. "The alleged killer. How do you figure this individual managed to get away, Ms. Randolph?"

Gillian knew the detective must have already considered every possibility himself, but she dutifully answered his question. "He could have hidden behind the thick growth of vegetation until he saw his chance to slip out, or—"

"What, Ms. Randolph?"

"There are venting hatches everywhere up there. I noticed them just after the two officers arrived. The murderer could have escaped that way and climbed down the steel framework of the dome." She leaned forward earnestly. "And I'll tell you something else. I think Charles Reardon must have been dead already when Cleve and I arrived at the dome. Otherwise, I would have heard more than I did."

"So that would make the gunshot you and Mr. McBride did hear mean—what?"

Cleve started to growl something, but Dan sent him a stern look and smoothly answered the question for them. "I think that's obvious, Lieutenant. It was probably intended to implicate Ms. Randolph while she was on the scene."

"It's possible," the detective agreed soberly. "Everything you suggest is very possible."

But Gillian feared he wasn't serious about any part of her conjecture. That he believed there had been no phantom figure in the fog. That she'd been alone with Reardon and that she had shot him. He hinted as much by what he said next.

"Of course, it's also possible the killer used one of those vents to get rid of the murder weapon. It could have been thrown out into the shrubbery and then retrieved afterward and taken away while the two officers were busy securing and searching the interior. What do you think?''

Dan's gaze this time warned both Gillian and Cleve not to respond. She could feel Cleve's mounting frustration.

The detective made a soft sucking sound with his tongue against his teeth as he looked down, consulting his notebook again. Then he flashed her another smile. ''I was just checking on my information here. The bullet that killed Reardon came from a .40 caliber gun. Now this is the interesting part—purely coincidence, I know—but it seems you have a .40 caliber semiautomatic Glock registered in your name, Ms. Randolph.''

Cleve stiffened on the sofa, prepared to angrily defend her. But Dan checked him again, this time with a satisfyingly sharp, ''You're crossing boundary lines here, Lieutenant. Gillian, I'm instructing you not to—''

''I need to settle this,'' she insisted. ''Lieutenant, I do have such a gun, and there's a very good reason why I bought it.'' She explained about Victor Lassiter. The detective expressed no surprise. He had obviously made himself familiar with this aspect of the case as well.

''But I can easily prove my gun was in no way involved in Charles Reardon's death,'' she continued. ''The gun is locked away in the glove compartment of my car, which is also locked. The car is in the parking garage downstairs and hasn't been out of its space since Friday morning.'' Opening her purse, she removed her keys and dangled them in front of her.

''What are you telling me to do, Ms. Randolph?'' he asked, wanting to be clear about her request.

''You have an officer with you waiting outside. I'd like you to send him down to the garage to get the gun. Then I want you to have it checked. A test will show the bullet that shot Reardon couldn't possibly have come from my semiautomatic.''

"You're sure about this, Ms. Randolph?"

"I am. Tell him it's the green Volvo on the far end."

Dan offered no further objection, but the look on his face told Gillian that he strongly disapproved of her action. Costello came forward, accepted her keys, and left the office to instruct the other man standing by in the reception area.

He was scarcely out of the room when Cleve exploded. "Damn it all to hell, Weinstein, he's trying to trap her! The guy means to crucify her, and you—"

"Cleve, please," Gillian begged. "I know what I'm doing. And, Dan, I realize you don't like it, but I have to give them the gun. It could be the one thing that puts me in the clear."

But her confidence was less certain when the detective reappeared. While they waited for the officer to return from the parking garage, he challenged her in another direction.

"I hate to keep making this more and more complicated, Ms. Randolph, but it seems there's another problem. We found and talked to Maureen Novak after you gave us your statement and, according to her, she never phoned you this morning to meet her."

Gillian wasn't in the least surprised. She had decided long before this that Maureen herself was in no way connected with the murder, but she had been reluctant to involve her client before it became absolutely necessary. It had just become necessary.

"And you're going to tell me she was nowhere near the dome, either."

He nodded with a reluctance that was less than genuine. "Afraid I have to. She's been working all day over in the formal gardens, right beside four other gardeners. So, who do you suppose it was that did phone you, Ms. Randolph?"

"The same person," she said decisively, "who called down to me from the top of the dome, pretending to be Maureen with a cold in case I wondered about the voice.

But why should I have been suspicious when he's always been able to use that voice and those hands to convince his audiences he's a woman, a child, even an animal? Oh, I know who it was all right, Lieutenant. I've had nothing but time since this morning to figure out exactly how foolish I've been.''

"And who was it, Ms. Randolph?"

"Victor Lassiter."

"The man you believe is stalking you."

"Yes."

He nodded slowly, considering her information. Gillian could tell by the faint curve of his mouth that he thought her claim was the far-fetched invention of a desperate woman. And how could she prove Victor *had* pretended to be Maureen when there was no one to corroborate her assertion? She was the only one who had heard the phone call this morning, as well as the voice at the top of the dome.

"Wouldn't you say this stretches the imagination a little?" the detective said.

The faint curve on his mouth widened into a full smile. A scornful one. And Cleve was no longer able to hold his fuming silence. Springing to his feet before Dan could stop him, he blew up like a boiler.

"Maybe it's time that closed mind of yours went to work, Costello, and came up with the full story!"

"Like what?"

"Like Lassiter determined to pin this murder on Gillian! Like his hearing enough of the exchange between her and Reardon at the Hutton Saturday night to invent this whole setup! And here's something else for your imagination to chew on! Maybe, just maybe, Lassiter learned Maureen Novak's voice by posing as a phone salesman! I don't know about you, Costello, but the rest of us get calls like that so often we don't think anything about them! Probably wouldn't even realize if they were being recorded!''

"And what else do you think my imagination needs to know?'' the lieutenant asked him dryly.

"That he could have lured Charles Reardon to that conservatory the same way he got Gillian to go up there. Phoning Reardon and pretending to be Maureen Novak, maybe offering to settle behind Gillian's back. Reardon would have gone for that.''

"And all this would have happened after Victor Lassiter practiced Mrs. Novak's voice from—what was it you said, Mr. McBride? A recording from a bogus phone marketing conversation?''

"Yeah, why not? And before you call any of this a fairy tale, Lieutenant, maybe you'd better check on Lassiter's alibi for this morning. Could be he wasn't on duty at the hotel like he was supposed to be. That is, if it's not too much to ask of your imagination.''

"Oh, it isn't, Mr. McBride.'' The smirk left his mouth, his freckled face hardened. "Because someone else in the department is handling that check for me right now.''

The door opened. The officer sent to the garage for the gun poked his head in. Lieutenant Costello excused himself and went out again to join him in the reception area. There was a taut silence in the office while they waited for his return.

The detective reappeared. He was empty-handed. "The officer searched your car carefully, Ms. Randolph,'' he reported soberly. "Your semiautomatic isn't there, and there is no sign of any break-in.''

Gillian stared at him in dismay. "It isn't possible. I—''

She didn't go on. What could she say? She had no proof that she had locked the gun in the glove compartment and hadn't touched it in days. And she knew her word wasn't enough.

The missing gun was a major blow to her courage. She felt suddenly as though a net had been dropped over her head and was slowly, relentlessly tightening around her.

His tone still grave, the detective asked her, "Do you have any idea where that gun is now, Ms. Randolph?"

"Lassiter, of course!" Cleve thundered. "Who else would have it? I don't care what your man didn't see down there. Lassiter must have found a way to enter the car and—"

He was interrupted by the ring of a cell phone. The detective removed the compact instrument from his pocket, flipped it open, and took the call. Gillian sat there numbly while the lieutenant listened, murmuring only occasional responses into the mouthpiece.

His expression was still solemn when he ended the call. "That was my partner over at the Hutton. Victor Lassiter has been there all day. He never once left the hotel. Which means he had no opportunity to kill Charles Reardon and, as far as I can see, no motive, either. On the other hand, Ms. Randolph, you—"

"Don't go any further, Lieutenant," Dan cut him off, "unless you're prepared to bring charges now. Because whatever you might have learned about Ms. Randolph's exchange with Reardon at the fund-raiser Saturday night, it does not constitute a motive."

"She was heard threatening him."

"With civil action, not murder."

Gillian held her breath in the long pause that followed. She released it with relief when the detective answered Dan's ultimatum with a quiet, "Relax, Mr. Weinstein. No one here is getting his rights read to them."

He didn't add, "Not yet, anyway." But his tone implied it. Gillian knew she was far from safe.

"Then this interview is ended," Dan said.

Costello got to his feet. "Whatever you say, counselor.

Just be sure your client stays available." He turned to Cleve with another of his deceptively friendly smiles. "Guess I don't need to remind you, McBride, that your P.I. license doesn't entitle you to interfere in our investigation."

"I'll try to keep that in mind, Lieutenant, if you'll do me a favor on your way out."

"What's that?"

"Don't tell us to have a good day."

When the detective had departed, Gillian rose from the sofa and walked over to the window where she stared down at the street repairs. "It doesn't look too good for me, does it, Dan?"

"It isn't that bad, Gillian," the lawyer tried to reassure her. "If he had any kind of worthwhile case, he would have come here with a warrant for your arrest or at least brought you in for questioning. Without any actual witness or the murder weapon, he doesn't have a case strong enough to bring to the prosecution."

"But he thinks I did it, and he'll try to prove it."

"Not without solid evidence," he insisted, and then frowned. "But I'm not happy about that missing gun of yours."

"I know. And I made it worse for myself by trying to produce the gun, but I never dreamed..." She laughed self-mockingly. "Sorry, Dan. It seems I didn't know what I was doing, after all. Have I gone and incriminated myself?"

"That depends on what happens if, and when, that gun turns up."

She nodded, then turned her head as she felt Cleve's intense gaze on her. His tawny eyes told her he needed to be alone with her. Dan didn't miss the message he silently conveyed. Offering a hasty excuse, the lawyer rounded his desk and left the office.

When the door had closed behind him, Cleve approached

her at the window. "I didn't want Weinstein hearing what I plan to do. What he doesn't know he can't object to."

She lifted her gaze to his face, searching his craggy features and understanding. "You're going after my missing gun."

"Remember how I swore to you back in the dome that we'd beat this thing?"

She hadn't forgotten. Even though gripped by fear and bewilderment in that moment, she had been deeply moved by the fierceness of his promise. "I remember," she said.

"So it's the gun that could help us to do that. Yeah, I think I need to find that gun."

"Why? You're not suggesting that, if we do manage to get our hands on it, we destroy it so it can't be used as evidence against me? Because if that is what you mean to do, I won't—"

"Who said anything about that? I just think we have to begin with the gun. We need to learn how damning a piece of evidence it is. Hell, we don't even really know if it was the murder weapon."

Gillian wasn't sure she liked his intention. "Why do you have to hunt for it? I can't imagine Lieutenant Costello won't be doing that himself."

"Sure, if he manages to get a search warrant he'll be looking for it. In your office here and then in your apartment. Probably everywhere but where he should be looking. Because we both know Victor Lassiter has the gun, and if we can prove it by locating it in his possession, then maybe Costello will start to listen."

Cleve paused, his brow furrowing in puzzlement. "Thing I can't figure out is why he'd risk hanging on to it. If he managed to get it out of your car, then why not put it back in your car after he shot Reardon? Assuming, that is, his motive is to have the murder pinned on you."

Gillian didn't answer him. He noticed she was gazing

into the street again, only she wasn't seeing the street repairs. There was a faraway look in her eyes.

"I understand it now," she said softly.

"What?"

"The expression on Victor's face Saturday night after he overheard me warning Charles Reardon. I didn't know what it meant then. Now it's clear. He was gloating. He recognized the opportunity he's been waiting for, and he was gloating."

"Have I missed something here?"

She turned to him. "Cleve, don't you see what he wants? Not to stalk and kill me. That was never it. He means for me to go to prison for the murder of Charles Reardon, just as he went to prison. That's what his revenge is all about."

"Okay, let's say it is his motive. But why all the rest? The snapshot he sent to you, the mutilated puppet, the graffiti on your door. And why is he holding back the gun?"

"Because he's a showman. A twisted one who understands that a climax is only successful if you've carefully built the suspense leading to it. That's what he's doing, building the suspense by tormenting me. Just like a matador playing with a wounded bull before the final—" She broke off, chilled by the deadly image.

"We can't let him do that, Gillian," he told her grimly. "We have to fight back."

She nodded decisively. "You're right. The gun needs to be recovered. But Lieutenant Costello... You heard him, Cleve. If you interfere in the investigation, you risk losing your license."

"Bull. The Chicago P.D. can't touch my license. The state issued it, and only the state can revoke it. There's only one thing that worries me."

"And that would be?"

"Working in the dark. I don't like it. Not one damn bit.

So what are you still not telling me about this case, Gillian? Because I can feel there's something.''

"Not again," she said impatiently. "I thought we settled this. I thought after Saturday night, when we walked out to Buckingham Fountain and I told you about Maureen—"

"That I'd be satisfied? You were wrong."

He hated to get tough with her. Not when she was like this, scared and vulnerable because of what was happening to her. But if he was going to save her, he had to know everything.

"Maureen Novak wasn't your secret. Come on, Gillian," he demanded, "what are you holding back?"

"Nothing! And you can just stop harassing me about it!"

There were glints of fire in those incredible violet eyes that glared at him. He glowered back at her, feeling the anger that palpitated from both of them. It was exciting, maybe because he was so aware of that other powerful emotion that constantly sizzled between them, like the relentless, sultry heat of the city. He knew with a smoldering certainty that they would have to do something about it one day. But until then...

"I guess," he relented, "I must have been imagining there was something. Sorry."

She visibly relaxed. "The gun," she reminded him, eager to change the subject. "Where are you going to look for it?"

"I'll start with the obvious, at Lassiter's address."

"Do you even know where he's living since he got out?"

"Not yet, but give me a phone call or two and I'll find out. It's amazing what you can dig up under the Freedom of Information Act. There are all kinds of sources out there a P.I. learns to access. And while I'm at it, I'll check in with my bellboy at the Hutton. Because if Lassiter is still on duty over there, it's an opportunity to visit his place while he's out of the way.''

He moved toward the phone on Dan's desk. Gillian headed for the door.

"I'll be in my office while you're making those calls. If we're going out again, I need to check my calendar to be sure I'm clear for the rest of the day.''

Cleve swiftly stopped her. "I think one of us isn't communicating here. *I'm* going out. I'm hunting for the gun. You're staying put.''

She paused at the door and turned. "I am not going to let you to go alone to Victor's place. Even if he is elsewhere, it's dangerous. You'll need me as a lookout while you search.''

"The only danger involved is getting caught and being charged with breaking and entering. I don't want you risking that.''

"Cleve, I've got a murder charge staring me in the face. Do you think I'm worried about a misdemeanor?''

"Then worry about your workload here. You said this morning you had a heavy one, remember?''

Gillian left the door and joined him at the desk. He recognized the signs of battle. Her head was angled to one side, and she wore that sweet little smile on her mouth that said somebody was in for trouble.

"I seem to remember something else from this morning,'' she said in a tone that was deceptively pleasant. "Something you reminded me of just a minute ago. About us beating this thing together. Wasn't that the word you used, Cleve? *Together.*''

"Yeah, but—''

"It's my fight, too, and that means I'm going to be there for it. Not cowering somewhere behind a locked door just so you can congratulate yourself that the little lady is safe.

Now, does that settle the issue, or do you want to go on debating the case?''

"Uh, I guess not. I guess this is a decision in your favor, counselor.''

"Thank you, your honor. Now make your calls.''

She was one hell of a woman, Cleve thought with a grin as he watched her leave the office, her pleated skirt swinging around a pair of legs that gave him any number of wicked ideas. But then, when hadn't he had those kinds of ideas about her? In fact, they were as strong now, maybe even stronger, than during those exciting weeks they had once shared.

Funny, he thought, that that past should continue to matter so much when it had been so long ago. But their time together, however brief and distant, had made such an impact on him that he was still carrying the emotional baggage from it.

Then why, he wondered, as he had so many times since that summer, had she walked out on him without an explanation? The puzzle continued to haunt him. He remembered how he had reluctantly left her in Chicago for a couple of days, working at her father's firm, while he handled an investigation downstate. When he'd returned, eager to see her, the receptionist had told him that Gillian was no longer at the firm and had left town. No other details.

Cleve had been stunned and then frantic. That's when Harmon Randolph, just back from an extended vacation with Gillian's mother, had appeared and taken him into his office.

"Cleve, I'm sorry,'' he'd informed him gently. "Gillian accepted an invitation from friends to spend what's left of the summer in Europe before she starts college in the fall. No, I don't know why she didn't tell you herself. I assumed she had.''

Her sudden, silent departure had been an agonizing blow.

Her father's disapproval, had it existed, might have offered an explanation. But Harmon Randolph probably hadn't learned of their relationship until his recent return to Chicago. He might have objected, among other things, to the age difference between Cleve and his daughter.

But the lawyer had been nothing but kind about Cleve's loss. He'd even provided him with a phone number and an address where Gillian might be reached. Cleve had made every effort to contact her, but there had been no response. He'd been out of his mind for days, and the sympathetic lawyer, in an effort to ease his pain, had kept him busy with investigations for the firm.

Gradually, Cleve had accepted Gillian's disappearance from his life. But he never understood it. And why should he still wonder about it after all these years, continue to punish himself over it?

All right, he decided, reaching for the phone, so he had to stop tormenting himself about the past if he was going to help her in the present. And as for what had happened to him this morning inside the dome... Well, he wasn't going to worry about that, either. He was convinced it was an isolated attack because of the extreme conditions in there and that it wouldn't occur again. With any luck, that is.

GILLIAN STRUGGLED with a familiar guilt as she walked back to her office. She hated having lied again to Cleve about what she continued to withhold from him. She had no choice. She had sworn to keep it secret, and she was not going to violate that promise. But her silence was growing more difficult to obey.

She was at her desk when Mason Campbell strolled into her office. He was the head of the firm, balding and slightly stooped.

"Can I see you for a minute, Gillian?"

He wore a smile, except there was something in his tone

that made her uneasy. She invited him to sit down. He did and proceeded to tell her he'd just spoken to Dan. And now he wanted her to know that, of course, everyone in the firm was sympathetic and on her side, but...

Mason went on to gently, but very firmly, suggest she suspend her practice. "Just temporarily, you understand. Just until this little unpleasantness is cleared up." And naturally her colleagues down the hall would be happy to handle her cases for her until she returned.

Gillian got the message. She thought about getting angry, telling him how unfair he was being. But she was afraid of the result. She wasn't a full partner yet, and she didn't want to damage her position beyond all repair.

She compromised instead with a cool, "I'll consider it."

That seemed to satisfy him. For the moment.

Cleve arrived in her office, passing Mason on his way out. "We're all set," he reported cheerfully. "Lassiter is putting in an extra shift at the Hutton and shouldn't be home until late. While I was at it, I did my own check on his alibi with my contact. I wish I could say I found a big hole in it, but my trusty bellboy tells me it came from the director of food services himself and the guy has impressive credentials. All the same, Lassiter managed somehow to be where he wasn't supposed to be, and in the end we'll prove it. Oh, and I got his home address, too, so—" He stopped, suddenly aware of the frustrated expression on her face. "What's wrong?"

"I would say, conservatively speaking, that I am not having a good day." She told him about Mason's visit. Wryly, she added, "There's something to be said for the situation. Now I don't have to worry about that heavy workload. Providing, that is, I agree to the little vacation the firm wants me to take."

"Gillian, I'm sorry."

"It could be worse. At least I'm not being disbarred. But if I don't clear myself, that could happen, too." Grabbing her purse, she got to her feet, a look of determination on her face. "Come on, let's go find my gun."

Chapter Seven

"It's not the Ritz, is it?" Cleve observed.

"I don't suppose he can afford any better," Gillian murmured.

"Or maybe it just suits him."

The seedy residential hotel was across the street from where they sat in Cleve's car parked at the curb. Surveying the place with its stained brick and cracked windows, Gillian decided it looked like something scheduled for demolition. The multistoried structure, located in a neighborhood that had known better days, was backed up against the north branch of the Chicago River.

There was one redeeming feature, she noticed. The first-floor windows boasted flower boxes that were obviously someone's pride and joy.

"What are we waiting for?" she finally asked.

"For me to decide how to get Lassiter's room number without making someone suspicious."

"Then you didn't—"

"No, only the street address was available. Well," he determined, reaching for the door handle, "I guess the best thing is to just march in there and ask for it. In a place like that, nobody is going to care."

Gillian started to leave the car on her side, but Cleve stopped her. "You stay here until I get the room number."

"Why?"

"Because I may need you as a backup."

Before she could ask for a better explanation, he was out of the car and striding across the street. She watched him disappear into the hotel. Then she waited, trying not to be anxious.

The street was deserted, except for a pair of teenagers in-line skating just up the block. The August sun beat down on the pavement. The only relief was a gusty wind, but even that was hot.

It was stifling in the car, even with the windows rolled down all the way. Cleve had left the keys in the ignition. She was thinking about turning on the engine so she could run the air conditioner when he suddenly reappeared.

Sliding back behind the wheel, he turned to her. "Time to go to Plan B."

"In other words, somebody in there does care."

"Yeah, the desk clerk. She must be 102 and as mean as a pit bull. When I asked her for Lassiter's room number, she laughed. When I showed her my P.I. identification, she bared her teeth. Then when I offered her a twenty, she…"

"What?"

"Well, she was reading a paperback when I roused her out of that cubby behind the front desk. I think it must have been an old Mickey Spillane, because when I tried to bribe her she said, 'Take a hike, gumshoe.' Quaint, huh?"

"For a guard dog, yes. So, exactly what is Plan B?"

"Damned if I know. Let me think."

There was silence in the car as Cleve concentrated on the problem. She noticed after a moment that he was looking at the hotel's flower boxes. Then he eyed the teenagers, who were still racing along the sidewalk on their skates. After a few seconds, his attention shifted back to the flower boxes.

"Got an idea," he said. "It involves sending in the second team. That's you, Gillian."

She learned why he'd had the foresight to save her as a backup as he outlined his intention.

"Wait until I'm inside," he concluded. "Then go into action."

"But can you get back into the lobby without the guard dog seeing you?"

"I think so. She was pretty involved in that paperback. I'm about to find out, anyway."

He leaned over and removed a fistful of something from the glove compartment. Before she could tell what it was, he was out of the car again. She watched him as he crossed the street and approached the teenagers. The two youths looked interested as he engaged them in conversation. They looked even more interested when he produced his wallet and handed each of them a bill. A few seconds later, Cleve turned and flashed her a high sign. Then he slipped into the hotel.

Gillian rolled up the windows, snatched the keys from the ignition, and scrambled out of the car, locking it behind her. The teenagers were already in position below the flower boxes, gleeful grins on their faces as she passed them and entered the hotel.

The dim lobby, with its cheap, shabby furniture, was deserted. Or so it appeared. She trusted that Cleve was safely concealed somewhere close by, waiting for the desk clerk to be distracted so that he could streak behind the desk and examine the hotel's register.

The desk was in an alcove at one end of the lobby. There was a tiny office just behind it. The cubby that Cleve had described. She could see through its open door the massive girth of the clerk settled in a chair, her attention focused on the book in her hands.

Gillian approached the scarred counter. She had to clear

her throat twice to win the woman's reluctant attention. Finally heaving herself out of the chair, she waddled out to the desk growling an unfriendly, "Yeah?"

"Your window boxes out front."

"What about 'em?"

This was the crucial part. Cleve's device depended on just how much the guard dog cared about the preservation of those flowers.

"I just thought you'd like to know there are a couple of kids out there helping themselves to bouquets."

"What!"

For someone her size and age, the woman could move with the speed of an athlete. Galvanized by outrage, she rounded the desk and charged toward the front entrance. Gillian followed close behind her.

By the time they reached the street, the teenagers had helped themselves to armloads of the bright blooms. The elderly woman began yelling at them. For a moment or two they gave her a hard time, laughing and dodging around her on their blades. Then they skated away, the desk clerk shouting after them, "The next time I call the cops!"

Examining the damage to her flowers, she muttered an angry, "Damn delinquents. Nothing is sacred anymore."

She ignored Gillian and shambled back into the hotel without a word of thanks.

Gillian waited for a long minute on the sidewalk, giving the woman a chance to get settled again in her cubby. Then she slipped back into the lobby, praying the paperback thriller had reclaimed the woman's attention. It had. Gillian caught a glimpse of her through the open door of the office, her nose buried in the book, as she stole past her line of vision.

Off the back side of the lobby was a corridor safely out of sight of the desk. Reaching it, she looked for Cleve. He wasn't there. She started down the gloomy passage. No windows, and the silence was a little unnerving.

She was nearing the far end of the dark corridor when a hand shot out of nowhere, hauling her into an enclosure. She squealed in surprise.

"Quiet!" Cleve whispered. "You want someone to hear?"

She slapped his hand away, whispering back, "Then stop playing Phantom of the Opera!"

"I thought you saw me."

"I can't see anything. It's like a catacomb in here. Don't they believe in lightbulbs?"

"Yeah, about fifteen watts apiece."

"No wonder I'm stumbling around, on top of which my eyes are still adjusting from the sun outside. Where are we? Oh." She realized then that he had pulled her into an elevator. "Where are we going?"

"Room 823."

"Then you were able to—"

"Like candy from a baby."

He stabbed a button, and the door rumbled shut. The ancient elevator began to creak upward.

By the time the sluggish elevator delivered them to the eighth floor, Gillian was seeing well enough to notice the bulge in Cleve's pants pocket. He must have stuffed into it whatever he had taken from the glove compartment. Not his gun. That was still in his shoulder holster under his lightweight sport coat.

"This way," he said, consulting the room numbers as they left the elevator.

They met no one as they followed the corridor. The hall turned. They were at the back of the hotel now.

"This is it," Cleve announced, stopping at the door of 823. "Let's be sure no one is in there."

He rapped on the door. Silence. Then he tried it. Locked, of course.

"How do we get in?" Gillian wondered, fearing the noise of a break-in.

"They teach us in P.I. school how to pick locks."

"Uh-huh. Just like they teach us in law school how to chase ambulances."

"Relax. In an old dump like this, one of these should do the trick."

He withdrew the bulge from his pocket. It proved to be a bunch of keys of every size and shape.

"Standard P.I. issue," he explained with a straight face.

As he began fitting one key after another into the lock, none of which tumbled the mechanism, she cast nervous glances along the hallway, fearful of discovery. What if one of the other doors along here should burst open and someone emerge to challenge them? What if—

There was a sudden, satisfying click.

"Ah, that did it," he said, pushing the door inward.

"Very resourceful of you, detective."

"Thank you, counselor."

He led the way into Victor Lassiter's quarters. Checking the hallway one last time to be sure no one was observing them, she followed, closing the door softly behind her.

They stood there for a moment inside the entrance, listening. The place wore the silence of desertion. It was more than just a single room. There was a sitting room here with a simple kitchen facility at one end. Behind this Gillian could glimpse a bedroom and a bath. The apartment's furnishings were as dingy-looking as those in the lobby downstairs.

"Let's see what the bedroom offers first," Cleve suggested, moving in that direction.

His immediate interest in the bedroom was in the window that looked out from the back side of the hotel. Gillian understood why when she joined him at the dirty glass. Just outside, practically overhanging the river, was an old-fashioned iron fire escape zigzagging down to a narrow alley.

"Never hurts to learn your options *before* you're cornered," he said. "Guess there's no question we're in the right place." He indicated a battered desk.

Spread across its surface were the tools and materials of a craftsman engaged in the art of puppet making. In itself it was an innocent occupation. But remembering who this collection belonged to, and what she associated it with, Gillian shuddered. Her gaze moved away from the unhappy reminder, locating a more promising discovery.

"Look."

On a small table next to the desk was a telephone. Beside the phone was a tape recorder and a stack of cassettes. They were still sealed, except for the one on top which had been opened and used.

"You think maybe...?" he asked.

She was afraid to count on it. She watched hopefully as he seized the cartridge and popped it into the recorder, punching the play button. If the tape revealed a telephone conversation with Maureen Novak, it could be enough to convince Lieutenant Costello that Victor *had* used this method to study her voice.

They listened carefully. Nothing. Cleve kept trying, using the fast forward to check other sections of the tape. But all of it was blank.

"He's erased it," he muttered, removing the tape and placing it back on the stack.

"Why did we think he wouldn't have been smart enough to do just that?" she said in disappointment.

"Don't give up hope. Remember it's the semiautomatic we came here to find."

"Where do we look for it?"

"Everywhere. You start with the closet," he directed, "and I'll take the chest of drawers over there. And, Gillian?"

"Yes?"

"Be sure you leave everything just as you find it. We don't want Lassiter knowing anyone was here if we can possibly avoid it."

She tried to obey his instruction as she thoroughly investigated the closet. It wasn't easy. Her emotions got in the way. She disliked handling Victor's belongings and was positively squeamish about the necessity of sliding her hands into the pockets of his clothes.

The contents of the closet were meager. He hadn't been out of prison long enough to accumulate much of a wardrobe. She finished with everything on the hangers, but there remained the shelf. It was too high for her to inspect the back of it. She'd need the desk chair to stand on.

Gillian started to drag the chair into position. But in her nervous haste, she lost her grip on it. It overturned, clattering on the floor. In the silence of the apartment it sounded like an explosion to her. She stared at Cleve in alarm.

"What if someone heard?" she whispered.

"So what? People drop things all the time."

"Not when they're not supposed to be at home. I'm sorry," she apologized. "I guess I'm not very good at this. I keep thinking that we're going to be discovered."

He nodded understandingly. "All right, maybe it's better if I handle the search while you play lookout."

Grateful for his suggestion, she left the bedroom and posted herself at the entrance to the apartment, cracking the door so she could hear if anyone approached. No one did. The hall outside remained quiet and empty.

The tense minutes passed as Cleve continued with the

search behind her. How long did it take to examine two small rooms and a bath?

He finally joined her at the door, shaking his head. "I've looked into everything, including light fixtures and the toilet tank. I guess we couldn't have expected it to be that easy, but I swear he's hiding the gun somewhere, just waiting to spring it."

It was another disappointment, but Gillian would deal with it later. Right now all she could think about was getting out of the apartment.

"Can we go?" she urged him.

"Yeah."

"Maybe," he said, "I haven't looked into absolutely everything."

"Cleve—"

"Just hang on for a second. I'm going to have a look inside that TV."

She watched apprehensively as he went to the television set. There was a thin manila file folder resting on top of the instrument. When he shifted the set around in order to reach its back side, the folder slid to the floor, strewing its contents across the frayed carpet.

"You'll never get that stuff back into the folder in the order it was arranged before," she cautioned him. "If he notices, he *will* realize someone was here."

"Can't be helped at this point."

Ignoring the spilled papers, Cleve used his pocketknife to remove the panel at the back of the television. He leaned over, peering into the set while she waited hopefully.

"Anything?"

He made a sound of disgust that told her he hadn't located the gun. "That's it, then," he said.

Replacing the panel, he crouched down and began to collect the scattered contents of the file. Gillian turned away to check the hall again through the cracked door. There was a sudden stillness behind her, and then he called to her, a note of excitement in his voice.

"We didn't find the gun, but I think we've discovered something just as good. Take a look at these."

Leaving the door ajar, she joined him on the other side of the room. He showed her the collection as she knelt beside him on the carpet where they spoke in hushed tones.

"He's been keeping a file on you. Clippings that go back years."

Gillian leafed through them in wonder. She was certainly no celebrity, but from time to time her legal crusades had earned her mentions in the newspapers. No matter how obscure the item, Victor had saved it, including an article she'd written for a professional journal.

"This proves he has been stalking me."

"Better than that," Cleve said. "Look at the ones that involve Charles Reardon and Maureen Novak. If our friend from homicide isn't interested in those, then I'm—"

"Wait!" she commanded, silencing him.

Lifting her head, she listened. Then, shoving the clippings into his hands, she got to her feet and rushed to the door. She could see through the slit that the hall was still empty. But no longer silent. Someone was around the corner where the corridor turned on its way to the elevator. Someone whose smooth, familiar voice chilled her.

"What are you doing out here, kitty? Are you lost? Yes, I know, you're looking for attention. You're a pretty kitty, aren't you? Yes, you are. All right, just a little rubbing, and that's all you're going to…"

Gillian squeezed the door shut, managing to make no sound, and flew back across the room where Cleve was standing, the restored file in his hand.

"It's Victor!" she whispered in a panic.

"What the hell is he doing back here when he was supposed to—"

"What difference does it make why he's home early? We have to get out of here!"

"Take it easy. We're not trapped. That's what the fire escape is for, remember?"

With Cleve at her heels, Gillian tore into the bedroom. The tall window looking out on the fire escape had a lock, which she snapped open without an effort. But the window itself was stuck, resisting her struggles to raise it.

"Here, let me," he commanded.

She stepped aside, giving him access to the stubborn sash. Gripping the handles while holding the file between his teeth, he exerted his strength and heaved. The window went up like a shot, the glass shivering in the frame.

Cleve swung himself through the opening and turned to help her out. She glanced swiftly back over her shoulder. She could glimpse the hall door in the sitting room. To her relief, it was still closed. Then, taking his hand and ducking her head, she scrambled onto the fire escape.

She found herself standing on an iron-barred platform a dizzy eight floors above the alley below. The wind blasted around them, whipping up her skirts. The sun was broiling. She gripped the rail to steady herself. The metal was hot to the touch.

"Want me to go first?" he asked, sensing her hesitation.

She shook her head and started down, moving as fast as her heels would let her. She wasn't dressed for a desperate flight down a rusty fire escape that trembled under their weight.

"The window," she remembered when they reached the next level. "We didn't close it."

"Doesn't matter," he said from close behind her, waving the file. "He'll know he had visitors when he discovers that this is missing. Can you move any faster?"

She made an effort to increase her speed, plunging down another flight of risky stairs. The wind off the river was a constant menace, the heat scorching. Where was Victor? Would he try to pursue them?

They must have been more than halfway down when one of her heels caught in the grating. It was only after she spent precious seconds freeing it that she realized Cleve was no longer right behind her. She looked up. He was there, stopped on the flight above her.

Something was wrong! He was hanging on the rail, his face contorted in pain!

"What is it? What's happened?"

He didn't answer her. He didn't seem to hear her. She started to go to him, and that's when he lost his support on the rail. The file slipped out of his hand, its contents scattering in the high wind. His body was suspended for an instant, and then in slow motion it started to pitch forward.

THE CAT BUMPED UP against his legs, wanting further attention. He nudged it away.

"That's all you're going to get, you greedy thing. On your way, now."

Victor liked cats. They were much easier to deal with than people. Though, of course, dogs were even better. You could train a dog to obey you. You could be in complete control of it. And that was a very desirable thing to him.

The cat followed Victor as he turned away and moved on around the corner to his apartment. He ignored it, no longer in the mood for anything but his own company.

It had been a long day, a *satisfying* day, but he was tired. It was a relief when the private party at which he'd been scheduled to serve this afternoon had been canceled. No longer needed at the hotel, he'd been allowed to leave. Now all he wanted was an easy chair and a chance to savor this morning's results.

Everything was shaping up just as he had planned, he

thought as he reached his door and inserted his key in the lock. And soon now…

He didn't finish the thought. He was distracted by a disturbing discovery. He knew he had locked the door on his way out this morning. It was no longer locked.

The only sound as he stood there listening was the purring of the cat. He made a threatening gesture with his foot, and the animal wisely retreated around the corner of the hallway.

Victor opened the door to his sitting room. He noticed its absence immediately. The manila folder was not where he had left it on the television set. He'd been in such a rush this morning to be where he needed to be for his complicated undertaking that he hadn't bothered with the file. For once it hadn't seemed important that it should accompany him everywhere. A mistake.

The second thing he was aware of was the current of warm air from the bedroom. The window in there was open!

Outraged over the invasion, Victor charged to the gaping window and looked out. They were somewhere below him on the fire escape. He could hear the clang of their feet on the iron treads.

Climbing onto the fire escape, he knelt at the edge of the platform and leaned out as far as he dared. They were visible now. He could make them out about five floors down, Gillian and that despicable P.I.

The sight of his file in McBride's hand infuriated him. They could use it against him. He mustn't allow it to happen. But what were his chances of overtaking them and recovering it? He had to try! He had to prevent them from getting away with material that could destroy everything he had so carefully designed!

He started to get to his feet, started to go after them. Then something unexpected happened. McBride came to an abrupt halt, clutched at the rail and started to sway precariously. Victor checked himself and watched.

What happened next delighted him. The P.I. lost control of the file. It opened as it dropped from his hand. The strong wind snatched its contents and carried them out over the river where the clippings began to flutter like wounded birds into the waters below. Nothing was saved. All of it vanished into the Chicago River.

Victor was satisfied. After all, the file had already served its purpose. He didn't need it anymore. And there had been nothing else in his rooms for them to discover. He'd seen to that.

As for McBride's condition... Well, Victor wasn't sure. The P.I. was obviously suffering some kind of seizure. He was in the act of collapsing when Gillian, with a startled cry, rushed up the steps to catch him. They teetered there for a moment midway on the flight, threatening to dive into space as she clung to his dead weight with a stubborn effort.

Then McBride seemed to rouse himself. In a dazed state, but able to function again, he permitted her to lead him down the remaining levels of the fire escape. They paused at the next platform, and she looked up. Victor enjoyed her alarmed expression when she discovered his livid face peering down at her.

He wondered if she knew what he was telling her in those brief seconds that their gazes clashed. *Yes, you're still free, but only because I want it that way. But before I'm finished with you, they'll lock you away. Put you where you watched them put me. Then it will be your turn to slowly suffocate.*

Victor didn't try to stop them from reaching the street. There was no need now. He waited until the thick shadows of the narrow alley swallowed them, and then he withdrew.

Back inside his shabby apartment, he thought about

McBride and his strange attack out there on the fire escape. Was the P.I. ill? He suddenly remembered something. Snatches of their conversation he'd overheard earlier while he'd been hiding at the top of the conservatory. Did they make sense now? Had McBride been threatened by a similar spell this morning?

Victor wanted to eliminate Gillian's protector. He was the only major obstacle to his scheme. Was this the answer? Because if the private investigator *was* vulnerable, and if he could turn that frailty against him...

But he couldn't count on it. Not yet, anyway. There was another method, however, worth trying. A risk, but if it got McBride out of the way long enough for him to fulfil the next step in his plan...

Victor went to the phone and dialed.

Chapter Eight

Gillian was frantic as she held on to Cleve. She had never seen him helpless before. Was he ill, or was she exaggerating the situation?

"What's wrong?" she demanded when he surfaced from what had seemed to be a momentary blackout.

He refused to explain. All he'd do was mutter urgently, "Let's get out of here."

"Are you sure that you should—"

"Look, are you going to help me down, or do I have to crawl?"

Offering her support, she managed to get him off the fire escape. He wasn't aware of Victor watching them from the landing outside his window. Nor did Gillian mention the unsettling sight of that gaunt figure above them.

They were in the alley now, making their way slowly toward the street. All either of them wanted was to reach his car.

She glanced at Cleve shuffling beside her. He looked awful. There were beads of perspiration on his upper lip that had more to do with the strain of his effort than the heat of the afternoon. He was tight-lipped and silent as she guided him through the endless alley. She could feel the tension in his body. A tension that was a result of his frustration.

He was angry about what had happened to him on the fire escape, and she was scared. Why was she so scared? But she knew why. He was at risk, and that made her admit to herself what she had tried to deny until now. She loved Cleveland McBride. Had, in fact, fallen in love with him that wonderful summer they'd first been together, even though she had never quite dared to name the emotion to herself. And all those years in between she had continued to love him on some subconscious level she had been afraid to acknowledge, because there had been no point in it—not when there was no hope of a future together.

But now Cleve was back in her life, and she could no longer ignore the truth. Her love for him had resurfaced and this time it was so deep and compelling that she was jolted by its realization. And she was terrified of losing him.

"We're almost there," she encouraged him as they gained the sidewalk in front of the hotel, her hand protectively clinging to him.

"Yeah." He jerked a nod as they started across the street.

When they arrived at the car, she released him long enough to hastily search for the keys in her purse. He leaned over, planting his fists against the hood as he waited. She found the keys and unlocked the car, holding the door open for him. He didn't object that it was the passenger side.

Swinging himself into the seat, he stretched back in relief. "Just give me a minute here, and I'll be okay."

Closing the door, she rounded the car and slid behind the wheel on the driver's side. There were maps in the pocket of the door. She took them out and began rapidly flipping through them.

"What are you doing?" he asked.

"Looking for a Chicago map. I want to know where the nearest emergency room is. Or would it be better if I just called for an ambulance? I probably should have done that right away, but—"

"Are you crazy?" He snatched the maps out of her hand. "Who said anything about a medical emergency? I don't need treatment."

His voice was much stronger. She was heartened by that, but still worried. "Cleve, you practically passed out. You almost fell to your death. Something is wrong."

"Just a severe headache, and it's going away. Stop looking at me like that. I'm not having a heart attack or anything like one. I told you I'd be fine. I just have to be quiet for a little while."

The way he said it, with a tone of almost casual confidence, immediately told her something. "This has happened to you before, hasn't it?"

He didn't answer her. He put his head back and closed his eyes.

"How frequently, Cleve? How recently?"

He still refused to answer her. And that's when she remembered something.

"This morning up in the conservatory. It almost happened to you there, too, didn't it? That's why you didn't come the rest of the way with me. I thought it wasn't like you to let me go on alone to the top. You were starting to have an attack of this—this thing," she accused him. "You were, weren't you?"

"Stop fussing," he growled. "And if you want to play nurse, how about some air-conditioning in here? It's sweltering."

She started the engine.

"That's better," he said as the first currents of cool air issued from the vents. "Now let's go home. And try not to wreck my car on the way, will you? Because if I remember rightly, you're a timid driver, and in Chicago traffic that's suicide."

"Cleve, don't you think—"

"Just drive."

He wouldn't talk about it. He was in a bad mood. Not because of what had occurred on the fire escape, she realized, but because she had been there to see it. He would regard that as humiliating. Cleveland McBride wasn't supposed to be weak. His foolish male pride couldn't deal with it.

Like it or not, she promised him silently, *you are going to discuss it once I get you back to the apartment.*

"Are you in any pain?"

"No, and stop asking." He immediately changed the subject with a question of his own. "Did you see any sign of Lassiter back there?"

"Yes, he was on the fire escape outside his window."

"I suppose he saw me lose all those clippings."

"I'm afraid so."

"Damn."

He said no more after that, but she knew he must be thinking it was his fault the vital file, which could have proved to the police that Victor did have a motive for murdering Charles Reardon, was gone. And without it... Well, whatever the next step was, it would just have to wait.

GILLIAN WAS concentrating on parking the car in a tight space in front of her apartment building and didn't notice that they had someone waiting for them. It was Cleve, fully alert now, who drew her attention to the figure who emerged from a vehicle across the street.

"Company," he said as Lieutenant Butch Costello approached them.

There was a grim expression on the homicide detective's face when he joined them on the sidewalk.

"You're in trouble!" he barked.

Gillian braced herself for the worst. Then, to her complete surprise, she realized he was addressing Cleve, not her.

"Damn, I knew I should have paid that last parking ticket."

"Don't be funny, McBride. I told you to stay away from this investigation."

"You have any proof I haven't?"

"How about a complaint of illegal entry? Would that be enough? Because Victor Lassiter made one to the department less than half an hour ago. You were in his rooms, McBride, searching his stuff."

He's accusing Cleve, Gillian thought in bewilderment. But he isn't including me. Why wasn't I named in the complaint when Victor clearly saw both of us leaving his apartment? Before she could object, Cleve nudged her with his foot to keep quiet.

"Come on, Lieutenant, you know you can't make a charge like that stick. A perp's got to be apprehended in the act of breaking and entering."

"Don't be such a wise guy."

"Hey, I'm just protecting my rights. And the way I see it, Lieutenant, it's my word against Lassiter's I was anywhere near his place."

Costello glared at him for a minute, his tongue making that unnerving sucking sound against his teeth that he'd made earlier in Dan Weinstein's office.

He finally made up his mind. "This is the last time I let you off with a warning, McBride. You interfere in my investigation again, I run you in."

He said nothing at all to Gillian. But his glance in her direction told her that he was far from finished with her, and that maybe the next time they met... She wouldn't let herself complete the fearful thought.

The detective turned around and strode back to his car. Cleve, watching him go, murmured thoughtfully, "Lassiter calling the cops on me that way... You know why, don't you?"

"I think I can guess now. He was hoping you'd be arrested, out of the way. But he isn't ready for me to be locked up yet. That's why he didn't mention me in the complaint. He wants me free so he can prolong my torment."

"Yeah, but we've got him worried that I'm here and helping you, and that's progress, Gillian."

She didn't care at this moment what Victor Lassiter was worried about. She was too busy with her own immediate concern for Cleve's health. And when they entered her apartment a moment later, she lost no time in expressing it.

"I think you ought to lie down."

"Is that a prescription or an interesting invitation?"

"Stop treating this like a joke."

"Maybe I will when you stop treating me like an invalid. Besides—" he crouched down to let himself be eagerly greeted by the black Lab, who was all over him "—I need to let Mike out into the yard. Yes, I've been neglecting you, haven't I?"

"*I'll* let Mike out. And if you won't lie down, then at least sit down."

Giving Cleve no opportunity to argue about it, she led the dog to the back door. She knew the Lab couldn't be desperate to use the yard, because her landlord on the first floor had promised to give him a break at noon. But she did feel sorry for the animal. He was used to running free in the north woods. Now he was penned up in an apartment all day. It couldn't be helped.

Releasing Mike, she returned to the living room. Cleve should have been settled in an easy chair by now. But, of course, he wasn't. He was standing by the table, restlessly examining her collection of Cubs mementos.

"I've made up my mind," she informed him decisively. "You're going to see a doctor."

He didn't answer her. He whistled softly through his teeth as he regarded a photograph of the legendary Ernie Banks.

"Cleve, talk to me. You might as well, because I'm not going to let you alone until you do."

He picked up a signed baseball, tossed it in the air a few times, then set it down. "Are you like this when you get a witness on the stand?"

"Yes."

Turning around to face her, hands shoved into his pants pockets, he leaned against the table. "I have seen a doctor," he said. "As a matter of fact, I've seen several doctors. There isn't a question I haven't asked or a test I haven't undergone. Want to know what they found out?"

"Yes."

"Not a thing. There is absolutely nothing wrong with me. I just get these little attacks. They start with headaches out of nowhere. *Blinding* headaches. Sirens going off inside my skull. Sometimes, if I don't push it or if I'm lucky, like this morning at the conservatory, that's all. Other times, like on the fire escape, I black out." He laughed bitterly. "I'm a damned medical mystery, Gillian."

He despised his condition. She could see it in his face, hear it in his voice. Cleveland McBride was a man who couldn't stand to be incapable of action in a critical moment. Wouldn't tolerate himself being weak and helpless. And yet that was exactly what he was dealing with.

"But there must be an explanation. If it isn't physical, then—"

"Don't say it, because I've seen that kind of doctor, too, and have undergone a thorough psychiatric evaluation."

"And?"

His broad shoulders lifted in a little shrug. "No answers.

The only conclusion was that these seizures are triggered by situations of physical stress, usually extreme ones. Hell, I knew that going in."

He described for her briefly several of his experiences over the past year or so, when the attacks had started for no reason anyone could determine, and how they had culminated with the almost disastrous chase on the el tracks.

"Am I wrong, Cleve, or is there an obvious pattern here? I mean, the el tracks, the mountain inside the conservatory, the fire escape...they're all high places."

He shook his head. "That's not the connection. I don't have a fear of high places, and never did. I don't suffer from classic vertigo, and believe me that was considered. There's nothing you can suggest that wasn't considered. Besides, the attacks don't always occur in high places."

Gillian suddenly felt as frustrated as he did. "Didn't they offer you any kind of remedy?"

"Sure. They all ended up advising the same thing. Get out of P.I. work. Settle into a pressure-free existence, preferably away from the pace of a big city. But P.I. work was all I knew or wanted. I ignored the advice. Until that kid almost lost her life. After that... Well, I realized it was one thing to risk myself, but I didn't have the right to risk others. So, in the end..."

She nodded slowly. "You closed your office and moved up north. Cleve, why didn't you tell me all this that day I came to the cottage?"

He didn't answer her. Raking a hand through his hair, he shoved away from the table and began to prowl around the living room.

"Why am I asking?" she said. "Of course, you wouldn't have told me. Because I might have realized you were actually vulnerable. I might have even understood and sympathized. Much better to just send me away thinking you were a heel than to admit something so unmanly as—"

"All right," he growled, "you've made your point."

"But you changed your mind about helping me after I left," she persisted. "Why?"

He had stopped at the front windows overlooking the street. He gazed down at the traffic, not answering her for a moment. "Because," he said finally, "it was a chance to overcome something I hated."

"And that's all?"

"Yeah," he said, refusing to admit it might also have been because she needed him so desperately.

"But what made you think that this time you could handle your problem?"

"I thought I'd licked it."

Not wanting to be cruel, but realizing the need for reality, she reminded him as gently as possible, "But, Cleve, you haven't licked it."

"Do we have to go on discussing this?"

"Yes, we do. Because I can't let you continue to work for me. It's too dangerous for you."

He swung away from the window, his craggy features taut with anger. "Weren't you listening? Headaches, Gillian, and maybe some short blackouts, that's all. And when I come out of them, except for being a little dizzy, a little shaky, I'm fine. Nothing else."

"And what happens to you during those short blackouts? Do you injure yourself, fall to your death?"

"Dumb. I was dumb to ever tell you. I should have figured this is how you'd react."

"Why wouldn't I? I'm a responsible person." Crossing the room, she stood directly in front of him so that he would be clear about the earnestness of her decision. "I'm sorry, Cleve, but I have to terminate our arrangement. If you'll give me a total for your fee and expenses, I'll write you a check."

"You're firing me?"

"Yes."

"Okay, so I'm no longer working for you. Doesn't change anything, Gillian, because you can't stop me from going after Lassiter on my own. I won't give up until I convince the cops he murdered Charles Reardon, and there's nothing you can do about it."

She searched his face. His features had hardened again. He meant it. "But why?" she appealed to him. "Just for the sake of your pride? Just to prove you can do it?"

His expression remained taut, but the tawny lion's eyes suddenly softened. There was a quality in his gaze that was unmistakable. It was tenderness, and it destroyed all of her resolve.

"You know why," he said, his voice so deep and husky that her insides dissolved.

She was unable to respond. Unable to breathe as his eyes went on challenging her. The apartment was air-conditioned. Then why was she so aware of the sultry heat that gripped the city like a heavy, swollen embrace?

Cleve didn't put his arms around her. Didn't touch her at all with his hands. He didn't have to. There was only one part of him she wanted in that moment. He understood and gave it to her. His mouth dipped and found hers in a slow, mellow kiss that deepened until their breaths mingled. Until she tasted his strength, inhaled the raw, forceful essence of him. She found it a richly moving experience, calling up a memory of that other summer when she had responded so eagerly to his long, lingering kisses.

There was no other contact. Just his mouth fused with hers, his tongue savoring hers. It was a long, searing business, and when it finally ended she was left without a defense. Except for one.

"All right," she whispered as he drew away from her, "you win. But there's a condition."

"Am I going to object?"

"Probably, but it won't do you any good. I'm going to do what the firm wants. I'm going to suspend my practice until Victor is behind bars again."

"And this little leave of absence is so you can...what?"

"Stick to you like glue."

"Yeah, I get the picture," he said dryly. "If I fall again, you're going to be right there to pick me up."

"Yes, and there will be no arguments about it, please."

"And what if I don't agree?"

"Then I'll help Lieutenant Costello to lock you up. For your own safety, of course."

"Oh, naturally. There's just one thing."

"What?"

"I'm not going to have any more attacks. Not before I see you cleared, anyway. Mind over matter, Gillian. Just a matter of willpower. I can do it. Then afterward..."

"What?"

"I guess I go back to my woods and water. That's the sensible thing, isn't it?"

Why did it hurt so much to hear him say that? "If that's the existence you want."

"You know it isn't, but it's probably what I'll have to settle for. Hell, it has its compensations. Life can be pretty pleasant in the wilderness."

"You can't give up. Just because a few doctors couldn't offer you a cure doesn't mean there isn't one."

"You have a solution? Because I'm ready to hear one."

"Maybe I do. Did any of your doctors suggest hypnosis?"

"It was discussed but not recommended."

"Why?"

"I don't know, I don't remember. Anyway, what difference does it make? It's not like I'm trying to quit a bad habit."

"But that's not the only use for hypnosis. There are others. Cleve, people under hypnosis reveal things they can't consciously recall. And once there's an explanation for what's happening, and the patient understands it..."

"Yeah, I know, then the behavior pattern stands a chance of being altered. But I don't have anything that my subconscious can be hiding."

"Why not? Why couldn't your subconscious be triggering something that tries to shut you down in moments of crisis? Something that it just can't face."

The subject made him uneasy, impatient. "So how come you know so much about this kind of treatment?"

"I don't, but I know of someone who does. A hypnotherapist who's achieved some pretty amazing results. She's been consulted a couple of times in connection with clients who have come through our firm. Cleve," she urged, "see her, hear what she has to say."

"I'll consider it."

"I have her card somewhere." She went to her desk against the wall.

"Does it have to be right now?"

"Yes." Dropping the lid, she began to search through the disorder that had accumulated inside the desk since the threat of Victor Lassiter. "She isn't listed. She only takes referrals, so I need to find her card."

"Gillian—"

"It isn't here. The bedroom. I bet anything I stuck it somewhere in all that mess in my bedroom."

Leaving the desk open, she headed for her bedroom. Cleve let her go. He didn't have the heart to tell her that he had no faith in her hypnotherapist, that he'd lost that kind of hope months ago.

All he cared about right now was making her safe from Lassiter. And once he had managed that, he'd go back to his cottage in Michigan, because he was no good to anyone like this. It was pointless to yearn for what he couldn't have. There was too much pain in that.

Mike was scratching at the back door to be let in. He went into the kitchen and obliged him. The dog accompanied him back to the living room, whimpering for attention. Cleve was too distracted to play with him.

His mind was back on the case. He regretted all over again his loss of the file that might have put Lieutenant Costello in their corner. And with that file gone, Lassiter must be feeling smug and safe. So where did that leave them? Still needing to find the gun. Where could Lassiter have concealed it?

The dog went on seeking his attention, circling around him as he paced the living room. "Don't look at me like that. I know I've been ignoring you lately. All right, we'll do the Frisbee bit in the backyard just as soon as— What is it, Mike?"

The dog had gone very still. He was gazing alertly in the direction of the front door, the rumble of a growl in his throat. Cleve heard it now himself. The low, rattling sound of a key being fitted into the lock. Someone was trying to get into the apartment! The landlord? No, he would have knocked before he entered.

Lassiter, Cleve thought. Could it be Lassiter?

Not willing to take any chances, Cleve whipped out his gun and flattened himself against the wall beside the door. Mike, though still growling softly, had the good sense to back away across the room.

Cleve waited tensely, the Colt in his upraised hand, as the lock clicked open. A few apprehensive seconds passed, then the door opened slowly. A figure came into the apartment.

Not Lassiter. It was a young girl. She couldn't have been more than twelve, and when she saw Cleve standing there with the gun she cried out in terror. Mike began to bark in a frenzy.

An alarmed Gillian rushed back into the living room. Taking in the situation, she flew across the room and folded the girl in her arms. "It's all right, sweetheart. He isn't going to hurt you. He's a friend."

The girl clung to Gillian, permitting herself to be soothed. Cleve stared at them in total bewilderment. What in the name of—

"Cleve, put the gun away. You're frightening her."

He obliged, returning the Colt to its holster. Mike was equally puzzled. He had stopped barking and was sitting on his haunches, gazing with interest at the newcomer.

The girl lifted her head from where it had been buried against Gillian's chest, reassured herself that the handgun was no longer in sight, and challenged Cleve angrily, "Who are you?"

"Cleveland McBride. How about you?"

"Sarah Randolph."

Shocked, Cleve drew a long, steadying breath. Gillian's daughter...? Was it possible?

The girl wanted answers. "What's going on here? Why does he have a gun?"

Gillian, one arm still around her, replied, "Mr. McBride is a private investigator, Sarah. He's helping me with one of my cases. It's nothing for you to worry about."

Cleve didn't think the girl was satisfied with that vague explanation. But Gillian didn't give her a chance to object. She was suddenly busy demanding her own explanation as she led Sarah toward the sofa.

"Sarah, what are you doing here? How did you—"

"You said I could use it if I had to." She held up the key that had gained her entrance into the apartment.

"Yes, but for emergency use only. Is this an emergency? Is something wrong?"

"I was worried. You haven't visited me or called in days. And when I tried to phone, there was no answer. Not even from the answering machine. I thought maybe something happened to you."

"Did I leave the answering machine off again? I—I've been kind of distracted lately. Busy with that case I mentioned. That's why I haven't visited or phoned. I'm sorry about that. But I promise you I'm fine."

"I was worried just the same."

The two of them, settled now side by side on the sofa, hugged each other. Cleve could see that they shared a bond of deep affection. And what else could he see? He wondered as he studied the girl. A narrow face framed in straight brown hair, a thin, coltish figure. Gillian might have looked like this at the same age. Was there a resemblance?

He suddenly wanted some answers of his own. A *lot* of them. Sensing his need, Gillian met his gaze over Sarah's lowered head. She shook her head and mouthed a pleading *"Later."* He had no choice but to settle for that, frustrated though he was. Gillian was still anxious about Sarah.

"How did you get here all the way from Lake Forest?" she asked, referring to the far northern suburb. For Cleve's benefit, she added a quick, "Sarah is a boarder at Saint Bride's Academy."

"Easy. I took the train to Evanston and then caught the el."

"All on your own? Oh, Sarah, that was wrong. What about the school? They don't know you left, do they?"

Sarah shrugged. "I told Shannon, so nobody would wonder and worry."

"Your best friend? That doesn't really count, does it?"

"Well, if I'd told any of the staff they wouldn't have let me go. Anyway, it's summer. It's not like I'm skipping out on any regular classes. Don't be mad at me, Gillian. I had to see you.''

"I appreciate that, sweetheart, but Saint Bride's must have missed you by now. They're probably sick with worry. I have to call them right away and let them know you're safe. Then you have to promise me never to do anything like this again.''

While Gillian was on the phone, reassuring the school that Sarah was safe and that she would drive her back to Lake Forest, the Lab came over to the sofa to greet the girl.

"What's his name?" Sarah asked, ready to forgive Cleve for scaring her as she bent down to stroke the dog.

"Mike," Cleve said, "and if you toss the Frisbee for him in the backyard he'll be your friend for life.''

Sarah looked up at him with an engaging smile that displayed the braces on her teeth. "Can I? Oh, but Gillian won't let me hang around. She'll probably make me go straight back to school.''

"I'll see what I can do about winning you a recess.''

"Really?''

Sarah's smile broadened into a delighted grin. Cleve could feel a piece of his heart being stolen.

GILLIAN AND CLEVE SAT side by side on the bottom step of the outside stairway that descended from the kitchen of her apartment. They talked in undertones while they watched Sarah romping with Mike across the fenced-in backyard.

"Is that true, what you told her about the answering machine?" he asked.

She shook her head. "No, I left it off deliberately. With Victor managing to get into places that are supposed to be secure, I was afraid to run the risk of his getting into the apartment and maybe hearing a message on the machine from Sarah.''

"You didn't want him learning of her existence. Or me, either," he said, unable to help his anger. "I knew you were holding something back. I could feel it all along. Why did you do it, Gillian? Why did you go on lying to me?"

"I had my reasons."

She didn't look at him. She went on watching Sarah tussling happily with the dog on the grass. There was a glow of protective love in Gillian's eyes.

"They must be damn good ones for you to keep your daughter a secret, to go and hide her in a year-round boarding school."

This time she turned her head to stare at him. "Sarah isn't my daughter. What made you—"

"She said her name is Randolph, so I assumed—"

"That she's mine. Well, it's true in a way, since I'm her guardian. But she's a Randolph because her mother was using her maiden name when Sarah was born. Just like I went back to my maiden name after Alan and I parted."

He twisted around on the seat to face her directly. "Are you saying what I think you're saying?"

"Yes. Sarah is my cousin's daughter. Molly had her after I helped her to relocate. She was pregnant with her when she left Victor."

"Does this have some connection with why he killed his wife?"

"No, he never knew she was pregnant."

"But if he's the kid's father…"

"He isn't."

"Then who? The man she was trying to divorce Lassiter for when he killed her?"

"No, that was someone else she met after Sarah was born. I don't know who fathered Sarah. Molly would never tell me, just that it was someone who was kind to her at a time when she badly needed kindness. It's my guess he was probably a married man with a family and that there was no question of a future for them together. Whoever he was, she kept Sarah's existence a secret from him."

"And from Lassiter."

"Yes, and it's going to stay that way," she vowed ferociously. "I shudder to think what that monster might try if he ever learned Molly left a child behind."

"Which, I'm guessing, is the reason why your cousin finally found the courage to leave Lassiter."

Gillian nodded. "Molly's pregnancy made her realize she had to get away. Victor was so totally possessive about her that she was afraid of what he would do. He didn't want to share her with anyone, and a baby that wasn't his... Who knows?"

"So she disappears and has her kid elsewhere without ever revealing the identity of the father, only she stays in contact with you."

"She had to count on someone. She made me promise to keep her secret and to take care of her daughter if anything happened to her. We arranged for it legally just after Sarah was born."

"Which," Cleve presumed, "is the real reason why a woman who, otherwise is strong and self-sufficient, goes to a great deal of trouble to hire herself the best private investigator she can get."

"I was desperate. I had to stay alive, and now I have to stay free. Sarah has to be looked after by someone who can keep on paying the bills. All I have is what I earn. My father made some bad investments, and what he left when he died went to my mother, who needed it. Sarah's education is very expensive."

"Does it have to be?"

"Yes. She has special needs, and her school is meeting them. But superior attention like that costs a great deal."

"You telling me she has a learning disability?"

"Nothing extreme, but enough to need the help of a

school like Saint Bride's. Otherwise, Sarah is a healthy, loving eleven-year-old that I wish I could have with me. I don't dare. It's risky enough keeping her this close to Chicago. But if I hadn't put her in St. Bride's Academy, she would have been too far away for me to visit, which I do as often as I safely can.''

"Okay," he admitted gruffly, "you're all she has. It still doesn't explain why you didn't trust me to know about her."

"It isn't my secret. It's Molly's, and I had no right to share it."

"She's dead, Gillian. Your cousin is gone, and you came to me for help. Which, as it turns out, is actually because her daughter needs protecting. Only I don't get told there is a daughter."

"You're not being fair."

"*Fair* is not holding out on the professional whose services you hire. As a lawyer, you ought to know the importance of that. A P.I. has a right to know exactly what's at stake in a case, because every piece matters."

"Doesn't that work both ways?" she said quietly.

He didn't like being reminded that he had withheld from her the knowledge of his seizures, but he knew she was right.

"Cleve, about Sarah…"

He watched the girl as she chased Mike across the yard, laughing over the dog's antics. It was a sight that moved him deeply. There was no way he could refuse Gillian.

"Don't worry," he said. "I'll do whatever it takes to help you protect Sarah."

And you along with her, he promised himself. Which brought him back to the subject of the gun that had killed Reardon. Just where the hell had Lassiter hidden it?

Chapter Nine

The rush hour traffic on the southbound expressway had thinned to a trickle, permitting Cleve to drive with his usual reckless speed through the gathering twilight. Gillian, seated beside him in his sporty red car, was too weary now to be nervous about that. This had been the longest day she had ever experienced. And probably the worst.

The only bright spot in the whole mess had been Sarah, she decided with a wistful little smile, regretting the necessity of having returned the girl to her school. And Cleve, too, she thought, remembering with a warm glow how kind and affectionate he had been with Sarah.

The two of them had bantered like old friends on the drive north to Lake Forest, happily insulting each other's taste in rock music.

"And who is Bruce Springsteen?" Sarah had innocently asked, pretending to Cleve's indignation that she had never heard of his favorite.

Gillian, listening to them, had loved Cleve all the more for caring about Sarah, for making her important to him.

But all that talk and laughter had occurred on the way to Saint Bride's Academy. There was silence now in the car. Cleve hadn't said anything for miles, and when she glanced at him there was a grim expression on his face.

"You can tell me, Cleve."

"Huh?"

"What Sarah whispered in your ear when she hugged you goodbye at the school."

"You didn't miss that, then."

"No, I caught it."

He nodded, keeping his eyes on the road. "I'm afraid you didn't fool her with that explanation back at the apartment about my being there because I was helping you with a case. She's guessed you're in some kind of trouble. She knew better than to ask what. She just wanted to be sure I would take good care of you."

Gillian felt a silly lump in her throat. Just thinking about Sarah, and how much she mattered, intensified her need to clear herself of Charles Reardon's murder. To be free of this shadow that Victor Lassiter had cast over her. But the outlook was as bleak as ever.

She would have discussed this with Cleve, but he was silent again, detached. Something was on his mind. She didn't learn what until a few minutes later when he unexpectedly halted the car in a pulloff that overlooked the lakeshore.

Gillian, mystified, turned to him for an explanation. She could sense his sudden excitement.

"I've been going crazy asking myself where Lassiter hid that gun. We know it's not in his rooms. Would he have it at work, maybe in his locker? No, too risky. So what else would be available to him where the gun would be safe until he was ready to spring it?"

"You've figured it out."

"I think so."

"Where?"

"Right where we're looking," he said, pointing south toward the winking lights of downtown Chicago. "Navy Pier, Gillian. The marionette theater at Navy Pier. The one you told me about when you came to see me up north. I remembered your saying that Lassiter operated it before he went to prison.''

She gazed at him in dismay. ''But that was years ago, and Navy Pier has undergone renovations since then.''

''All of it?''

''No, they're still working on it, and there are unused sections that haven't been touched yet, but—''

''Gillian, I have a gut feeling about this. I think that theater is still there and if we search it, we'll find your missing gun.''

She hated to deflate him, but it was time to face reality. ''Cleve, even if all this is true, if the place is still there in its original state and Victor was somehow able to hang on to his key for it and we manage to get inside and find the gun…''

''You trying to say we shouldn't bother now chasing it down?''

''What can it prove except that it was the weapon used to kill Reardon and, since it's mine, that only makes it worse for me?''

''You're forgetting what we set out to do. To show Costello that Victor Lassiter has the gun in his possession and that he used it himself. Look, if we can lead Costello to where the weapon is and convince him to put a tail on Lassiter, then sooner or later Lassiter will retrieve the gun in order to plant it against you. When he tries that, Costello will know it was Lassiter who put it there and why and even if that fails, there's always the chance of finding other evidence in the theater. Just like we did in his apartment.''

''That's true.''

''Gillian, we can't give up. If I learned nothing else in my years as a P.I., I learned that.''

He was right, of course, and she told him so. Then she added, ''But you're not proposing we try to go there tonight?''

"I suppose not. Tomorrow should be soon enough."

"But not until after I report to the firm. I'll need to let them know my decision about a leave of absence. Which will mean spending some time handing my cases over to the other lawyers."

"That's no problem. It'll give me a chance to check out the pier, find some way to get inside that theater. Then, after I'm sure Lassiter is at work—"

"You're not to try to go in there on your own," she said quickly, fearing his vulnerability to another stressful situation. She meant to be right beside him.

"All right," he reluctantly agreed. "I'll come back for you at the firm."

"No, I'll grab a cab and meet you at the pier. Don't look at me like that. I'll be safe. Victor isn't going to come after me. He's going to let the police do that now." Before he could argue about it, she turned to another sensitive matter that had gotten sidetracked by Sarah's appearance at the apartment. "I did find the hypnotherapist's card in my bedroom, Cleve. Will you make an appointment with her?"

"Sure, right after we clear you of this—"

"No, call her tomorrow."

"I guess I can manage to fit it in."

She knew he wouldn't. He would go on evading the issue. She wouldn't let him. She would make that appointment herself in the morning from her office. That left only one problem. How to convince him to keep the appointment.

IT WAS LATE afternoon before Gillian was able to join Cleve at Navy Pier. Handing her cases over to her colleagues had been more involved than she'd thought.

When Cleve had checked in with her earlier by phone, they'd arranged to meet outside the distinctive front entrance with its matching brick towers. He was waiting for her impatiently.

"We're in business," he reported as she reached his side.

Cleve had learned from his paid informant at the Hutton that Victor Lassiter was safely out of the way at his job. She didn't remind him that Victor was supposed to have been elsewhere when he caught them in his rooms yesterday. She knew that a risk was necessary.

"Have you managed to figure out how we're going to get inside?" It wasn't necessary to ask him if the puppet theater still existed. He had already assured her on the phone that it did. His instincts had been right. So far.

"You'll see," he said, and would say no more until they reached their objective.

They began to walk along Dock Street, which edged the south side of the facility. The broad pier that carried them toward their target extended nearly a mile straight out into Lake Michigan. It was crowded with novelty shops, restaurants, a giant Ferris wheel, and a variety of recreational pavilions. On clear summer weekends the place was mobbed with visitors. But it had rained earlier in the day and the outdoor arcades were nearly deserted. Nor were there any lines waiting to board the sightseeing boats that cruised the lake.

The scene was drab, the air stifling. It was hard to breathe. They didn't talk, saving themselves for what waited for them at the far end of the pier.

To her surprise, Cleve stopped outside a shop that sold posters and T-shirts. "Wait for me," he said. Then, without an explanation, he disappeared into the store. Gillian couldn't imagine what he intended.

Cleve reappeared. He was carrying three posters, rolled up and with the plain sides out.

"Souvenirs?" she asked.

"Maybe."

"Why do you always have to make a mystery out of everything?"

His only response was a big grin. But she didn't mind his slyness. Not really. Because even when he was being aggravating like this, she appreciated him. She supposed that's what it meant to be in love, to care for someone so deeply that his flaws were as endearing as his virtues. But with the trouble she was in, love was a dangerous emotion, something she couldn't risk dealing with right now.

They moved on, and she remembered that she was guilty of her own secrets. Like not telling him yet about the appointment she'd made for him with the hypnotherapist. She had decided to keep that little bomb to herself until after they investigated the theater. If he was in a good mood because their search produced results...

No, don't count on anything.

But hope sharpened inside her as their long walk brought them within sight of their goal at the end of the pier, which terminated in a grand ballroom from another era. Attached to it was an enormous, three-level exhibition hall. Gillian knew that the puppet theater was located on the lower level below the street.

The entire structure had changed little since the pier was built early in the century. But now this section was undergoing its own extensive remodeling. She could see and hear the sounds of activity as they approached. Sawhorses were lined up on the sidewalk, barricading the entrance to the public.

Cleve drew her aside to explain the situation. "The theater downstairs hasn't been touched yet. Probably won't be for another year. But they're using its lobby to store materials for the job upstairs."

"You haven't been inside?"

He shook his head. "Didn't have to. I had lunch back at

that little café there. There were workers from the job at the table next to me. They love to talk. I love to listen.''

"So how do we get in there without being turned away?"

"Just smile and follow me."

With an anxious Gillian at his heels, Cleve marched boldly past the barricades and through the gaping main doors. They were immediately challenged by a burly electrician.

"This part of the pier is off-limits to the public, sir."

Cleve held up one of the rolled posters he'd just purchased and waved it like a baton. "My assistant and I are delivering specs to the foreman. Changes for the next job site."

Were all P.I.s this resourceful? Gillian wondered. Or just the brazen ones?

"Well, don't ask me where he is," the electrician said. "You'll have to find him on your own."

He turned away, no longer interested in them. And now that they were safely inside, none of the other workers bothered them. The crews were all occupied, the area loud with the noises of their construction that echoed in the great hollow hall.

"Over here," Gillian said, remembering the route from her several visits to the theater when Molly had been here.

She led the way toward a marble stairway at the side of the hall, moving swiftly around crates and equipment before anyone else decided to stop and question them. Reaching the stairs, they checked behind them. No one was looking their way. They ducked down the flight, leaving all the commotion behind them.

The steps turned on a landing and descended again. They arrived in a narrow foyer. Two pairs of heavy doors stood open to the theater's lobby just beyond. The area was silent and deserted.

"Looks like we're in the clear," Cleve said, preceding her into the lobby.

Providing a worker doesn't come down here for any of these supplies, Gillian thought, following him into the lobby and through a maze of lumber, boxes of tile, and coils of electrical cable.

There were no windows anywhere down here. However, the lobby was lit because of the materials stored in it. But when Cleve cracked open one of the swinging doors into the auditorium, they met a well of blackness. Dropping the posters, he extracted a thin flashlight from his pocket.

"Wait here," he said. "I'll go see if I can find some house lights."

He disappeared into the auditorium, leaving her alone in the lobby. She eyed its ornate embellishments. They were tarnished and dirty from more than a decade of disuse. The air at this level was close and musty, adding to her nervousness as she waited for Cleve to return.

Maybe this isn't so smart, she thought. If someone from upstairs catches us here...

She kept glancing in the direction of the stairs through the open doors, but no one appeared. Nor could she hear any sound from inside the auditorium. What was keeping Cleve?

Seconds later, a swinging door opened and his head poked around it. Gillian wasn't encouraged by the sight of the cobwebs in his hair, but he wore an expression of success. "It's safe now to come in."

She joined him inside the auditorium, making certain that the door was tightly closed behind her. If there were any unexpected arrivals in the lobby, she didn't want them spotting lights in the auditorium.

She needn't have worried. The place was so dimly lit that she could scarcely distinguish Cleve standing beside her in the aisle.

"I know," he apologized, "but it's the best I could do. I found the electrical panel backstage, but it looks like most of the bulbs in here are burned out."

There would have been no need to replace them, Gillian realized as her eyes adjusted to the gloom. The small, intimate theater, which over the years had been home to every entertainment from a repertory company to a popular magician before Victor had converted it to his own use, hadn't seen an audience since its last occupant had gone to prison.

His marionette stage, with its raised bridge and leaning rail from which the puppeteers operated, was still there where he had left it on the front center of the larger stage. The masking curtains on either side had been removed, revealing in the shadowy wings the ghostly shapes of scenery and props. There was an eerie stillness in the once elegant theater, its air stale and smelling of old memories that were better left undisturbed.

Refusing to be haunted by the past, Gillian briskly turned to Cleve and asked, "Where do we begin?"

"You take the house out here. I'll start with all that clutter on the stage." He pressed the flashlight into her hand. "You'll need this. The light's a little better on the stage."

They parted. Gillian began with the first rows down front, working her way slowly toward the back of the auditorium. There was dust everywhere but no sign of a revolver. She carefully checked each seat, knowing that the gun could be anywhere in here. Or nowhere.

The long minutes passed as she moved from row to row, trying not to worry but all the while fearing they'd be discovered. To prevent that, she searched as quietly as possible. There was no sound from Cleve, either.

She was at the rear of the auditorium, her back to the stage, when the silence behind her was blasted by a voice booming out a terrifying, "You have trespassed in a sacred place, and for that you must pay the penalty!"

Gillian whipped around with a startled gasp. The stage was no longer in gloom. Light blazed from the heart of it, dazzling her, and from the darkness behind the light the cruel voice went on, "You will never leave here! It will be your tomb!"

For a moment she felt as if she were in a bad horror movie and that a hand from the grave had just clutched her by the throat. Then a merciful reality kicked in. The glow was nothing more ghostly than the foot and border lights on the marionette stage. As for that melodramatic voice— laughing harshly at this point—she could tell now it was a recording. But chilling all the same, and in this place, under these conditions...

Cleve! Where was Cleve? She called to him. No reassuring answer. No movement from the shadows. He had vanished.

What was going on here?

Her heart, which had slowed, began to race again. She made an effort to calm herself. Logic told her that the menacing voice was just a character from a fairy tale. One of Victor Lassiter's tapes that accompanied his marionette productions. And that there had to be a sensible explanation for why it was playing, why the lights were on.

But for now she must ignore them. All that mattered was finding Cleve. She had a sinking feeling that he was in need of her.

Steeling herself, but feeling none too confident about her courage, she headed for the front of the auditorium. It wasn't until she mounted the stage that she was able to hear Cleve's voice over the volume of the recording, which now had the heroine begging for her life. But he sounded muffled and far away, as though he'd been trapped inside a pit.

"Where are you?" she shouted.

"Down here behind the puppeteers' bridge. And be careful, or you'll fall in like I did." His warning was followed by a mutter of frustrated, very explicit curses.

Fall into what? she wondered, cautiously approaching the back side of the elevated marionette stage. The flashlight he had given her revealed the answer in the form of a yawning, two-foot-square cavity. The trapdoor was located in the floor of the main stage directly behind the bridge.

Kneeling on the edge of the opening, Gillian directed the flashlight into its depths. Its glow disclosed the astonishing sight of Cleve suspended on his back in a net several feet below her.

"Are you hurt?"

"No, this thing caught me, but now I can't get out of it. With hardly any light down here to see, I've gone and tangled myself up in it."

He began to twist again in frustration, making his situation worse. Then he stopped thrashing, glaring up at her with a sudden suspicion.

"Are you laughing?"

"Absolutely not."

But she was laughing. Mostly in relief. He was all right. He wasn't having one of his attacks. Her joy in knowing he was safe was so sweet a sensation that, had the situation permitted it, she would have hugged him fiercely. Oh, this was crazy! What was he doing to her? Every time she got near him, her emotions started to churn.

"I think you are laughing. You gonna go on having a good time up there, or are you going to help me out of this booby trap? What's it doing here, anyway?"

She collected her wits and managed to answer him. "I think it's a stage trapdoor. You know, magicians and disappearing acts."

"Figures it'd go and collapse under me."

"Hold on. There must be a stairway down."

"Before you go looking for it, you'd better shut off that tape player before someone upstairs hears it. Guess I tripped a switch somewhere when the floor dropped out from under me."

Gillian looked around with the flashlight and located what he suspected. It was close to the edge of the open trapdoor, a foot lever that controlled both the lights on the puppet theater and the tape player tucked under its stage. Cleve must have struck the thing as he fell.

She reached out and smacked the lever, killing both the lights and the creepy music that had begun to issue now from the speakers.

"That's better," Cleve called from the hole. "That stuff was beginning to spook me. Hurry up, will you? I'm starting to get claustrophobic in this hammock."

Getting to her feet, Gillian went backstage and found a narrow stairway that led her to the area under the main stage. The light down here was even weaker than in the auditorium, but there was just enough of it to direct her to the net in which he floundered above her.

"Have you any suggestions for how I'm supposed to cut you out of that snarled mess?"

"Must be a way to lower the net to the floor. See anything?"

She aimed the flashlight at the ceiling, playing its beam in a slow circle. "Uh…yes, there's a rope from the net that goes over a pulley, and this end of it—" she followed the rope down along the side of a post, discovering the place where it was tightly lashed around a cleat "—is tied to a thingy down here."

"That's it. Untie the rope and let me down. Gently, if you please."

Gillian laid the flashlight on the lid of a nearby trunk to free both of her hands and unwound the line from the cleat.

But controlling the sudden weight of him once the tension was released was an impossibility. Though she meant to ease the net to the cement floor, he was too much of a load for her. He came down on the hard surface with a thump. There was the ominous sound of something cracking.

She knelt beside him in concern. "Are you hurt? Did you break something?"

"Get me out of this thing, and we'll see."

It took another anxious moment to unwrap the folds of the net. Finally liberated, he got to his feet with a groan. "Now I know what a fish feels like. Thanks for the rescue." Reaching around behind him, he withdrew his compact cell phone from his back pocket. "Dead," he said after testing it. "That's what we heard cracking."

"Better the phone than one of your bones. Or did you—"

"No, I'm fine," he insisted, though she noticed him rubbing a backside that was probably sore.

Reassured, she got to her feet. "I don't know about you, but I've had enough. Let's get out of here." Scooping up the flashlight from the trunk, she started to leave.

Cleve stopped her. "Hang on for a minute."

"Why?"

"This trunk. We're here, so let's look inside it. Hold the flashlight so I can see."

"All right, but if bats fly out of it..."

He raised the lid. Faces gazed up at them. The trunk was packed with them. Each of them had been carefully bagged in clear plastic, their control boards at their sides.

"Marionettes," she murmured. "He stored his marionettes in here. Come away, Cleve."

She didn't like looking at them with their wide, staring eyes. There was something weird about seeing them piled here in layers. Like bodies that had been entombed.

"Maybe he's stored more than just puppets in here," he said.

He began, one by one, to remove the marionettes from the trunk, placing them in rows on the floor. An unwilling Gillian aimed the flashlight and watched nervously as he burrowed through the layers. He was more than halfway down when he uncovered it. Like the marionettes, it was wrapped in clear plastic and nestled between Aladdin and a wicked sorcerer.

They stood for a moment gazing down at the semiautomatic Glock. And then Cleve, needing to be certain of their discovery, asked her softly, "Yours?"

"Yes. At least it looks just like mine, so I suppose..."

She started to reach for the revolver, wanting to verify its identity, but he held her back. "No, don't touch it. It's evidence, and we might be contaminating it. We'll get Costello over here to handle it."

She nodded. "Then we'd better try to leave everything just as we found it." She began to help him to return the other marionettes to the trunk. "You were right, Cleve. Victor did use this place to hide the gun. What do you suppose he intended doing with it?"

"I think it's like you said earlier. This is all calculated to make you suffer. To keep you wondering day and night just when and where the revolver would turn up to be used against you. Then when Lassiter felt you couldn't take any more, he would have come back here for the gun and planted it somewhere associated with you and where the cops would be sure to find it."

"Yes, that's just how that twisted mind of his would work."

The last marionette went into the trunk. Cleve was lowering the lid when they heard the slam of a pair of doors being closed. They looked at each other in alarm. Before either of them could speak, a second pair of doors banged shut. Then there was an ominous silence.

"It came from the direction of the lobby," Gillian whispered. "You don't suppose…"

"Come on."

He grabbed her by the hand, and they raced up the stairway, tore through the auditorium, and reached the lobby on the other side of the swinging doors. It was dark. The lights in the lobby had been doused. Both sets of outer doors had been fastened.

The flashlight's feeble glow permitted them to find their way through the stacks of construction materials. Arriving at the first exit, Cleve thrust his shoulder against the solid double doors. They gave just slightly. Then there was resistance, the rattle of a strong chain.

"Padlocked," he said.

Moving on to the other set of doors, he heaved against them and met the same result. He swore under his breath.

"Sorry, Gillian. I should have remembered this was a possibility. One of the work crew said at lunch his boss was complaining about supplies down here disappearing and that, if the theft continued, he was going to lock up the stuff every night. I guess he decided not to wait."

"But it can't be that late." She focused the flashlight beam on her watch. "It's not anywhere near five o'clock."

"I guess they quit early."

"What do we do?"

"It's a theater. There must be emergency exits. Let's find them."

They did locate them a moment later, one on either side of the auditorium. But with the theater no longer in use, both of them had been sealed tightly from the outside. Not ready to give up, Cleve led them on a thorough search from one end of the facility to the other. They found themselves back in the lobby, having found no other usable exit.

"Can't we try rousing someone?" Gillian suggested. "It won't matter now if they discover we're in here. The police are going to have to know we entered the place anyway when we tell Lieutenant Costello about the gun."

"I suppose we'd better."

Pressing against the doors, he began to shout through the thin crack. There was no answer.

"Cleve, it's no good. Either they've all left already, or they're too far away to hear us. You have your gun, don't you? Couldn't you—"

"Shoot off a lock? Not when it's on the outside, Gillian."

"Then we're trapped in here!"

He eyed her shoulder bag. "I don't suppose there's any chance that you're carrying your own cell phone."

"It's still in my car where I keep forgetting it."

"Uh-huh, I know. And your car is still in the parking garage at work. That's it, then. So, how do you feel about spending the night in here?"

The prospect of huddling in the theater, enduring the long hours until morning when the work crews arrived, was anything but a welcome one. "Do we have a choice?"

"Doesn't look like it," he said, making an effort to improve his mood. "Well, we might as well wait it out in the auditorium where there are lights and comfortable seats."

She put a hand on his arm. "Cleve, let's not go back in there." She suddenly couldn't bear the thought of returning to the auditorium with its uneasy atmosphere. She'd had enough of the place.

"Guess it doesn't have very pleasant memories for you. All right, we'll manage here. Let's see what I can do about restoring the lights."

He took the flashlight from her. Its batteries were almost finished, but there was just enough power left to enable him to locate a wall panel in a corner of the lobby. Behind its door were the switches for this section of the theater. Within seconds, the lobby glowed again with light.

"That's better," he said.

He selected a long, low carton from the construction supplies and dragged it over against a side wall. They settled on it side by side, their backs against the wall.

"Too bad the rest rooms are off the foyer out there instead of in here," he said. "It's going to be a long night."

His observation reminded her of something. "Mike," she said, worrying about the Lab back at her apartment.

"He'll survive."

She nodded. There was a long moment of silence between them. The situation was such that Gillian couldn't seem to resist the depression that closed around her like a suffocating shroud. Without realizing it, she spoke her fear aloud.

"Is there no way out?"

"Look," he assured her with a lopsided grin. "If they don't open those doors tomorrow morning by a reasonable hour, we'll sue the city. Anyway, it could be worse. If this were Friday, we'd be in here the whole weekend."

She smiled at him forlornly. "Being locked up in here isn't what I meant."

"Yeah, I know. Lassiter, huh?"

She nodded. "I think it's going to take a miracle to get out of this web he's woven around me. And I'm afraid finding my gun in there just isn't that miracle."

"It's a start. A damn promising one."

"I'm trying to believe that, but..." She shook her head.

"Come here." He slid an arm around her and drew her close against his side. "Better?"

"Yes."

She loved the feel of him holding her protectively. Of his hard, warm body being there for her in her desperation. Loved the clean male scent of him in her nostrils and the way he rested his stubbly cheek against her head so that his breath gently stirred her hair. Loved everything that was so uniquely and forcefully Cleveland McBride.

"Gillian?" he said hoarsely.

She lifted her head, searching his face. Their gazes met and locked. She could read his soul in his eyes, knew that he wanted to kiss her. *Needed* to kiss her.

She experienced the same hunger for him. And when he dipped his head, when his mouth captured hers in a heart-stopping kiss, she responded with a reckless exuberance. It was exhilarating, intoxicating, with sensations that she never wanted to end. It was the kind of kiss that should have been followed by an impassioned commitment.

But Cleve didn't express the commitment she longed for when his mouth finally lifted from hers. How could he, she thought, clinging to him in despair, when their situation was such an impossible one? So many depressing ifs standing in their way. *If* she went to prison for the murder of Charles Reardon...*if* Cleve couldn't overcome his strange seizures...*if* he left her and went back to his lonely lakeshore cottage...

She couldn't stand this unending threat of separation. Not now when she had found him again, when he had become so precious to her. She had lost him before, and to repeat that terrible anguish... No, it was too much.

I won't go through that again, she thought. I *can't*. But there was a very real possibility that she would have to.

They were silent for a moment, and then in an abrupt change of mood Cleve asked, "Does Sarah know that her mother was married to Victor Lassiter and that he killed her?"

She was immediately wary. "Why are you asking?"

"Gillian, the kid is eleven years old. She must have asked you something about her past."

"I told her everything about her mother. Everything that was safe for her to know."

"Yeah, I get it. You left her believing that Molly was killed by a stranger. Gillian, you lied to her."

"If I did omit the truth," she countered defensively, "it was only to protect her. I won't have her hurt by knowing that her mother was married to someone like that."

"You can't hide it from her forever. Sooner or later, she's going to have some serious questions. And what about her father? She must have wanted by now to learn who he is."

"I shared what I know, which is nothing. How could I tell her who her father is when Molly never revealed him?"

"And she accepted that?"

Gillian stiffened, pulling away from him. "She had no choice. Why do you ask?"

"Because even if Lassiter isn't her father, she's entitled to know about that part of her mother's life."

She didn't answer him. She was angry. But underneath her anger, she knew he was right. Sarah would eventually demand the details about her mother's death, and she feared what might happen when that day arrived.

"All right," Cleve apologized, hauling her back into his arms, "I shouldn't have pressured you like that. Hell, you've got enough to deal with. Forgiven?"

She resisted him for a few seconds, then she relaxed and submitted to his embrace. She needed the security that only his arms could provide.

They were quiet after that. He went on holding her. Gradually, with her head on his shoulder, she felt a welcome drowsiness steal over her. She knew that Cleve was already asleep. She could hear his slow, even breathing. They were both tired, worn out. Sighing, she dozed off.

When her eyes opened again several hours later, the freckled face of Lieutenant Butch Costello was looming above her. She knew by its expression that they were in trouble.

Then Cleve and Gillian finish their conversation from
moment ago as if nothing has been... Tagline this pointing
conversation, thank them being surprised Did they were a
nothing to it—

Chapter Ten

"You don't listen very well, do you?" the homicide detective growled at them. "I tell you to stay away from the investigation. I tell you if you're caught breaking and entering again—"

"Uh, excuse me, Lieutenant," Cleve interrupted him, struggling up from the low carton on which they had seated themselves, then helping Gillian to stand beside him, "but if I could just amend that. We didn't break in. No sir, we simply strolled in through doors that were unlocked and wide-open. Now that's not the same as breaking and entering, is it?"

"Always have to be a smart aleck, don't you, Mc-Bride?"

"Hey, Lieutenant, don't be mad. I'm not mad. In fact, I'm damn grateful for your rescue." He eyed the two figures standing behind the detective. One of them was a young officer in uniform. Gillian recognized him as the man who had accompanied Costello to her firm's offices. The other was an elderly man jangling a set of keys. "Speaking of which, how did you, um—"

"Night watchman here doing his rounds spotted your lights through the door joints. Phoned the police. Morelli—" he indicated the young officer "—answered the call. And having a brain, which apparently you don't,

McBride, Morelli figured after getting a peep at you two sleeping beauties that I'd be interested and contacted me.''

"My, my, and we snored through it all.''

"Satisfied? Good. Now it's your turn to satisfy me. What are you doing here?''

"Same thing we were doing in Victor Lassiter's rooms, Lieutenant. Looking for the gun that killed Charles Reardon. Know what? We found it.''

"Where?'' he demanded.

Cleve jerked his head in the direction of the auditorium. "In there. Don't worry, Lieutenant, we didn't disturb it. Left it just where Lassiter concealed it. Now, aren't you pleased?''

"Morelli, go with him. Have him show you where the weapon is and take charge of it.''

Cleve and the young officer disappeared through the swinging doors. The homicide detective turned to Gillian.

"Your missing semiautomatic, Ms. Randolph?''

"Yes. At least I think it is.''

He didn't comment any further. He just gazed at her in silence as they waited for the return of Cleve and Officer Morelli. She didn't like the speculative look in his eyes and was relieved when the two men returned. The officer was bearing the gun still wrapped in plastic. He handled it with caution, and Costello was equally careful when he took possession of it.

"We'll see what the crime lab has to tell us about this.''

"You know what the results are going to be,'' Cleve said. "It'll show that the bullet that killed Reardon came from that gun. But it won't have Lassiter's prints on it. He would have seen to that. But he used it just the same and then afterward hid it away where he thought nobody would ever search for it. Because in case you didn't know it, Lieutenant, Lassiter operated this theater before he went to prison. All his stuff is still here.''

"As a matter of fact, I did know it. But the part of your little scenario I have trouble with—assuming it's remotely worth anything in the first place—is Victor Lassiter's reason for concealing the weapon at all."

"Come on, Lieutenant, it's obvious. He was waiting for an opportunity to plant the gun somewhere in connection with Gillian and where you'd be sure to find it."

"And you don't find anything at all far-fetched about this theory of yours?"

"No, I don't," Cleve insisted.

"Uh-huh. Well, here's another interesting possibility." The detective paused, making that annoying sucking sound again with his teeth as he turned his head to look at Gillian. She wondered if he did it consciously and deliberately to unnerve his suspects. "Maybe you and Ms. Randolph brought the gun here yourselves. Maybe you sneaked in here and put it with Victor Lassiter's things in order to incriminate *him.*"

Cleve laughed cynically. "You don't seriously believe that's what happened?"

"Why not?"

"Because if we didn't find the gun here just like I said we did, that would make me a liar. And if I'm a liar, I would have sworn at the beginning of this whole thing that I was with Gillian at the top of the conservatory and that she didn't kill Charles Reardon. Then that would have made all of our efforts since then unnecessary."

"Or cunning." He stared at Gillian, then nodded decisively. "Seems to me I've got enough reason here to make an arrest."

She caught her breath, then released it in a rush. "If you're charging me, Lieutenant, I assume you have a warrant and that my attorney, Dan Weinstein—"

"Not you, Ms. Randolph. Not tonight, anyway," he said mildly, and then jolted her by swinging in Cleve's direction. "It's your friend here I'm taking in. I told you yesterday, McBride, no more warnings about interfering in my investigation. You didn't listen, so maybe a night in the lockup will teach you I meant it."

"On what charge?" Cleve demanded.

"I don't need a charge. I can hold you overnight without one. No, Ms. Randolph," he cautioned her as Gillian started to object, "no arguments about it. Unless you plan to join him. I don't think a judge, if it came to that, would have any problem with it since you're both guilty of illegally trespassing."

"He's right, Gillian. Won't prove anything if he runs you in, too. And somebody needs to give poor Mike his supper. Hey, don't worry. It won't be the first night I spent in the slammer." He tossed her his car keys. "Okay, Costello, I'll come quietly, but I want your promise Ms. Randolph gets a safe escort home."

The detective agreed, ordering Officer Morelli to follow her back to her apartment in his cruiser. Then he led Cleve toward the exit. Gillian, watching them go, felt sick about his arrest, even if Cleve was maddeningly cheerful about the whole thing.

THE EIGHTEENTH DISTRICT Police Station was on West Chicago Avenue. Gillian was lucky enough to find a parking space across the street from the unimposing, granite-faced building.

As early as it was, the air was already uncomfortably sticky. It promised to be another stifling day. There wasn't much relief inside the police station. Its window air conditioners were insufficient.

When Gillian presented herself at the front desk, the policewoman on duty told her that Lieutenant Costello wanted to have a word with her before Cleve was released from the lockup. She tried not to anticipate what the detective was going to say or do while she waited for him to arrive from his desk in the homicide division. But she couldn't help being tense about another encounter with him. Was this it? Was he going to charge her?

Lieutenant Costello with his sandy hair and deceptively boyish face finally appeared. He took her into a tiny, impersonal office where he could speak to her in private. She refused his offer of a chair. He perched on the edge of a scarred desk and gazed at her in bland politeness.

"Couple of things I thought you'd like to know, Ms. Randolph."

"Yes?" she asked him, rigid with anticipation.

He didn't miss her apprehension. "You can relax. For the time being," he added dryly. "I don't have the report back yet on the semiautomatic. Crime lab is slow this month with people on vacation."

Whether he intended it or not, she understood the implication. She had a reprieve. But once he had the results of the tests from the lab, proving conclusively the bullet that killed Reardon came from her gun, he would have sufficient cause to arrest her. She and Cleve *had* made a mistake in locating the revolver. Their effort had ended up backfiring on them, because Costello plainly believed they, and not Victor, had planted the semiautomatic in the theater.

But why had the lieutenant told her about the delay with the lab? What did he hope to accomplish by sharing inside information with his chief suspect?

"Anything you'd like to tell me, Ms. Randolph?"

Gillian had no response for him. Costello must be hoping the strain of waiting would be unendurable for her. That she would betray herself somehow, even confess in order to find relief. She knew that silence was her only defense. She was at risk here without Dan Weinstein at her side. What concerned her was that Costello was also taking a chance. He could compromise his case by meeting with her like this. Which meant he must be very confident of her guilt.

"I have nothing to say, Lieutenant. Is there anything else before I collect Mr. McBride?"

"Yeah. We checked with Victor Lassiter. He said he hasn't had any rights to the theater at Navy Pier since he went to prison ten years ago and that he kept no key to an outside entrance."

"And you believed him."

He shrugged. "No reason not to."

"Of course. Can I have my private investigator back now, Lieutenant?"

"He's all yours, Ms. Randolph. But from now on keep him away from my case."

"I'll see what I can do. Funny thing about Cleveland McBride, though. He seems to have a mind of his own."

The detective's jaw tightened, but he offered no other reaction. To Gillian's relief, he wasn't present when Cleve arrived several moments later at the front desk where she went to wait.

When they finally saw each other their concerns were expressed simultaneously.

"You okay?"

"You all right?"

"I'm fine," she assured him with a smile, choosing not to tell him that she had spent a restless night because of him. All he had to know was that Victor hadn't tried anything in his absence.

"Me, too."

He didn't look fine, even if he was his usual jaunty self. In fact, he looked awful. Bleary eyes, unshaven jaw, rumpled clothes.

"Yeah, I know," he said, raking a hand through his tousled, golden-brown hair, "I'm a mess. I'd look a lot better if I hadn't had a cell mate who kept me awake half the night describing his talents in detail and telling me exactly how much his lady clients paid him for each of his spectacular feats."

He pocketed his belongings that were returned to him by the policewoman behind the desk, then cupped Gillian's elbow. "Let's get out of here."

Cleve waited until they were in the car and on the way back to the apartment before he asked, "Anything develop while I was being entertained by the city of Chicago?"

"Yes, an interesting little session with Lieutenant Costello." She filled him in on what the homicide detective had shared with her, ending her account with an anxious, "You know what's going to happen when he gets the results from the crime lab. He'll have his official evidence then."

"But he can't act until he does, and that buys us more time."

Unless Victor provides him with something else, Gillian thought. It was a strong possibility. Either way, she was convinced she would be charged. Until then, she had—what? Another day? Maybe two days? And if she and Cleve couldn't manage to clear her...

Sensing her fear, he found her hand and squeezed it reassuringly. He would never know how much she appreciated that simple gesture, even though she was skeptical of his promise that followed. "We'll find a way out of it."

She waited until they stopped at a traffic light to mention the other subject that had been worrying her since last night. "Any problems while you were a guest of the Eighteenth District, other than your male hooker, that is?"

She tried to be nonchalant about it, but Cleve wasn't deceived by her light tone. He scowled at her from his place behind the wheel.

"I knew I shouldn't have told you about my blackouts. Now I suppose you'll be watching me like a mother hen.

No, Gillian, I didn't have any problems, and I don't want to be coddled."

This was definitely not the moment to tell him about his appointment with the hypnotherapist.

Once they were inside her apartment door Cleve announced suggestively, "I need a razor, a shower, and breakfast in that order. Which one are you going to help me with?"

"Eager to experiment with some of your cell mate's techniques?"

"Only the ones that seem anatomically impossible to me. He assured me they weren't, not if you have a roomy shower stall and the right partner. You willing?"

"I think it's safer if I handle the breakfast part."

That didn't turn out to be completely true. She had coffee, bagels and juice on the table, and was dishing up scrambled eggs, when he strolled into the kitchen wearing nothing but the terry cloth towel he had snugged around himself after leaving the shower.

It wasn't much of a cover. A pair of long, muscular legs protruded from its short length while Cleve's hard, hair-roughened chest was bared. Stripped of his whiskers and smelling of soap, his hair in damp spikes, Cleveland McBride was a tantalizing sight.

The breath caught in her throat. She swallowed it and managed to achieve a casual tone as she said, "I can keep this warm if you'd like to get dressed first."

"Clothes can wait," he said, either unaware of his tempting state or secretly enjoying its effect on her. She suspected the latter.

Sliding onto a chair, with Mike curled up near his bare feet, he tucked into the eggs. Gillian, sipping from a mug of coffee she didn't want but needing to keep her hands occupied, sat across from him. This morning's talk was going to be difficult under any circumstances, but with him looking like that...

Better get it over with, she thought, summoning her courage and launching into her explanation.

"I have something to tell you, Cleve. It's something I should have cleared up right away."

Alerted by her sober tone, he glanced at her sharply. "I thought all the secrets were out."

"There's one more. It's about what happened fourteen years ago."

His tawny eyes darkened. "I thought we agreed to leave that in the past."

"I can't do that anymore. I need for you to know the truth because... Well, I just do. So please let me explain why I walked out on you that summer. No, don't look at me like that. I know it's painful. It's painful for me, too. It was painful when I left you, but it was necessary."

"Look," he muttered, "it's obviously what you chose to do, so why can't we just—"

"I didn't choose it. I was *forced* to do it."

He put down his fork and stared at her. "Who?"

"My father."

"That's nuts. Harmon liked me. He liked the work I did for him and his firm. And when he and your mother came back from that vacation and learned we were keeping company, he never once complained about it. Never spoke a word of disapproval about my seeing his daughter."

"Of course he didn't tell you how he felt. It was because he did value your work and didn't want to risk losing you. You wouldn't have been so easy to replace. And, yes, he even liked you. But not for me. He hated our relationship. He felt the age difference was too great and... Well, other things."

"Yeah, I can guess. I wasn't from the right side of town. Okay, so he didn't want me hanging around his daughter.

Only he's afraid to tell me that, so he demands that you end the romance. What did he threaten to do, Gillian? Cut you off without—"

"It was never about money!" she informed him angrily.

"All right, that wasn't fair. Not when I know better these days. But what else could he do to make you run off to Europe without so much as a postcard to explain it? Sure you were young, but even then you were your own mature woman. An adult free to make her own choices."

Gillian drew a slow, steadying breath. This was the hard part. "That's just it. I wasn't."

"Huh?"

"Cleve, I wasn't of legal age."

He pushed his plate away and leaned toward her, a shocked expression on his craggy face. "Are you telling me you weren't eighteen? That I slept with a minor? Just how old were you?"

"Seventeen. But—"

"Good Lord! Why didn't you tell me? Why did you let me think you were of age?"

"Because I needed to be with you. Because you were everything I wanted, and it didn't matter to me how old I was. I knew my own feelings. But I thought it might matter to you. That you'd think I was too young, and somehow eighteen seemed more acceptable."

"Didn't you ever stop to consider there was a risk?"

"Not until my father used my lie as a weapon. He gave me an ultimatum, Cleve. If I didn't leave you, and do it in silence so he wouldn't lose your services, then he'd expose my real age and you'd be prosecuted for being intimate with a minor."

"You believed he would have actually done that?"

"I was scared. I thought he'd ruin you and that it would be my fault. Cleve, I was young. I didn't have any knowledge of the law then. It wasn't until long afterward I learned that in Illinois, as far as the age of consent is concerned, seventeen is a gray area. You probably couldn't have been charged. Daddy must have known that, too, but he knew *I* didn't.''

"So you walked away to save my neck. And you let me think all these years that you..."

He didn't go on. He didn't have to. The expression on his face, gratitude mingled with regret and yearning, said it all. It was a look that made her go soft inside.

All that changed a second later when his whole body went rigid with a bitter resentment. "You sacrificed yourself for me, and your father made you do it. He didn't stop to care what he was doing to us, how he was cheating us of something special. My existing for months afterward as though I'd been kicked in the gut, our losing each other like that...all so that bastard could satisfy himself that his daughter wouldn't be wasting herself on some—"

"Cleve, no! You have to understand him, just like I had to in the end. What he did was right in his eyes, a father who was convinced he was protecting his daughter. He did eventually regret it, though. He told me as much just before he died. He asked me to forgive him, so I told him it no longer mattered.''

His earnest gaze sought hers. "Were you telling him the truth?"

"I was married to Alan then, remember?"

"But you're not married now."

She was still clutching the mug of coffee, untouched except for those first few sips. She set the mug on the table and met his direct, demanding gaze. "I never stopped caring about you, Cleve. Even when I convinced myself I loved Alan, I never stopped caring."

He left his chair, rounded the table, and crouched down in front of her. "Gillian," he said solemnly, taking both of her hands in his, "this is important. Why have you told me all this?"

"It was something I could no longer stand to have between us."

"But why now?"

"Because if I have to leave you again, if they lock me up..."

"Closure?"

She shook her head emphatically. "Not that. Not like you mean. I just need you to know how much you matter to me before it's too late."

His hands tightened on hers. "You're not going anywhere," he promised her fiercely. "I won't let that happen. Why won't you believe that?"

"But if—"

"No. Don't say it. Don't think it." He released her fingers. He reached up, his big hands gently framing her face. "Understand?"

She searched his face below her, her eyes misting over at the caring, loving intensity of his expression. "Yes," she whispered.

"Then no more doubts."

And that's when he drew her face down to his. He began to kiss her with a raw longing that left her breathless and aching for him. She suddenly couldn't get enough of him. She wanted the taste of him in her mouth, the male scent of him in her nostrils, the feel of his flesh against hers. She wanted to be absorbed by him.

She had no awareness of joining him down on the floor. But that's where she found herself, with both of them kneeling face-to-face on the tiles. Clinging to his strength, she filled herself with the essence of him, flames curling inside her as he deepened their kisses. His tongue stroked hers, his fingers seared the sensitive sides of her breasts.

His towel was no longer a barrier. It loosened with their

feverish activity, the ends falling away, exposing his hardness which surged against her with a demanding urgency. That's when she knew where they were headed, when she addressed the consequences of their recklessness.

Resisting his embrace, she pulled her mouth from his. Her voice was ragged as she murmured, "What about the promise we both made? That there would be no sex?"

"I say to hell with it," he said, his voice husky with need.

She smiled at him. "I guess I didn't really believe it was a promise we could keep. But I have one condition."

"Name it," he said, suffering over the delay and ready to agree to whatever she wanted.

"Not here on the kitchen floor, please."

"Deal."

He stood and then leaned down to eagerly scoop her up in his arms, but Mike got in his way. The indignant Lab dodged to one side with a little yelp.

"The path to true love is never a smooth one," Gillian said cheerfully as he carried her into her bedroom.

"Quiet," he ordered, smacking her playfully on the bottom.

Kicking the door shut behind them, he placed her on the bed. She stared at him in fascination. She had forgotten how virile a figure he was with his broad shoulders and lean hips.

Excited by her admiration, he crawled onto the bed and reached for her impatiently. He helped her to dispose of her shirt and bra, then to free her of her cotton slacks. She stopped him when his hand began to drag at the waistband of her panties.

"I have one further request."

Cleve groaned. "What now?"

"There will be," she said with as solemn a tone as she

could muster, ''no law-related puns about things like briefs and plea bargaining.''

He grinned. ''Okay, counselor, if you want to play this straight, then I have my own demand.''

''Which is?''

''No cracks about my cell mate last night. Like did I pick up any interesting tricks from him? Or did he happen to share the age-old secret of all-night endurance? You know, stuff like that.''

''Agreed.''

''Then can we proceed? Because I gotta tell you I'm in serious need here.''

Gillian laughed and held out her arms to him. He answered her invitation with a swiftness that took her breath away. His mouth and hands suddenly seemed to be everywhere at once. Tugging the buds of her breasts with his caressing tongue, tenderly stroking her thighs with his skillful fingers. All humor fled from her as he awakened sensations she hadn't known in fourteen years. Inflamed by his sensual assault, she strained against him with a longing to have his body joined with hers.

For one unbearable moment he denied her that completion. Rearing back, he gazed down at her with eyes that slowly cherished her naked length.

''I used to dream of you like this,'' he whispered. ''I used to drive myself crazy with the images. I thought I remembered everything about you. I was wrong, because I'd forgotten just how beautiful you are.''

She glowed with his words. And that's when he lowered himself and merged with her. She opened for him in a slow, deep fusion that was an accompaniment to his swollen kisses. Then his hardness rested within her softness until neither of them could endure the agony of their stillness.

Gillian stirred under him, pleading for fulfilment. He responded with long, lazy strokes that intensified to a blinding rhythm. Clasping him with her arms and legs, her body begging for the release that only he could provide, she mounted the pinnacle with him.

There was a roaring in her ears, and then she was rocked by spasms that felt as if her very soul were being consumed. Seconds later Cleve joined her, soaring into the sweet radiance.

Afterward, flushed and happy, squeezed against his side with his hand resting possessively on her hip, she savored their togetherness. The interlude must have been equally precious to him because he murmured drowsily, "I missed us like this. And when I think of all those years that were wasted..."

She smiled, her fingers stirring through the hair on his chest. "Wouldn't you say we just made a darn good start in making up for them?"

When he didn't respond, she lifted her head to look down at him. Exhausted by his long, sleepless night and their bout of lovemaking, he had drifted off. She let him sleep while she went on gazing at him, taking pleasure in the sight of his wonderful, compelling face.

But there was a shadow on her joy that she couldn't ignore. She had given Cleve every opportunity this morning to express his love for her. He hadn't. He'd once told her she was the only woman he wanted. But fourteen years was a long time. Maybe...

No, that wasn't the problem. She sensed how much he still wanted her, that she was just as vital to him as he was to her. But they could do nothing about it as long as this murder charge stared her in the face.

Even then it might be too late for them to recover what they'd lost all those years ago. Because Gillian knew, with a depressing certainty, that Cleve would never commit himself to her while he lived with the threat of his blackouts.

And that was when she remembered she had yet to tell him about the appointment with the therapist.

Chapter Eleven

"You did *what?*"

The bed shook as Cleve shot up against the carved headboard. He was explosively angry. She had just told him about the appointment with the hypnotherapist.

Gillian tried to defend her action with a persuasive argument. "She's in demand, usually booked up weeks in advance. But she had this opening because of a cancellation. It's first thing Friday morning, so I thought—"

"You had no right! No damn right at all!"

"I know I didn't," she agreed softly. "I know it was wrong of me. But if I hadn't arranged for the appointment, if I hadn't been so anxious to see you get help—"

"Didn't I tell you I'd make the appointment myself? That I'd do it right after this mess with Lassiter is settled?" He swung his legs to the floor and reached for his robe. "What happened, Gillian? You decide not to believe me?"

That was exactly what she had decided, but she didn't tell him that. Instead, she argued, "And what if the case isn't cleared up? What if it goes on, while every day you're vulnerable?"

"Then I live with it." He got to his feet, slid into his jeans, and headed for the door. "So what *you'd* better do," he added gruffly before he stormed out of the bedroom, "is phone your therapist and cancel that appointment, because I'm not planning to be there Friday morning.''

She gazed after him, resenting his stubbornness, fearing that the only therapy he trusted was to bury himself again in the wilderness. And if that happened, she would lose him. Her life and career were here in Chicago. Providing, that is, she still had them when all of this was over. So, even if she chose to join him in his cottage by the lake, even if he wanted that himself, she knew he would refuse to let her share his existence up there. He would be convinced she was sacrificing herself. He would walk away, and—

No! She wouldn't let him go! He had to listen to her!

Scrambling off the bed, she found her robe and slipped into it. Then she followed him out into the living room. He was sprawled in an easy chair, absently scratching Mike who had flopped down on the floor beside the chair.

She went and stood in front of him. He didn't look up. There was a sulky expression on his face. It wasn't like him to pout. It took her a long moment of staring down at that lowered head with its tousled hair to realize what was going on in his mind.

Dear God, why hadn't she seen it before? Cleve was afraid to see the therapist. This strong man, who would face any physical danger without hesitation, was scared to death. Not because he risked another disappointment if the session failed but because of what he might learn about himself. He would never admit it, but he was terrified of what could be uncovered while he was under hypnosis. Of being told about some terrible secret buried in his subconscious, of having to confront it and deal with it. That was what his anger was all about.

She understood, she was sympathetic, but she wouldn't let him run away from himself. She loved him too much for that.

He lifted his head and glared at her. "Did you make the call?"

"No," she said gently. "You'll have to do that yourself, only I hope you won't."

He stared at her, saying nothing. Gillian knelt on the floor between his parted legs. She reached for his hands, holding them tenderly between her own.

"Listen to me," she said, appealing to him as earnestly as she knew how. "I want you to promise me something. I want you to tell me that you won't cancel the appointment, that you'll try at least one session with the therapist."

He started to pull his hands away. "Haven't I already told you—"

"No," she insisted, hanging on to him, "I won't let you refuse me. Cleve, I'm not asking anything else of you, just this one thing. And I have to ask it now, because when Friday rolls around I may not be here to argue with you about it. I could be behind bars by then."

Cleve went very still. His gaze met her wide eyes pleading with him. His anger evaporated, leaving an ache inside him. It broke his heart to see her like this.

"I thought we agreed there would be no more doubts about getting you cleared. What's it going to take to convince you that—"

"I'm trying to be confident," she interrupted him. "But, Cleve, we have to be realistic. And the reality is I face arrest when Lieutenant Costello gets back that report."

"But until he does…"

"What? What else is there to try? We found the gun, and that didn't help. So where do we go from here?"

Freeing his hands, he dragged her up onto his lap where he held her in a fierce embrace. "I don't know, sweetheart. I just don't know, but I'll think of something." She started to speak, and he silenced her with a quick, fervent kiss.

She wasn't to be diverted. When his mouth lifted from

hers, she was ready with another urgent plea. "Cleve, please—"

"Yeah, I know. All right," he said reluctantly, "I promise to keep the appointment."

"Good."

He expected to see complete satisfaction on her face, but there was something else bothering her. He could read it in her eyes. "What is it now?"

"I lied," she said solemnly. "Because there is one more thing I'd like to ask you to do."

"Name it."

"It's about Sarah. If the worst should happen, and I'm no longer able to be here for her, would you take care of her for me?"

"Gillian, don't say that. We're *both* going to be here for Sarah whenever she needs us."

Striving to prove that, he began to kiss her again.

"Heaven and earth," he murmured between kisses. "I'll move heaven and earth to get you out of this jam. Just gotta come up with a plan."

Breathless from his assault, Gillian relented. "Well, until you do…" Slipping off his lap, she got to her feet, forcing herself to be cheerful, teasing. "I expect to hear an exciting inspiration by the time I'm out of the shower and dressed."

An inspiration, he thought as he watched her turn and move toward the bedroom. Hell, that's just what he needed. But he'd run out of inspirations. Nothing occurred to him. He had nothing but his resolve to save the woman who meant everything to him, and it wasn't enough.

Damn it, he was a good P.I., wasn't he? There must be something he could try.

Lassiter's alibi, he thought suddenly. That was the key now. Somehow he had to find a way to break Lassiter's alibi for the time of the murder. If he could convince Costello that the bastard hadn't been working at the hotel when

Charles Reardon was slain, they stood a chance of getting the detective to seriously listen to them. Of winning him over to their side. How? The bellboy at the Hutton, who was Cleve's paid informant, had no idea how Lassiter could have been in two places at the same time. But there had to be an explanation and a means of obtaining it.

What was it Harry Rosinski used to say? The words of his mentor, who had taught him all the essentials of private investigation, came back to him.

"The answers don't come in blinding revelations, Cleve. Not very often, anyway. When you finally get some answers, it's only after hard work. And that means research. Yeah, you research a subject to death. You go back into his history, and you dig for every detail, because you never know when some little discovery is gonna lead to just what you're looking for."

Solid advice, Cleve thought. Okay, so what particular portion of Victor Lassiter's history had he not yet looked into? The answer to that one was clear and simple. And with it came a swift decision.

Gillian was blow-drying her hair when he found her in the bathroom. One glance at his face was all it took.

"You're on to something," she said eagerly.

"Could be. We'll see. How does a drive over to East Moline appeal to you?"

She understood his intention. "You want to go to the correctional center where Victor was an inmate for the last years of his sentence. But why? What can you possibly hope to learn there?"

"Don't know yet. Maybe nothing. Or maybe something valuable. Anyway, I figure it's worth the effort. It's still early, and it's interstate all the way. We should be able to make the place by afternoon, then get back here sometime tonight. You up for it?"

"Of course. But why not just call East Moline and ask your questions over the phone?"

Cleve shook his head. "People have a way of turning you down on the phone. It's less easy to say no when you're face-to-face."

"That's true, but do you really think any of the authorities there will give out information on one of their ex-inmates without some court order?"

"Probably not, but I have to try. If I could just pick up some lead, some connection..." He shrugged. "I don't know. Call it a P.I. itch. Whatever it is, I need to scratch it."

"And I suppose it's useless to point out to you that you just spent a night in jail for ignoring Lieutenant Costello's warning about not pursuing the investigation?"

"Yeah, that would be useless all right."

She made up her mind. "Give me twenty minutes, and I'll be ready to go."

"Time enough for me to get into some clothes and gas up my car."

He was anxious now to get on the road and didn't want to stop once they were underway. That impatience was still with him when he returned to the apartment after visiting a filling station two blocks away. But it was momentarily forgotten by the sight of Gillian waiting for him in the living room. He could tell that something had happened in his absence.

"What is it?" he demanded.

"I had a phone call from Maureen Novak. With Reardon dead, the company is willing to settle the suit out of court and clear her husband's name. Bless her, she still wants me to handle the negotiations for her. But, Cleve, they're asking for a meeting this morning."

"Which means you wouldn't be free to go to East Moline."

"Well, my situation being what it is, I can't handle the actual negotiations, but I would like to sit in on the meeting."

He didn't miss the hopeful look in her eyes. Maureen Novak's request was a vote of confidence at a time when Gillian badly needed someone other than himself to believe in her. He couldn't deny her that.

"Okay, you stay, but not on your own. I'm going to hire Moody Jackson to stick with you while I'm gone."

"And Moody Jackson would be...?"

"A bodyguard I know. He's dependable. Only thing is he doesn't have a car. The two of you will have to get your Volvo out of the garage downtown."

She knew better than to waste time arguing with him about the necessity of a bodyguard. But there was something she didn't like and *was* prepared to discuss. And by the look on her face, he could easily guess what it was.

"Don't look at me like that," he growled before she could bring it up. "I'm not going to have any blackouts on thc way to East Moline."

He hadn't meant to snap at her, but her concern was irritating. He could feel her watching him all the time, worrying about him. He appreciated that she cared, but it put a strain on their relationship.

More than ever now he hated his condition. He'd longed to tell her after their lovemaking just how he felt about her. But how could he commit to her with this thing hanging over him? As for his appointment with the hypnotherapist on Friday... Well, he wasn't going to think about it. It would panic him if he did. He couldn't afford to concentrate on anything but saving Gillian. Because if he couldn't clear her, nothing else mattered.

"GET WHAT YOU WANT?" she drawled, flicking ash from her cigarette.

Cleve, who had just emerged onto the street after leaving the correctional center's administration building, glanced at the receptionist. She had thick glasses and a smile that showed too many teeth.

His disappointment must have been easy to read because, after gazing at him between puffs, she laughed. "Never mind. I can see you didn't. Told you so going in, didn't I?"

"How do I get out of here?"

"You don't until the guard that admitted you comes back to usher you out to the gate. It's a prison, hon. The security is as careful as the staff is about the records of the inmates." She dragged on the cigarette, blowing out a cloud of smoke before teasing him with a casual, "Course, there are always exceptions."

Cleve forced himself to smile at her persuasively. "Are there? Like what?"

She considered him for a moment, then shrugged. "What the hell. I was given two weeks' notice this morning, so what have I got to be loyal about?" Dropping the cigarette, she crushed it underfoot. Then, looking around to make sure they were still alone, she murmured a quick, "Try Bill Jerome."

"Who's Bill Jerome, and where do I find him?"

"Ex-guard. He retired end of last week. Guards in this place know a heck of a lot more than the warden does about the inmates. And as I recall, Bill had some pretty strong feelings about your man. Maybe he'd be willing to answer your questions. Here comes the guard to show you out."

"Thanks, but where—"

"Place called Blues. It's a sports bar down near the river, and I never told you."

As SPORTS BARS WENT, Cleve thought, Blues was nothing out of the ordinary. It had the usual giant TV screen, pool table, and walls mounted with basketball hoops, football jerseys from another era, and some battered looking hockey sticks.

He decided the most welcome fixture in the place was the air-conditioning. Moline was experiencing the same heat wave as Chicago.

At this hour, Blues was empty except for the bartender, a stocky guy with almost no hair and an affable face. Cleve guessed he was somewhere in his late fifties.

"What can I get for you?" he asked as Cleve parked himself on a stool at the bar.

"I'll start with a cold draft beer."

The bartender drew the beer and placed it in front of him. "You one of our regulars? I'm trying to learn the names and faces of all the regulars. I just bought a partnership in the place after retiring, so it's all new to me."

"No, I'm just passing through," Cleve told him. "Looking for someone, and I think I may have found him. Would you be Bill Jerome?"

"Uh, yeah, but how did you…"

Cleve introduced himself, displayed his P.I. identification, and explained what he wanted and why. "I'd appreciate anything you could tell me about Victor Lassiter."

The ex-prison guard shook his head. "I dunno. I wouldn't want to do anything to risk my pension, and answering a bunch of questions—"

"No one will ever know where the information came from but you and me," Cleve urged him. "That's a promise you can trust, because a P.I. never reveals his sources. If he does, those sources dry up on him, and he's out of business."

Bill Jerome sniffed and considered his appeal. "Yeah, well, I always said Lassiter never should have been released." He hesitated. "And you say he's already killed someone again?"

"I'm convinced of it. I just need enough evidence to bring to the police, and then he can be put away again where he belongs."

Bill nodded, making up his mind. "I don't know about evidence. I don't have anything like that to give you. All I can tell you is that I've seen a lot of bad cons come through East Moline. Maybe not as hardened as what they get in other prisons, but some of them bad enough. Not one of them, in my opinion, could match Lassiter."

Cleve sipped his beer. "How do you mean?"

"Most of the men inside aren't smart. That's why they're in there. But Lassiter was bad *and* smart. In a creepy way, if you know what I mean."

"I think I do."

"Smart enough to control people, when he could get away with it. He sure had that cell mate of his just where he wanted him."

"Tell me about that."

"Rudy Martinez. A nervous little guy who blinked all the time. I think he'd been convicted of shooting his wife's boyfriend. Something like that. Anyway, he and Lassiter were cell mates in Joliet and also here in East Moline. Way I heard it, Lassiter saved his butt when some tough con threatened to tear Rudy apart. They were all scared of Lassiter. After that, Rudy would do anything for him."

Rudy Martinez, Cleve thought. Why did that name ring a bell? "Is this Rudy Martinez still inside?"

"No, he got out some time back. Don't know what became of him. His sentence was revoked after a lot of lengthy appeals. Meant he wouldn't have been a parolee when he left, so there was no one to monitor him. He was free and clear."

"What did he do in civilian life?" Cleve knew that an individual's occupation could provide a wealth of information about him.

"Let's see…" The ex-guard frowned, trying to remember. "Something around food services, I think. Yeah, that's it. He'd trained as a chef and then spent a lot of years managing kitchens and restaurants. Pretty experienced at it, too, I guess."

Cleve suddenly thought he knew why the name of Rudy Martinez sounded vaguely familiar. He had heard it in connection with Lassiter's alibi. Probably from his contact at the Hutton Hotel. But he would need to make certain of that.

He leaned forward, a note of excitement in his voice. "You're sure you have no idea what became of Rudy Martinez after he left East Moline?"

Bill Jerome shook his head. "Afraid not."

Cleve nodded and raised his glass, swallowing another mouthful of beer as he gave himself a moment to think. He was convinced that he had just struck gold. But he would need to verify his discovery.

"You have a pay phone in here, Bill?" he asked, setting the glass back on the bar.

"Over there by the door."

Cleve went to the phone on the wall and used his card to call the Hutton in Chicago. He was put on hold until his contact at the hotel was free to come to the phone. He was tense with impatience waiting for the bellboy to get on the line, though *bellboy* in this case was something of a misnomer. Sammy Gates was just shy of qualifying as an octogenarian, and still going strong, bless him.

Be there for me, Sammy, he silently prayed.

A second later the bellboy was.

"Sammy, it's Cleve McBride. I have a question for you. Do you have a Rudy Martinez employed at the hotel?"

"Yeah, he's the director of food services. Seems to me I mentioned that to you already."

Yes, you did, Sammy, and I committed the unpardonable

P.I. sin of failing to check it out. Cleve damned himself for trusting until now that the provider of Victor Lassiter's alibi was all that he was supposed to be: the Hutton Hotel's director of food services, above suspicion and having no possible past connection with Lassiter.

"Sammy, there's something else I need you to find out."

"Like?"

"Does your director of food services hire the waiters and is he in charge of scheduling all their shifts in the dining rooms and room service. Think you could check that out for me?"

Sammy grunted. "I don't have to. I already know. Martinez does do the hiring and he does handle the scheduling for the servers."

Cleve promised the bellboy he would take care of him as soon as he got back to Chicago. Hanging up, he thanked Bill Jerome for his valuable help, paid for the beer, and added a generous tip. Seconds later, he was in his car and headed for the interstate.

It fits, he thought with a sense of triumph as he wove through the traffic. It all fits.

Lassiter had convinced Rudy Martinez to take him on as a server at the hotel. Then Victor had used him again when he murdered Charles Reardon. Martinez must have given him his alibi, somehow covering for him on the schedule and then swearing he'd been on duty at the hotel when Victor had gone to the conservatory to meet Reardon.

Only there were still a couple of puzzles here. Since Martinez was responsible for hiring the waiters, the Hutton's upper management wouldn't necessarily have to know that one of their servers was an ex-con. Or maybe, since waiters were badly needed, they would give a parolee a chance. But Rudy was also an ex-con, and he wasn't a mere waiter. He was the director of food services. Why would a reputable hotel give an ex-con a position like that? How had Martinez managed to secure it?

And there was something else. Why would Rudy Martinez, even if he was grateful to Lassiter, risk both his job and his freedom by providing Lassiter with an alibi for murder?

They were questions demanding answers. But this time Cleve wouldn't be doing the digging. He was convinced Lieutenant Butch Costello would be more than willing now to handle that side of the investigation himself. He was eager to confront the homicide detective with his discovery. And Gillian...he could picture Gillian's face when he told her. The image had him glowing inside.

He needed gas, and he also needed to contact Gillian. There was something she had to do. He found a station, filled his car, and used a pay phone to call her at her office.

"Cleve! Where are you? Are you all right?"

"I couldn't be better." Then, anxious for her safety, he asked, "How about you? You okay? Is Moody still with you?"

"Right here. The First Lady couldn't have better protection. But you haven't said—"

"I'm at a filling station just off the interstate. Headed home."

"Any luck in East Moline?"

He hesitated, then decided he didn't want to try to explain the results of his effort over the telephone. "Tell you when I see you."

"You sound excited. Is it—"

"Gillian, it's complicated." *And I want to see your face when I tell you.* "But I guarantee you're going to be pleased. Now before you blow me a kiss, counselor, and give me a sweet goodbye, there's something I need you to do after you hang up."

"You realize how keyed up you've just made me, don't

you? All right, stop chuckling about it and tell me what you want.''

"Contact Lieutenant Costello. Ask him to meet us in the lobby of the Hutton. I should be there in—'' he consulted his watch ''—say two hours from now.''

"How do I convince him to—''

"Tell him it's important, that he's got to be there.''

"I'll manage it,'' she promised him.

"See you at the Hutton then.''

Satisfied, he rang off. He couldn't wait to be with Gillian again. To touch her, hold her in his arms. He thought about how warm and wonderful their lovemaking would be tonight, how freely they could give themselves to each other once she was free of this pressure that had been building around her like a violent storm. The prospect of their intimacy excited him.

Everything is going to be okay now, sweetheart. I know it is. I can feel it. And then you and I...

But it was bad luck to count on something as important as this until the victory was final and official. Because the game still had crucial seconds to be played.

Chapter Twelve

Gillian kept her eyes on the homicide detective's freckled face and prayed. Except for the taut line of his jaw, he wore no expression that told her what he might be thinking as he listened to Cleve's story. She had trusted every word of Cleve's exciting deduction when he had shared it with her a few minutes ago while they'd waited for the plainclothesman to arrive. But would Costello go for it?

The lieutenant sat back in the easy chair that faced them after Cleve was finished with his explanation. The three of them occupied a small, private alcove off the vast lobby of the Hutton Hotel. There was a tense silence in the alcove while they waited for Costello's reaction.

Cleve was seated close beside her on the sofa. Gillian found herself seeking his hand and squeezing it. He returned the pressure, communicating his confidence.

The detective finally spoke, asking brusquely, "Who told you all this?"

Cleve shook his head. "You know I can't tell you that. But you can trust it comes from a reliable source."

Costello leaned forward, thumping his knuckles on the surface of the coffee table situated between his chair and the sofa. "I ought to lock you up again for this."

"But you won't, because you know I've got something this time."

Costello said nothing for a minute. He made the familiar sucking sound with his tongue against his teeth. Gillian breathed easier. She could tell now that he was interested.

"Maybe," he conceded.

"How about it, Lieutenant? I bet if you went right now to Rudy Martinez and faced him with this, he'd crack. From what I was told about him, he'd be too scared not to."

The detective made an impatient gesture with his hand. "What you learned about Lassiter and Martinez might be true, but this business of their manufacturing an alibi is pure conjecture. *Your* conjecture."

"But worth testing, isn't it?"

"We'll see."

Without another word to them, Costello got to his feet and left the alcove. Gillian kept her gaze on his retreating figure, expecting him to turn in the direction of the kitchens where Rudy Martinez's office would be located. But to her dismay, the sandy-haired detective strode without pause toward the hotel's street entrance.

"He's leaving!" she cried. "He didn't believe you!"

Cleve shook his head. "No, I'd say he's going out to use the radio in his car. I think he's going to have headquarters do a fast check for him on my information. He wants to make certain that Lassiter and Martinez *were* together at East Moline before he tackles the assistant director of food services."

"Then maybe..." she said hopefully.

"Yeah, I think this could be it, Gillian. I think we stand every chance now of getting Costello in our corner."

But Gillian was far from ready to celebrate. She waited restlessly for the return of the detective.

Cleve, aware of her painful suspense, drew her into his arms, murmuring a husky, "Public place or not..."

He kissed her. A long, slow kiss that was so reassuring,

so compelling that she almost forgot where they were and why they were here.

She was still clinging to him, still savoring the promises his kiss conveyed when they were interrupted by the pointed sound of a throat being cleared. Gillian, removing herself from Cleve's embrace, looked up to see an elderly bellboy standing over them. He wore a wicked-looking grin as he regarded them.

"You interested in registering for our honeymoon suite?" he asked them in a gravelly voice. "Because it sure looks like you could use one."

Gillian felt herself blush. Cleve merely laughed. Getting to his feet, he introduced his contact, Sammy Gates. The two men compared notes, with Sammy reporting that Lassiter had finished his shift and left the hotel for the day, but Rudy Martinez was still in his office.

Cleve was paying Sammy for all his help when Lieutenant Costello reappeared in the alcove, accompanied this time by another officer. They couldn't tell by the detective's expression what he had learned. Nor did he share his decision.

But though he confided nothing, Gillian was encouraged when he turned to the bellboy and asked tersely, "Can you show us to the director of food services' office?"

"My pleasure," Sammy answered without hesitation.

The bellboy led the way toward the service regions of the hotel, Lieutenant Costello and the other officer at his heels. Cleve seized Gillian by the hand and followed them. If the detective objected to their presence, he didn't indicate it.

For all his years, Sammy was astonishingly energetic as he conducted them through a bewildering maze of corridors at the rear of the hotel. Gillian found herself growing breathless as she struggled to keep up with him.

The smell of fresh paint assailed them. Gillian understood why when they turned a corner and arrived in a long passageway. The area was being repainted. There was a work crew in the hall, busy with their buckets and brushes.

Sammy stopped and pointed toward a small, dark man who was standing in the doorway of an office talking with one of the kitchen staff.

"Rudy Martinez," he said and left them without another word, returning to his duties in the lobby.

Weaving through the paint crew, Lieutenant Costello and his man approached the director of food services, with Cleve and Gillian close behind them. Martinez looked startled when they reached him.

"Uh, something I can do for you folks?" he asked them in a breathless, nervous voice as his rapidly blinking gaze traveled from one face to another.

The detective offered quick introductions and then displayed his credentials. "I need to speak to you, Mr. Martinez. In private."

There was no mistaking the alarm on Rudy's face, though he tried to hide it when he politely indicated his office behind him. "Sure. Come on in."

"You two stay out here," Lieutenant Costello instructed Cleve and Gillian.

They knew better than to argue with him. The detective, his officer, and the director of food services disappeared into the office, the door closing behind them. The member of the kitchen staff had already melted away. The painting crew went on with their work.

Gillian and Cleve waited in the hall, their tension mounting again. They were silent now, busy wondering what was being said behind the office door. The long seconds crawled by.

RUDY WOULDN'T BE expecting him, Victor thought with satisfaction as he arrived at the employees' entrance off the rear of the hotel. The little man would be relaxed, confident he was free of his nemesis until Victor's next shift tomorrow morning.

Victor had planned it that way. This was the quiet hour for the food staff, that period between lunch and the bustle of dinner preparations. He knew this was when Rudy was most likely to be alone in his office, probably working on menus.

Victor's intention was to surprise him. Rudy would be vulnerable that way, more easily handled. He was concerned about Rudy. The little man had grown increasingly fearful about their arrangement, becoming a potential danger. Victor needed to remind him in the privacy of his office just how much he would lose if he failed to keep his silence. That was why he had returned to the hotel.

Victor met no one on his way to the office of the director of food services. It wasn't until he turned a corner, smelled the fresh paint and saw the crew busy on ladders that he remembered this section of the service region was being repainted.

It was no problem for him. The painters were too occupied with their work to even notice his approach. He was just one more faceless hotel employee. But several of them were in the process of repositioning their ladders and drop cloths. They blocked the route to Rudy's office, which was now a few yards away along the corridor. He had to stop and wait until he could get by them.

A few seconds later there was an opening for him to squeeze through. But Victor didn't move. Now that his view was no longer obstructed, he could see the figures of a man and a woman standing just outside Rudy's office door. They were not painters.

Even with their backs to him, Victor recognized them. Gillian and her private investigator! Why were *they* here? What were they waiting for?

But this was no time for speculation. At any second one of them could swing around and discover him standing here. And Victor's instinct for survival told him this was something he needed to prevent. Increasingly uneasy about their presence, he began to slowly and carefully back away.

Then he realized this was no good. A considerable length of corridor stretched behind him. There was every possibility that before he could reach the end of it and vanish around the corner he would be spotted.

There was a closed door directly to his left. He knew it was kept locked. But since it was a storeroom containing equipment for room service, he had been provided with a key. Fishing in his pocket, he produced his keys.

The painting crew, discussing their work, ignored him as he unlocked the door and slipped into the room. He was in such a hurry that, when he snatched his keys away from the lock, they flew out of his hand and went sliding across the floor of the storeroom.

Victor waited to recover them until he had safely closed the door behind him. Then, finding himself in a thick gloom, he realized that, unless he turned on a light, he would never find the keys. He wasn't prepared to risk that. There was a transom above the door, and any glow in the storeroom might be noticed and investigated by a passing member of the hotel staff.

It was safer to remain here quietly in the dimness, then search for the keys later. Victor was prepared to wait, no matter how long it took. Even if he could escape now, he wouldn't. He was determined to learn what Gillian Randolph and her protector were doing outside Rudy's office.

The framework of the transom over his head had been painted and then the window left open so it would dry without sticking shut. That meant he could hear the painters out in the hall. But he wasn't interested in what they were saying. He was worried. He wondered how long it would take until Gillian and McBride left the area so he could corner Rudy in his office and demand an explanation.

GILLIAN'S NERVES were in a state of advanced turmoil by the time the office door finally opened. Lieutenant Costello emerged, followed by his officer and the food director.

One glance at Rudy Martinez told the story. Or at least the first part of it. The man was trembling, his eyes wide and frightened. In custody of the police officer, he was led away down the corridor.

"We're taking him in for further questioning," the homicide detective informed Gillian and Cleve. "His lawyer will probably have him out in a couple of hours, but by then it'll be too late for him to warn Lassiter. Not that I think at this point he'd want to."

"Then he did talk?" Cleve asked the lieutenant.

Costello started to answer him, but then he became aware of the painters. By this time the crew had worked its way up the corridor and was ready to deal with the area outside the office where they stood.

"We're in the way here," the detective said. "Let's move down."

He led them along the corridor. The three of them stopped outside a closed door that was labled as a storeroom. They were out of hearing of the painters.

"So tell us," Cleve demanded impatiently.

"It took a promise of leniency, but Martinez finally cooperated. We got a full explanation out of him."

Gillian searched the detective's face. His whole attitude had changed. He was no longer gazing at her with accusation in his eyes. But she wouldn't feel genuine relief until she had heard everything. Cleve, aware of her apprehension, squeezed her hand with encouragement.

"Lassiter doesn't know it yet," Lieutenant Costello went on, "but his alibi has collapsed. Martinez admitted he was lying when he swore that his former cell mate was here at the hotel at the time Charles Reardon was murdered. Lassiter was on duty that day, but he was able to slip away for a few hours while Rudy covered for him.''

"Why would Martinez risk everything to do that?'' Cleve wanted to know. ''His job here, going back to prison. Was he that scared of Lassiter?''

"Yes, but not like you think. Lassiter was blackmailing him. Rudy had made the mistake of confiding to him back in East Moline that he had a cousin in Memphis who'd just gone under on a hotel he owned there and needed money. For the right price, the cousin would write a glowing reference for Rudy.''

"I get it,'' Cleve said. ''Rudy was supposed to have been the director of food services in this Memphis hotel. A lie to cover those years he was actually in prison. No wonder the Hutton here hired him. They never knew he was an ex-con. They thought he'd just come off this impressive job in Memphis.''

The lieutenant nodded. ''The Hutton checked, of course. Phoned the man they didn't know was Rudy's cousin and were assured that Rudy Martinez had been a fantastic director of food services in his hotel.''

"And Victor used his knowledge of that fabricated reference,'' Gillian said, ''to force Rudy Martinez into giving him a job here and then afterward into providing him with an alibi. And the alibi was for murder.''

"Looks like it,'' the lieutenant acknowledged, ''although Rudy claims he didn't know what the alibi was actually for.''

"But we know better, don't we?'' Cleve pressed the detective. ''If Lassiter goes to the trouble of inventing an alibi for that morning, that means he's your killer and Gillian is in the clear. What about it, Lieutenant?''

"We'll see if Victor Lassiter is it,'' Costello said cautiously. "*After* I've had him picked up and brought in for questioning. I'll keep you informed. With all that's happened, I think you have that right. In the meantime—" he turned to Gillian, favoring her with an expression of apology "—I'm sorry, Ms. Randolph, but everything did point to you. Consider yourself no longer my chief suspect. That satisfy you, McBride?"

And without waiting for a reply, he turned and strode off along the corridor.

Gillian gazed after the detective until he was out of sight. Then she turned to Cleve, a joyous expression on her face. "I'd be going with him, and in handcuffs, if it hadn't been for you and your refusal to give up until you solved the case."

Cleve grinned at her. "That's right. What's my reward?"

"A bonus with your fee?"

"Not good enough."

"What will you settle for?"

"A real expression of your gratitude. Let's see if this works."

He took her face between his hands, leaned forward, and angled his mouth across hers. His kiss was deep and searching, leaving Gillian swaying weakly when he finally released her.

"Not bad," he said. "As a down payment."

He would have kissed her again but, aware of one of the painters gaping at them, she held him off. "That poor man is about to fall off his ladder."

"What? He's never seen a victory kiss? All right, I'll save the rest until later." His eyes gleamed with enthusiasm. "Hey, I know what we should do. Let's drive up to Lake Forest and get Sarah. She can go out with us and help us celebrate. The kid would love that."

She considered his offer a moment and then shook her head. "After Sarah's truancy the other day, I'm not sure

how much Saint Bride's would appreciate that. Besides—''
her expression sobered ''—I think that, until Victor is
caught and Lieutenant Costello is fully convinced of his
guilt, I'd feel better keeping Sarah in school. Just as a pre-
caution.''

Cleve nodded. "You're probably right."

Besides, he had just decided that he had a much better
celebration in mind for the coming evening. One that did
not include Sarah. It involved a bottle of good wine, some
soft music, and Gillian's king-size bed. Oh, yeah, *definitely*
the king-size bed.

He slid an eager arm around her waist. "Come on, counselor, let's go home."

THERE WAS silence now outside the storeroom door. But
Victor didn't stir. He went on standing there in the gloom,
his mind seething with a black rage.

He had heard it all through the transom, and he knew he
was finished. The bitch and her boyfriend had destroyed
his plan for her. She would remain free, and he would go
back to prison. But they had to find him first, and until
then...

It wasn't too late, he realized with a growing excitement.
He could still hurt her, could still make her suffer.

Sarah. There was someone called Sarah in a school in
Lake Forest. Victor had heard a deep devotion in Gillian's
voice when she'd discussed the girl. Her daughter? Victor
had never heard about a daughter. Why had Gillian kept
her a secret? But it wasn't important. This Sarah obviously
mattered to her a great deal, and that's all he needed to
know.

He would have his revenge, after all. He would use the
girl to punish her.

Saint Bride's. She was at Saint Bride's Academy. He
knew it was a private boarding school in Lake Forest. He

had presented one of his marionette productions there years ago. He hadn't forgotten.

It was time to leave. There were several things he had to accomplish. The minutes were suddenly precious, but he wasted a couple of them trying to find his lost keys. He couldn't locate them, so he gave up the effort. After all, the keys were really no longer of any use to him.

Careful to make sure the corridor was deserted now, except for the painters who were too occupied with their work to pay any particular attention to him, Victor left the storeroom and hurried to the nearest back exit. He met no one until he was on the street where he lost himself in the crowds.

Chapter Thirteen

Church bells. Gillian could hear them a few blocks away as she surfaced from a restless sleep. This was Thursday morning, not Sunday. They were probably tolling for a funeral service. She found them disturbing and didn't know why. After last night, nothing should be troubling her.

She and Cleve had made love. He had been infinitely tender. And insatiable. The memory warmed her. Then why was she so unsettled?

Probably because Lieutenant Costello had yet to phone them that Victor was in custody. That was what was bothering her. She needed to know the outcome of Victor's arrest before she could begin to feel easy. And until then...

Turning her head on the pillow, she searched for the comforting presence of Cleve on the other side of the wide bed they had shared. He wasn't there. She was alone in the room.

The bells stopped pealing. In the quiet that followed she caught the husky murmur of Cleve's voice through the half-open door. At first she thought he was talking to Mike in the living room. Then she realized he was on the telephone. She couldn't hear what he was saying, but her sense of misgiving deepened.

A moment later there was silence. Cleve must have hung up. Gillian was sitting against the headboard when he entered the bedroom. He was already dressed. One glance at his somber face told her that she hadn't been imagining things. Something was wrong!

"What is it?" she demanded, trying not to be alarmed as he perched on the edge of the bed and reached for her hand.

"I just got off the phone with Lieutenant Costello. Something has come up. It could be serious."

"Victor! It's about Victor, isn't it? Has he—"

"The police went to his hotel late yesterday to bring him in. He wasn't there and didn't show up, not then or anytime during the night. And he's failed to report for work at the Hutton this morning. They have the net out for him, but no result so far."

Gillian was puzzled. "If Victor has disappeared, that means he's aware the police are on to him. But how could he have learned he's wanted?" She suddenly became conscious of the comforting way Cleve was holding her hand, as though he had yet to tell her the worst. "There's more, isn't there? Tell me," she urged him.

"The Hutton Hotel contacted Costello early this morning to report a set of keys that were found by the painting crew. They were clearing out the storeroom near the food director's office, getting it ready to paint next. The keys were identified by a manager there as Lassiter's, and one of the kitchen staff thinks she spotted him leaving the hotel yesterday afternoon. The time would have been shortly after we were in the hallway outside that storeroom."

Gillian stared at him. "Are you telling me that Victor was hiding in the storeroom, that he somehow overheard what we were saying?"

Cleve nodded soberly. "It looks like it."

She struggled to recall exactly what they had said. Lieutenant Costello had informed them of Rudy Martinez's confession, which meant Victor would have realized he was finished. Then the detective had departed, leaving her and Cleve to— Oh, dear God! In sudden horror, she remembered the rest.

"Sarah! He knows about Sarah!"

"I'm afraid so. There was nothing we said to indicate she's Molly's daughter, but it was enough to reveal Sarah's importance to you."

Gillian had another terrifying thought. "We mentioned her boarding school and Lake Forest, which means Victor knows exactly where to find her!" In a panic now, she pulled her hand away from his. Throwing aside the bedcovers, she started to swing her legs to the floor. "I've got to alert Saint Bride's! I've got to warn them that Sarah may be at risk!"

Cleve put a hand on her arm to stop her. "Easy, sweetheart. That's all being taken care of. I explained to Costello about Sarah, and he's phoning the school himself. He's even arranging for the police up there to send an officer out to Saint Bride's. Sarah will be protected."

She should have found comfort in the realization that Lieutenant Costello would do everything he could to safeguard the girl. That he was now ready to believe Victor, and not Gillian, had murdered Charles Reardon. But this was no longer a vital issue to her. She could think of nothing but Sarah.

"I've got to go up there myself," she said, scrambling off the bed. "I've got to be there for her. With Victor on the loose out there somewhere..."

She couldn't finish her thought. It was too frightening.

Cleve understood. "Get dressed. I'll take you."

Snatching up some clothes, she headed for the bathroom and a quick shower. When she emerged fifteen minutes later, ready for their drive to the northern suburb of Lake Forest, Cleve was waiting for her. She knew immediately by the worried expression on his craggy face that there had been another development while she'd been under the shower.

"What's happened?"

"Costello phoned again. Saint Bride's told him that two of their teachers took some of the girls out in the school van. They left an hour or so before he called. Something about a hike and a picnic in one of the nature preserves."

Her heart sank. "Sarah—"

"Yeah, she's with them. Gillian, it's going to be okay. The local police are on their way now to the nature preserve."

She tried to convince herself that Cleve was right. That nothing could happen to Sarah. The teachers at Saint Bride's Academy were responsible individuals, always concerned about the well-being of their charges. This picnic was evidence of that. During summer vacation like this, when so many of the students were at home with their families, the school kept its remaining boarders content with a variety of entertaining and instructive activities.

That was what Gillian told herself, but she couldn't shake her fear. It stayed with her as she and Cleve climbed into his car and headed north along the lakefront. There was a haze out over the waters, the result of the sultry heat that continued to hold the city in its tight fist.

Gillian felt like the weather, heavy and feverish. She was sick. Sick with dread over the welfare of Molly's daughter.

"If he can't destroy me one way," she said, referring to Victor, "he'll use another. He's evil, Cleve. Evil *and* demented. He'll take Sarah if he gets the chance and use her to hurt me."

"Stop torturing yourself. She may be safer off at this nature preserve than at the school itself where Lassiter would assume he'd find her. Try to keep that in mind."

"I hope you're right. The thing is…"

"What?"

"I keep thinking he must believe Sarah is mine. Maybe Molly and I made a terrible mistake in keeping her existence a secret from him. If Victor knew Sarah wasn't my daughter, that she was Molly's—" She broke off, shaking her head in doubt and self-reproach. "But even then, being what he is, it might not matter. Not when she isn't his. Not if he's convinced I love her as much as if she were my own. Oh, Cleve, I couldn't stand it if anything were to happen to her."

"It won't. Just hang on."

They sped up the expressway in the direction of Lake Forest, weaving in and out of the weekend traffic. And for once, Gillian didn't concern herself about his reckless driving.

GILLIAN'S BREATH quickened as they turned in at the gates of Saint Bride's and rolled up the drive through the shaded, spacious grounds. There was a sober scene in progress when they arrived at the front entrance. The school van had returned from the nature preserve. She could see it parked under the trees. Behind it was a patrol car, its light flashing.

People had gathered on the sidewalk. Gillian recognized several school authorities exchanging information with two uniformed officers. They were all adults. Sarah was not among them.

Lieutenant Costello was also there, and when she and Cleve emerged from his car, the detective detached himself from the group and came to speak to them. There was a grim expression on his freckled face that told her she was about to hear something awful.

"It's not good," he said, coming straight to the point. "We think Lassiter managed to snatch her."

"How in the name of heaven could something like that happen?" Cleve demanded angrily, his arm around Gillian, who was so stunned she couldn't speak.

Costello shook his head regretfully. "No one saw anything definite, so it's only guesswork. But we think Lassiter must have arrived here at the school last night when they were loading the van. One of the girls thinks she remembers seeing a man strolling across the lawns out there. But that's not unusual. That part of the grounds is a public park, and people are always out walking."

"Why weren't the teachers in charge more alert?"

"You can't blame them, McBride. Remember, this all happened before they knew there was anything to worry about. It's not as though Lassiter looked threatening or tried to approach them. But he must have been close enough to hear Sarah respond to her name when one of the teachers corrected her about some bit of mischief. That's probably how he was able to identify her."

"What then?"

"He must have been on hand this morning and followed the van to the nature preserve. No one saw him out there, but he had to have been nearby and waiting for his chance. The teachers were busy setting up for the picnic before they organized a hike. The girls were told to stick close, but you know how kids are. One of Sarah's friends told us that she and Sarah wandered off just into the edge of the woods. Then they got called back. The friend ran on ahead, and by the time anyone noticed that Sarah wasn't right behind her—"

"She was gone," Gillian whispered, her heart feeling as heavy as stone.

"They were starting to look for her when the local police arrived," Costello continued. "The officers sent the van back to the school. The preserve has been thoroughly searched, but there was no sign of Sarah or Lassiter."

"So he has her," Cleve said, his voice hoarse with fury. "What happens now?"

"We do everything we can to get her back. We're getting out an APB right now with full descriptions."

Gillian roused herself from her shock and grief to offer the detective information that might be important. "Lieutenant, I don't know if it will make a difference, but there's something you ought to know...."

She went on to explain about her relationship with Sarah, but that Victor didn't know any of it. Nor would Sarah be aware that her captor had been her mother's husband and murderer in another life.

The lieutenant was sympathetic, sensing the effort it cost her to confide the secret. "We'll do our best for Sarah, Ms. Randolph. Meanwhile, McBride, I think you should take Ms. Randolph home and stay with her. There's nothing either of you can do here. Besides, Lassiter may try to contact you there. And if he does, no heroics, McBride. You call immediately and let us handle it."

IT WAS AFTERNOON by the time they returned to the apartment.

Gillian, frantic over Sarah's disappearance, stood by the living room window and looked down into the street.

"You know why he's kidnapped her, don't you, Cleve? He failed to send me to prison, so now Sarah has become the instrument of his revenge."

"Don't keep punishing yourself. It won't help."

She rounded on him angrily. "What am I supposed to do? Just sit here and wait?"

"Look," he said awkwardly, "can I get you something? How about a glass of your special iced tea?"

She smiled at him apologetically. "No, Cleve, I don't want anything."

"You're worn out."

"I didn't sleep very well last night."

"Then lie down."

"I couldn't possibly sleep."

"I know, but you can at least rest."

Not giving her a chance to object, he took her by the hand and drew her into her bedroom.

"Come on," he urged. "I'll join you."

Kicking off their shoes, they stretched out on the bed. Cleve gathered her close. Turning on his side, he began to massage the nape of her neck. It was meant to offer her a small measure of comfort, a tender expression of his concern. She was touched by it. She loved the feel of his strong, skillful fingers and the way his tawny gaze caressed the contours of her face with a sadness for what she was suffering. His gentleness made her want to cry.

Cleve searched his mind for a course of action. He had promised to help her protect Sarah, and he had failed. But it wasn't too late. Whatever Costello had ordered, there must be something he could try. If only—

The extension rang on the bedside table, startling both of them, even though they had been waiting to hear it. Cleve rolled over and reached for the phone. Gillian watched with wide, anxious eyes as he took the call.

"It was Costello," he reported to her after he hung up a few minutes later. "They found the car Lassiter rented yesterday, empty and abandoned in a parking lot. So far nothing more than that. He's decided Lassiter is probably too smart to make any contact by phone. But, just in case, he's trying to arrange for any calls here to be traced. He says it's a problem, though I don't know why it should be."

"Because," Gillian explained, "even with my permission, the police need a court order for that. Trying to find a judge willing to issue one on short notice..."

He nodded. "I guess." He didn't add that a desperate P.I. wouldn't have bothered with the legality of it.

The afternoon stretched on. Costello didn't call again.

The phone remained silent, the useless waiting unendurable.

IT WAS THE KIND of place that asked no questions. And looked it. The walls were in need of fresh paint, the fixtures stained, the furniture shabby from hard use. It was an ugly motel in a run-down neighborhood.

None of that was important to Victor. All he needed was a safe hideout for a few hours. He had paid cash for the room and moved in with his essentials.

Now, with the drapes closed, he was seated at the solitary table. His materials he'd acquired at the craft shop yesterday were in front of him. He worked rapidly, handling the tools with skill and confidence. From time to time, he glanced at the motionless figure stretched out on the bed near the table. With her hands folded across her chest, she reminded Victor of a fairy-tale princess on her funeral bier.

But the girl was not dead, only unconscious. She would stay that way for hours. The drug was as reliable as he had been promised by the ex-con he had known back in Joliet. The same unsavory character who had supplied him with the handgun and the car, which was now parked out of sight behind the motel.

He directed his attention back to his work on the table. This would be the last marionette he would ever produce, and he wanted it to be right. Time didn't permit the kind of careful detail he prized in his creations, but it would serve his purpose.

Much later, when he was finished, he sat back and examined his effort. He was satisfied with it. He looked at his watch. Time to go out and find a safe public phone away from the motel. He had two calls to make, one now and then another a bit later on.

Pushing back from the table, he got to his feet and glanced at the girl on the bed. There was no sign of her stirring. He could leave her for a few minutes. But to make certain she remained quiet, he tied and gagged her. He would remove the restraints when he returned.

Slipping out of the motel room, he locked the door behind him, pocketed the key and went off to put his plan into motion.

CLEVE HAD YET to settle on any possible course of action when the phone finally rang again. This might be it! The call they had been waiting for!

He snatched up the receiver with a quick, "Gillian Randolph's apartment."

"Is this the private investigator?"

The tone was breathless, on the nervous side. He couldn't imagine who it was, though the voice did sound familiar. Gillian was hovering at his elbow, waiting for him to identify the caller. He shook his head, indicating to her it was neither Lieutenant Costello nor Victor Lassiter.

"Yeah, this is Cleve McBride. Who's calling?"

"It's Rudy Martinez over at the Hutton."

He recognized the voice now, even though he had heard it only briefly yesterday in the hallway outside the food director's office. Martinez's lawyer must have won his release. But why on earth was he calling here?

"I remember. What do you want, Rudy?"

"To get clear of this mess Victor got me into."

"Didn't Lieutenant Costello promise you yesterday that if you cooperated—"

"There was no guarantee I wouldn't go back to prison. Well, I want to make sure I don't. And maybe I can do that by helping you. I hear you can't find Victor. Suppose I know where he's hiding and that I can lead you to him."

"Where?" Cleve demanded.

"Uh-uh, I'm not giving away anything over the phone. I called because I wanted to be sure you were interested.

If you are, then there's another call I'll make when I hang up. And never mind who or where. All you need to know is that after that call I should know for certain just where Victor is.''

"Why aren't you taking this straight to Lieutenant Costello?''

"No more cops,'' Rudy insisted, his voice rising on a note of slight panic. "I'm taking enough of a chance as it is. If any of this gets back to Victor before he's caught—''

"All right,'' Cleve interrupted him impatiently, "I get it. You're scared, and you want me to play the go-between.''

"That's the deal. You willing?''

How could he not be? At this point he was ready to risk anything to locate Lassiter. "What do you want me to do?''

"Meet me in a half hour,'' Rudy instructed him.

"Where? At the hotel?''

"Not here. There was enough of that yesterday. I got my job to think of. Make it the edge of Grant Park right across the street from the hotel. And, McBride?''

"Yeah?''

"You'd better be on your own, or I don't talk.''

Returning the receiver to its cradle, Cleve rapidly described the conversation to Gillian.

"Can you trust him?'' she asked.

"There's not much choice, not when it's a chance to find Lassiter.''

"That's true.''

He eyed her in concern. "I don't like going out and leaving you here, but somebody needs to stay by this phone.''

"I'll be all right.''

He made up his mind. "Yes, you will be, because I'm phoning Moody Jackson to join you. He said he'd stay available for the next few days, if we needed him again.''

"And what if Lieutenant Costello calls again wanting to know where you are?"

"If he does, I guess you'd better fill him in. Tell him I'll contact him as soon as I know anything. He won't like that, but I'm not stopping to worry about it. And if Lassiter should phone you—"

"I know," she said. "I'll let the police handle it."

Satisfied, he called Moody Jackson. The bodyguard promised he would come immediately.

"I'm not crazy about leaving you alone before he gets here," Cleve said, slipping into his shoes, "but if I don't leave now, I won't be in time to meet Rudy Martinez."

"Don't worry. I'll keep the chains on the doors until Moody arrives. Cleve?"

"Yeah?"

"Take care of yourself. I don't want you vanishing along with Sarah."

"You'll get me back," he promised, "and I'll have Sarah with me when I return."

He parted from her with a quick, reassuring hug. Not long after he was gone, her front door buzzer sounded, sending Mike into a frenzy of barking. Silencing the dog, she went to answer it.

She was prepared for Moody Jackson and was surprised when a young voice on the intercom identified himself as, "Chicago Courier Service, ma'am. I have a package for a Ms. Gillian Randolph."

She wasn't expecting a package. Was this something in connection with Victor? If so, it was an unexpected form of contact. She couldn't ignore it. "Second floor apartment," she instructed him, buzzing him into the house.

She had the door pulled back on its chain when he arrived on the landing outside, ready to slam it if there was anything suspicious about him. But he was wearing a delivery uniform and a cheerful smile. He looked legitimate.

"Just a second." Closing the door, she released its chain and opened it again to receive the package he was carrying.

"Do you know where this originated from?" she asked him as she signed for it.

"I just deliver them, ma'am."

She thanked him and secured the door behind him. Mike stood there with his tail wagging, watching her quizzically as she gazed down at the package in her hands.

It had no return address on it, but she was certain now who had sent it. The shape and size of it were familiar. Somewhat larger than a shoe box, it was wrapped in brown paper and tied with cord. Gillian had received one almost exactly like it at her office directly after Victor Lassiter had been released from prison. Its contents had been chilling.

She was trembling now, afraid to open the delivery but knowing she had to if it meant helping Sarah. She carried the package out to the kitchen, Mike at her heels. Setting it on the counter, she removed a knife from a drawer and slit the cord. Then, with hands that shook, she pulled off the brown paper and lifted the cardboard lid.

For a long, stricken moment she gazed at the marionette inside the box. It was not as accurate as the figures he had created of Molly and herself, but it was recognizable. Enough like Sarah to convince her there was no shred of doubt about it. He had the girl.

What sickened her was how he had clothed the marionette. It wore the familiar blue-and-white uniform of Gillian's beloved Cubs. Probably removed from one of those Cubs dolls that were sold in souvenir and craft stores throughout Chicago.

She thought the uniform was a form of Victor's twisted humor, his way of gloating to her that he had stolen something from her she greatly prized. But there was a definite purpose in his vile joke, one she discovered only after she lifted the marionette out of the box.

At the bottom was a note. Unfolding it, she started to read it, but the writing was so cramped she needed her glasses. She fumbled for them in her purse on the kitchen table, slipped them on, and with her pulse racing, read the message.

Do you still love those doubleheaders? They're playing one today. We're going to be there enjoying the final innings. Why don't you join us? I'll look for you out in center field after the crowds have all gone home. Then, when it's quiet, we'll play our own game. Just you and me, Gillian. If you bring anyone else, anyone at all, your favorite little player will be out before she ever comes to bat. But if you follow the rules, she could be safe on base. Who knows, maybe she'll even get a home run.

He was challenging her to rescue Sarah, and his instructions were clear. Gillian was to come to Wrigley Field where the doubleheader was now in progress, then discover a way to stay behind after the ballpark had emptied. And if she was alone—no Cleve, no police—he would make a trade. Sarah would go free, while she, herself…

Gillian shuddered over the probable outcome of such a bargain. Of course, if she did obey Victor, she couldn't trust him not to harm Sarah anyway. But if she could convince him that Sarah wasn't her daughter, maybe he wouldn't sacrifice her.

Gillian had no illusions about her own survival once she surrendered herself to Victor, but that was a risk she was prepared to take. There was no other way. She saw that now. Bringing the police into the ballpark would condemn Sarah. Victor wouldn't hesitate to kill her, even if it meant his own death. And to involve Cleve… No, she wouldn't let the man she loved be a target for that lunatic.

She had to go. And she had to leave now before Cleve—

The door buzzer sounded again, startling her as she was removing her glasses. Moody Jackson! She had forgotten about him!

This was a new problem. If she ignored the buzzer, the bodyguard would think she was in trouble and break in. She had to admit him. But then how was she going to get away from the apartment without him?

The buzzer called to her again impatiently. Mike started to bark. In a panic, Gillian slid Victor's note into the pocket of her cotton slacks. Then, snatching up the marionette, she dropped it into the wastebasket, shoving the wrappings on top of it to hide it.

Mike sniffed suspiciously at the bodyguard when she opened the door a minute later, then licked his hand in acceptance.

"Hey, he remembers me," Moody said with a cheerful grin. Then the big man turned to her with a frown on his bearded face. "You sure took a long time answering. You okay?"

"Fine," Gillian assured him, afraid her breathlessness would betray her. "I was in the bathroom."

"Oh."

"Would you like something?" she offered quickly, wishing she didn't sound so nervous. "There's beer in the refrigerator, and I have those pretzels you like."

"That would be good."

Within minutes, Moody was happily installed on the living room sofa, watching TV and sipping a cold beer. And Gillian was still searching for a way to escape from the apartment. Mike provided her with the opportunity. The Lab had his nose pressed against the closed door to the kitchen.

"What's he want?" Moody asked.

"I think he needs the backyard. You stay put. I'll let him out."

The bodyguard nodded. He was deeply engrossed in an old movie when Gillian left him. Grabbing her purse off the kitchen table, she unlocked the back door.

Mike was reluctant to go out. It must have been something else in the direction of the kitchen that had interested him, maybe his water dish or his food bowl. She had to tug him by the collar to get him out on the landing. But once the door was shut behind them, he followed her willingly down the stairs.

"Moody will let you back in," she whispered to the dog, who began to sniff around the yard.

And by then she would be long gone. She hated to trick the bodyguard like this, but she had no choice.

Hurrying across the yard, she let herself out by the side gate, gained the sidewalk and began to walk rapidly in the direction of Wrigley Field. She left her Volvo where it was in front of her building. Parking was a problem at the ballpark. Anyway, it was only a few blocks south from here. She could cover the distance easily on foot.

She was no longer nervous. Perfectly calm now, she was ready to do whatever was necessary.

Chapter Fourteen

Gillian couldn't stop herself from thinking about Cleve. He would be frantic when he returned to the apartment and found her gone. She couldn't dwell on that, though. She would be sick with guilt and regret.

If she had to think about him, it was much better to remember what she cherished. All those little things that made him the man she loved. The way his bronze-colored hair, with its sprinkle of silver, curled at the nape of his tanned neck. The sensual timbre of his husky voice. And how he carried himself so erectly.

The images came crowding into her mind. His anger with her followed by his gentleness. His wonderful hands teasing her flesh. The way he sometimes gazed at her so possessively when he thought she wasn't looking.

She embraced each of these images, because she might never experience them again. They gave her courage to face what lay ahead of her in the ballpark.

She crossed a busy street, aware of the headlights on most of the cars. The afternoon was fading. The sun was already behind the buildings on the other side of Clark Street, the first shadows of twilight gathering in the alleys.

She was passing Graceland Cemetery when another change occurred. The wind shifted. It no longer moved in from the southwest. The turning breeze blew now off Lake

Michigan to the east. And as it increased, it lifted the thick heat that had blanketed the city for days, dispersing it in a matter of seconds.

The difference was very sudden and very extreme, as the weather often was in Chicago. A welcome relief, except Gillian wasn't dressed for the cool lake wind. Shivering in her lightweight slacks and summer top, she quickened her pace.

Graceland Cemetery was behind her now. Another couple of blocks and she reached a corner where she had to wait for the light to change before she could cross. Wrigley Field was directly on the other side.

Gillian had never thought of the ballpark, one of the oldest in the country, as anything but homey and friendly, a beloved Chicago landmark. But now, in the dwindling light, it loomed in front of her like a massive fortress, its soaring walls solid and forbidding, daring her to penetrate them.

The light changed. She crossed the street toward the nearest gate, steeling herself for what waited for her inside.

WHERE THE HELL WAS HE?

Cleve stopped his pacing on the sidewalk that edged Grant Park to consult his watch. It was well past the time Rudy Martinez had set for their meeting. Something must have happened.

Eyeing the entrance to the Hutton across the street, Cleve decided he had waited long enough. Whether Rudy liked it or not, he was going after him inside the hotel.

Dodging the traffic, he crossed Michigan Avenue and strode through the lobby. No need to ask for directions. He remembered the way to the office of the assistant director of food services.

Rudy wasn't in the office when he arrived. There was a young woman there talking to a chef about the last minute details of a banquet scheduled for that evening. She gazed at him in surprise.

"Can I help you, sir?"

"Is Rudy Martinez around?"

"Mr. Martinez is no longer with the hotel, sir."

That wasn't what Rudy had indicated on the phone. "He came in to clear out his desk?"

The woman shook her head. "Mr. Martinez hasn't been anywhere near this office today."

Cleve stared at her. For a few seconds he was baffled, struggling to understand. And then all at once, like the hard jolt of a fist in his gut, it struck him.

Lassiter! It must have been Lassiter himself who had phoned him! With his talent for mimicry and his knowledge of his former cell mate, Victor would have had no trouble imitating Rudy's nervous voice. And Cleve, in his eagerness to locate Sarah, had believed his performance.

He had been a prize fool! Lassiter had succeeded in separating him from Gillian, leaving her vulnerable! A target for that sociopath! He had to go to her! And pray that Lassiter hadn't managed to reach her yet!

Cleve knew he was violating a half dozen traffic laws in his race back to the apartment. He didn't care. His only concern was in reaching Gillian. And his one comfort on that wild drive was Moody Jackson. At least he'd had enough sense to arrange for the bodyguard's presence at the apartment. Moody would protect her.

But, to his dismay, when he arrived in front of the building he found Moody alone out on the street. Something was wrong!

The bodyguard was built like a wrestler, but he blubbered like a child when he told him.

"She's gone, Cleve. Walked out on me when my back was turned. I been chasing all over the neighborhood searching for her. Figured she has to be on foot because her car is still parked over there. Why would she go and walk out like that, and where did she go?"

Cleve didn't know. Moody kept insisting there had been no sign of Lassiter, no evidence of a struggle. Unless Lassiter had been waiting for her down in the yard, she had simply let the dog out and then failed to return.

"Her purse," Cleve remembered. "She had her purse on the kitchen table. Is it still there?"

Moody didn't know.

"You wait here. I'm going to find out. Because if her purse is missing, it means she wasn't grabbed. She left by her own choice."

Which, Cleve thought as he hurried into the building and up the stairs, is probably exactly what happened. Lassiter wouldn't have kidnapped Sarah without a plan. He must have somehow used the girl to lure Gillian away from the apartment. Gillian had gone to help Sarah. But *where?*

It was Mike who provided the answer. Cleve had just reached the kitchen, and assured himself with a glance that the purse was gone, when the Lab trotted around the table to meet him. There was a toy in his mouth. Except this was no doggie toy that Cleve remembered. Mike surrendered it with reluctance.

Teeth marks and dog slobber had damaged the object, but he identified it immediately. A marionette of a young girl. He knew who the figure must represent. The overturned trash can on the kitchen floor told the rest of the story.

There had been a delivery in his absence, probably accompanied by instructions. Gillian must have buried the marionette in the can, hiding it from Moody under the wrappings from the package. And Mike, unable to resist the temptation, had later claimed it for himself.

The wrappings were still there on the floor where the dog had dragged them. Cleve examined them, but they told him nothing. In the end, it was the costume on the marionette that gave him what he needed. He knew now where Gillian had gone.

Moody was waiting for him on the front steps when he charged out of the building. He passed the bodyguard without a pause, yelling over his shoulder an urgent, "Call the cops, Moody! Send them to the ballpark!"

But there was something Cleve failed to remember as he flung himself behind the wheel of his car and tore off down the street, tires squealing. For Moody Jackson there was only one ballpark. The one near which they'd both grown up and where the White Sox played. Comiskey Park on the South Side.

Not Wrigley Field.

THE MAN IN the ticket window was chewing gum. He looked at Gillian as though she were slightly crazy.

"They're into the top half of the ninth," he informed her. "The game is almost over. The *second* game. Why would you want to—"

"Please, it's very important. There's someone inside I have to meet. I promised him I'd be there."

He shook his head, but to her relief he sold her the ticket. Gillian hurried through the gate and along the curving, brick-floored concourse. Seconds later, she emerged into the open on the vast stands that embraced the playing field like a giant boomerang.

The combination of fair weather and a doubleheader had attracted an enormous crowd. Victor and Sarah could be anywhere among the thousands that swarmed the stands. Or he could be hidden with Sarah deep within the bowels of the park. Gillian could never hope to locate them. All she could do was wait until Victor found her.

Her seat, the only ticket available, was in the section over the visiting team's dugout above the first-base line. She settled into it tensely, ignoring the noise and stir of the people packed around her and, for the first time in her life, indifferent to the action down on the field.

Gillian was interested in only one thing at this moment. Obeying Victor's subtle instructions, which meant she had to determine where she could conceal herself when the game ended and the stands emptied. It wouldn't be easy. She knew there was a large security staff that checked carefully after a game to be sure everyone was out.

But Gillian was familiar with Wrigley Field. She had joined tours through the facility on several occasions. She tried to remember the layout and any possible hiding places as she scanned the sweeping terraces and upper decks.

She dismissed the banks of seats. Nothing in those immense stretches offered a likely prospect.

Dragging her gaze away from the stands, she focused her search in the other direction, out over the playing field itself. She had to hurry. A glance at the board informed her there were already two outs in the top half of the ninth. The Cubs were ahead by one run. If the visiting team at bat failed to score before their third out, there would be no bottom half to the last inning. The game would be over.

Her gaze drifted away from the scoreboard, and then went back to it speculatively. It was behind center field, soaring above the narrow bleacher section. Gillian knew the structure was hollow in order to permit the team stationed inside it to operate the board manually. What were her chances of climbing that ladder after the team departed and hiding herself inside the scoreboard?

No. Too many drawbacks. Then *where?* Where could she conceal herself until—

Her attention was suddenly captured by a movement in the wall below the bleacher section. An inconspicuous door had opened. One of the players emerged, closed the door, and sauntered away along the perimeter of the field.

The batting cage, Gillian remembered. There was a batting cage behind that door. It was tucked out of sight under the bleachers. The players went there sometimes to practice. But most of the time, she had been told, it was deserted. Silent and empty. And it was directly behind center field where Victor had instructed her to—

The crowd came to its feet with a roar, startling her out of her absorption with the batting cage. The game was over. The Cubs had won. And Gillian was forced into a quick decision.

The throngs began streaming toward the exits. She struggled against them in the opposite direction. Expecting at any second to be challenged, she managed to get down out of the stands and onto the graveled walk that framed the field.

A moment later she reached the door in the wall and slipped inside. Hopefully, her swift action had gone unnoticed in the mass exodus from the park.

Adjusting her eyes to the dimness, she saw that the area contained more than just a batting cage. All the apparatus used to so carefully maintain the lush turf of the playing field was stored here. She selected a large mowing machine and crouched behind it.

The long, unnerving minutes passed as she waited in the stillness, praying no one would come to investigate, or worse, lock the door from the outside. But there was no movement, no sound except the muted flow of the street traffic on the other side of the outer wall. She tried not to worry about Sarah, tried not to wonder where Victor had hidden himself with his young captive while she huddled down here in the chilly gloom.

The seconds crawled by, an eternity of them. When Gillian could stand it no longer, she got to her feet. The shadows had deepened. She couldn't see her watch, but she judged that a good forty minutes had passed, maybe even more than that. It should be safe by now for her to appear on the field.

Cautiously cracking the door, she listened. Nothing. Spreading it wider, she slid out into the open.

The blankness that greeted her was a rude shock. They were gone, all the sights and smells and sounds of a ball-park with a game in progress. No cries of the food vendors, no odors of onions heaped on steaming hot dogs, no restless crowds in the stands. The terraces and decks were deserted.

The sun had also entirely vanished. It was twilight. A raw twilight, Gillian discovered as she moved toward center field. Without the shelter of the back wall, she was exposed to the wind from Lake Michigan. A cold, searching wind.

The falling temperature hadn't mattered earlier in the stands. All those bodies packed around her, together with the sinking sun, had produced sufficient heat. Now there was nothing to keep her warm.

Hugging herself against the gusts that buffeted her, she came to a stop behind second base. Her nerves didn't help. She was shaking from them as much as from the cold.

This was far enough. All she could do now was wait again, a lonely target in the bleakness of the half-light. She had never felt so helpless, so vulnerable.

Nothing stirred in the vast silence of the park. Where was Victor? Watching her from the heavy shadows? Why didn't he come? She couldn't stand this torment much longer.

A moment later she saw them. Two small figures high in the upper terrace section. They began to descend the steep expanse, moving toward her in the gray light. Gillian drew a deep breath, preparing herself for the confrontation.

TOO LATE!

Cleve swore savagely as he reached Gate F. The stout mesh screen was already locked in place across the entrance. No sign of anyone behind it. No one to rouse. But he tried anyway.

"Hey, someone, *anyone!*" he shouted through the grille. "Open up! It's an emergency!"

No response. Not a sound.

He guessed the other gates would also be blocked and abandoned. But he had to try them. He had to find a way inside.

Moving off at a trot, he began to circle the huge structure, his frustration mounting as he found nothing but sealed gates and blank walls. All of them too high and solid to climb.

He was on fire with worry. If Wrigley Field operated like Comiskey Park, and he figured it did, then he knew it was staffed with a large security force. During a game they were all over the place, handling crowd control. But once that crowd was out, and the park secured, the teams departed along with players and other staff.

Behind them they left a solitary night watchman in a windowless room buried somewhere under the stands. There'd be all kinds of monitors in that room. But the watchman on duty there would be interested only in the electronic eye beams that triggered alarms if the perimeters were invaded by any attempted break-ins. He wouldn't bother with the areas those perimeters embraced. They were unoccupied. Nothing was supposed to be happening in them.

But Cleve knew they weren't empty. Not this evening. Gillian was somewhere in there. And Sarah, together with that lunatic, Victor Lassiter. He had to get in there. He had to help Gillian. But how, *how?*

He was at a point of desperation when he reached the back side of the ballpark. And then he saw it. A paneled truck parked close to one of the service doors. The door was wide open, and as he approached it two men emerged wheeling a cart. The cart bore containers that they began to load into the truck.

Has to be one of the food concessions that cater parties in the private boxes, Cleve thought.

What were his chances of getting through that service door? He pretended to be waiting for the traffic to clear so he could cross the street. The men were paying no attention to him.

"Let's get that last cart," he overheard one of them say, "and then we can get out of here."

Out of the corner of his eye, he watched them turn and go back inside. They left the service door open, which meant they were returning almost immediately. Cleve moved like lightning, following them into the park.

He saw the backs of the two men as they climbed a ramp in front of him. He could hear them talking, grumbling about being so late, then the rattle of the second cart as they reached it and began to move it into position. In another second the heavy cart would be turned around. They would roll it down, and they would discover him.

A narrow, short passage paralleled the side of the ramp at ground level. Cleve dived into it and raced to the door at its end. It was locked. No way through it. But the shadows here were heavy. He crouched down into a tight ball, hugging the wall of the ramp.

The cart clattered down the ramp, was pushed through the service door without pause. And then the metal door clanged shut, followed by the snapping of a lock. There was silence.

Exhaling in relief, Cleve got to his feet. He was inside, though caught in an enclosed area. What now? He made his way through the gloom and mounted the long ramp. At the top were dimly lighted corridors branching off in several directions, a bewildering maze of them.

He paused, trying to determine which passage would take

him out into the open. And where the hell were the cops he had asked Moody to send? They should have been here by now.

He would just have to manage on his own. Gillian needed him.

Removing his Colt .38 Special from its holster under his jacket, he checked the revolver to be sure it was loaded. He was ready. He chose the corridor on the far left.

VICTOR HAD A GUN in his hand. Gillian could see it when they reached the lowest seating section where the club boxes were located. He used it to nudge Sarah, to keep her moving in front of him.

The girl kept stumbling, her steps dragging as they made their way down onto the playing field. Even from this distance, and in the fading light, Gillian could see there was a dazed expression on Sarah's narrow face. What had happened to the lively eleven-year-old she loved?

She's in shock, she thought, outraged by Victor's treatment of the girl. She wondered if he had drugged her to keep her quiet.

Victor was in no hurry. He took his time. There was a satisfied little smile on his thin mouth as he maneuvered Sarah into position just behind home plate. He murmured something into her ear, and she came to an obedient halt. Her chin was down, as though she hadn't the strength to lift her head.

"That's far enough," he called out in his cold, dead voice. Then he added a slow, silky, "For now, that is."

Gillian knew he was speaking to her this time, not his captive. She hadn't realized until this second that, in her need to reach Sarah, she had drifted forward from second base and was now standing on the pitcher's mound. He waved the gun at her warningly, and she stayed where she was.

"Victor," she cried, begging for Sarah's release, "let her go. Send her out of the park. You don't need her anymore. You have what you wanted. I'm here."

At the sound of her voice, Sarah raised her head, as though aware for the first time that Gillian was present. There was a confused, frightened expression on her face. "Gillian?" she asked, appealing to her.

Gillian felt as though her heart were being squeezed.

Victor muttered something into the girl's ear, and she dropped her head again and was silent. "You see," he boasted, "she does what I will her to do. She's just like one of my marionettes. All I have to do is gently tug a string, coax her with a word, and she dances for me."

He's a monster, Gillian thought angrily. Only a monster would enjoy something like this.

She wanted to shout curses at him, wanted to tell him that he was without a shred of humanity. But she resisted that urge. She stood there on the pitcher's mound, with the cold lake wind sweeping over the field, and fought for self-control. Struggled to find the words that would free Sarah, keep her safe.

"Victor, listen to me."

"Ah, you're about to pitch something. Why not, when you're in the appropriate spot for it."

"You have to listen to me," she pleaded.

She was dealing with a jury. The most difficult jury she had ever faced. The case required all of her persuasive powers as a lawyer. It had to be argued with conviction, and she had to win it. Sarah's life depended on it.

"There's something you don't know," she said earnestly. "Something you were never told. It's about Sarah."

Victor laughed harshly. "I was wrong. We're not on a baseball diamond, are we? We're in a court of law."

Gillian ignored his sarcasm and pressed on. "Sarah isn't my daughter. She's Molly's daughter. Molly was pregnant with her when she left you. Do you understand what I'm telling you, Victor? You're her father. She's *your* child.''

There was silence from the direction of home plate. A terrible silence. Gillian knew the risk of the part lie, part truth she had just revealed. Sarah must be as stunned by it as the man who held her, but she couldn't stop now to concern herself with the consequences of that.

Victor's denial was sharp and violent. "You're lying!"

"It's true. Look at her. Open your eyes and look at her. She has Molly's coloring and eyes, but they're in *your* face. You can't hurt her. Whatever you do to me, you can't hurt your own child."

There was another long, indecisive silence. No sound but the rush of the wind in the deepening twilight. Would he believe her lie? Both he and Sarah happened to have narrow faces. Was that enough to convince him there was a resemblance? When the jury of one finally arrived at his verdict, Gillian knew with a sick lurching of her stomach that she had lost the defense.

"Shut up!" he snarled viciously. "Shut your lying mouth before I do it for you!"

As proof of his intention, he stretched out his arm to its full, lethal length. The gun clutched at the end of it was aimed directly at her. Gillian went rigid. This was it! He was going to kill her!

Refusing to surrender to death, even when all hope was gone, she swung her head from left to right. Searching wildly for some means of help. Not expecting to find it. And unable to believe it when she did.

Cleve! Cleve was crouched there in the stands above third base, his revolver in his fist!

Not stopping to wonder how he'd managed to be here, she whipped her gaze back to home plate. Victor hadn't discovered Cleve's presence in the murky light. His attention was focused entirely on her.

Joy swelled inside her for a brief second, and then was cruelly deflated by a sudden realization. He can't bring Victor down with that revolver, she thought. If he tries, he risks hitting Sarah next to Victor.

Handguns, she knew from her instruction on the firing range, were inaccurate at any distance. And Cleve was too far away, with no time for him to close the gap.

She could see Victor's teeth gleaming in a grin of triumph, could sense his finger beginning to squeeze the trigger. She started to shout a furious, ''No!'' But before she could utter even that much, a gun barked.

Cleve's revolver. And the bullet found its mark. Not Victor's body. Cleve had known better than to attempt that. But the gun in Victor's outstretched hand had been a possibility. Cleve's only choice.

There was a flash at home plate. Sparks from struck metal. Then Victor's howl of rage as the gun jumped out of his hand and went soaring like a foul ball outside the third-base line. Victor went after it.

''Gillian,'' Cleve yelled down to her, ''take Sarah and get the hell out of there!''

She didn't hesitate. She rushed toward home plate, like a desperate runner determined to steal a base. In her race to reach Sarah, she was aware of Cleve firing again and again. Trying to cut Victor down from a difficult angle calculated to prevent harming her or Sarah. Trying to prevent him from recovering his weapon. And all the while Victor was leaping and dodging, screaming curses.

Gillian arrived at home plate. Grabbing Sarah by the hand, she permitted herself a fast glance along the third-base line. Cleve's revolver was silent. He had emptied its chambers, and Victor was still on his feet. There had remained too wide a separation between Cleve and his target. Unhurt, Victor started to pounce on his gun.

She had to take Sarah and find a cover before he could

use that weapon on them. The nearest refuge was the Cubs dugout. The girl, still bewildered, resisted for a second when Gillian pulled her toward the trench. Then, finally shaken out of her trance by the reality of their danger, Sarah fled with her down into the dugout.

Knowing they couldn't pause here, that Victor would reach them before Cleve could stop him, Gillian dragged Sarah into a tunnellike passageway.

"Where are we going?" the girl demanded.

"Wherever he can't find us," Gillian answered, urging her forward through a steel door.

The narrow corridor led away from the playing field, sloping upward under the stands, like a long gallery buried deep inside an ancient pyramid. A few weak security lamps lighted the way. Otherwise, it was dim and silent. The only sound was the echo of their hurrying steps on the cement floor.

Sarah, unable to hold her silence, asked breathlessly, "Is it true what you told him? It *can't* be true!"

Gillian glanced at her. There was no longer a vacant expression on her young face. The girl had been shocked out of her numbed state.

"Sweetheart, I promise you it isn't true. Not for a minute. But I had to tell him something to keep him from hurting you."

She was thankful when Sarah seemed to accept her reassurance. They were silent again, saving their wind for their climb through the tunnel. Gillian listened for the slam of the door behind them, the slap of pursuing feet, but she heard nothing. Where was the hunter?

The passage turned. There was another metal door, then a flight of stairs. It was like a subterranean cavern, and she was relieved when they finally emerged into a spacious area lined with open cubbies.

"It's the Cubs' locker room," Sarah whispered.

And of no help to us, Gillian thought, remembering from one of her tours that the clubhouse contained offices, a weight room, and other facilities. But they would be cornered if they stayed anywhere in the suite.

They had to go on. They had to keep climbing. Had to escape that fiend behind them.

Cleve, she wondered as she led Sarah away from the locker room. Where was Cleve at this moment? Battling one of his frightening blackouts? She prayed for his safety. It was all she could do.

VICTOR, with his gun back in his hand and ready to plunge into the dugout after Gillian and the girl, hesitated. No, he decided. He would make better time climbing up through the open stands. He'd cut them off at the top.

They wouldn't get away from him. Whatever it took, he would destroy that bitch. And the girl along with her. His daughter? No, he refused to consider even the possibility.

His only problem was Cleveland McBride. The P.I. had been forced to stop and reload his revolver, giving Victor a chance to regain the stands behind home plate. But now he was trying to intercept him, weaving rapidly through the boxes off third base.

Victor bounded up the cement stairs of the wide aisle, making an effort to outdistance him. It was like attacking the side of a mountain, steep and treacherous. A bullet pinged into one of the rows he was passing, then another near his feet. McBride was gaining on him.

Enraged, Victor swung around, lifting his gun to fire back at him. Nothing happened when he squeezed the trigger. The bullet that had struck his weapon at home plate must have damaged the mechanism. With a savage oath, he flung the useless gun off into the twilight.

McBride fired on him two more times as he turned and ran. Neither shot came anywhere near him. The failing light? A moving target at a difficult angle? Neither of these explanations was the correct one, as Victor learned when he glanced swiftly behind him.

McBride had missed him because he was no longer on his feet. He had sunk to his knees in the aisle. Bemused, Victor stopped and turned. As he watched, ready to bolt if this was a trick, the P.I. struggled to raise his gun. And failed. The arm dropped. McBride collapsed on the steps and was still.

Of course. Victor remembered it now. How the P.I. had blacked out on the fire escape outside his rooms. How he had stored the knowledge of that curious frailty in a corner of his mind, because eventually he might be able to use it against McBride. That opportunity had arrived.

Wasting no time, he retraced his steps and bent cautiously over the investigator. He remained unconscious. Victor wrenched the revolver out of his hand and aimed it at McBride's head, intending to kill him. Then he thought of the last four bullets fired at him from this gun. He checked the chambers. Yes, only two bullets left, and he would need those for Gillian and the girl.

No time to search the P.I. for the possibility of further ammunition. The woman and the girl would escape if he didn't hurry. Whatever the explanation for McBride's seizure, he was in a deep shock, no longer capable of interfering. Just to be certain of that, he delivered a brutal kick at the P.I.'s head. McBride never stirred.

Victor, gripping the Colt, left Cleve sprawled there on the steps and went after his quarry.

"CAN'T WE GET OUT of the park?" Sarah asked.

"No, every exit will be sealed."

"Then what can we do?"

Gillian didn't answer her. She wasn't sure. They had already wasted precious time trying to locate the park's security center and possible help. But they had failed. They were still on their own.

The best thing she could do now, she decided, was to conceal Sarah where Victor wouldn't find her. Then she wanted to go back and look for Cleve. She was worried about him, convinced that he needed her. In this situation of extreme stress he could have been overcome by one of his blackouts. If so, he would be a helpless target. Her plan probably made no sense, but in her desperation she couldn't think of a better one. In any case, she had to hide Sarah. But where?

"He made me wait with him somewhere up here until the park closed," the girl said, referring to Victor. "It was a dark place that wasn't being used. A kitchen storeroom, I think."

Probably off the dining room used by the press corps, Gillian thought, remembering her tours. The facility, along with the booths occupied by the media during games, was above them on the upper deck.

"Well, we can't use that. He'd be sure to check the spot."

By this time, she and Sarah had climbed to the top of the ballpark and were on the mezzanine. The entire level consisted of reserved sky boxes suspended far above the playing field. Each of the enclosed suites contained a private bar and a seating area behind glass.

If the doors can be barred somehow from the inside, Gillian thought, I can leave Sarah in one of the boxes.

"This way," she said, leading them into a long, curving corridor as she explained her intention to the girl.

She waited until the ramps were out of sight behind them before she tried one of the doors to the overhanging boxes. Locked. They moved on, testing some of the other doors. All of them had been locked up after the game by the security force.

This was no good. If they remained here in the corridor, they could be trapped in a dead end.

"We have no choice," Gillian said, hurrying Sarah toward the ramps. "We have to go back."

"Then where?" Sarah asked, her voice quavering now with her growing anxiety.

"We'll have to try the upper deck, after all."

There was no other place left for them to go. If they descended, they risked running into Victor. They had to evade him as long as they could.

Gillian kept Sarah behind her when they neared the ramps, where she paused to look and listen. No sign of Victor, no sound from below. Perhaps Cleve had managed to stop him, but she couldn't count on that. Where were the two men, what were they doing? This suspense was unbearable.

"All right," she whispered, "let's go."

They mounted the zigzagging flight with as much speed as possible. Sarah didn't complain, but Gillian was aware that she was tiring. If they didn't find a refuge for her soon...

They arrived on the upper deck. There was an outside door with a window in it. And an unexpected, blinding glare from the other side where there should have been nothing but the darkness of the evening sky.

"What is it?" Sarah demanded, alarmed by the glow through the glass.

"If I'm not wrong, it could mean something good. Let's find out."

Gillian tried the door and was relieved to find that, since it wasn't an entrance to a private area, it had been left unlocked. Tugging it open, she took Sarah by the hand and drew her out into the open.

The wind, much stronger at this height, brought tears to Gillian's eyes. Pushing the hair away from her face, she gazed around her in recognition. She knew this place. It was the outdoor patio where a concession served snacks to the public before and during games.

"Look!" Sarah said, pointing with excitement to the roofs above them.

The batteries of huge lamps, mounted on high steel frameworks in order to illuminate the playing field for night games, were burning like brilliant suns. The whole park was blazing with light. It was a welcome sight, but Gillian was afraid to trust it. Not until she knew for certain.

With Sarah at her side, she made her way through the scattered tables to the steel railing. Six floors below them was the street, where they could see people from the neighborhood gathering on the sidewalks. They were gazing up at the park, wondering why it was dazzling with light when no night game was scheduled.

"Listen!" Gillian said. "Hear it?"

Above the wail of the wind came the sound of rapidly approaching sirens. This confirmed it. The night watchman, finally aware of trouble, must have called the police and lighted the park.

"We're going to be all right now, Sarah. Help is on the way."

"But too late for either one of you," came the menacing voice from behind them.

Gillian whipped around from the railing, her heart leaping into her throat. Victor stood there in the open doorway across the patio, his usually bloodless face flushed with triumph.

For a moment Gillian was too paralyzed to move. Then, keeping her eyes on Victor, she grabbed the girl and shoved her behind her. There was nowhere to run, but she squeezed back against Sarah, trying to protect her with her body.

As their enemy began to approach them, gun in hand and his features contorted with hate, Gillian experienced fear and anger at the same time. And something else. A clinging hope, which had her casting her gaze in the direction of the doorway.

Victor, understanding her silent prayer, laughed as he continued to advance on them relentlessly. "I'd forget that if I were you, because McBride has had another of his seizures in a crisis. He's lying unconscious down in the stands. Poor choice for a protector, Gillian. He's of no use to you now."

"The hell he isn't!"

The startling bellow came from the shadows just beyond the gaping doorway. And right behind it appeared Cleve, who staggered out onto the lighted patio.

As a shocked Victor started to swing around, Cleve recovered his strength with a massive effort and launched himself into space. He struck Victor below the waist with all the impact of a linebacker. Tables and chairs clattered and were overturned. Locked in combat, the two men went down on the tiles.

There was a furious struggle for possession of the gun, which involved grunts, curses and sickening blows to the flesh. The revolver fired once, twice, the first wild shot striking the wall, the second shattering the glass of a window.

In the end, it was Cleve's fist landing like a hammer on Victor's bony jaw that destroyed his death grip on the weapon. The revolver went spinning across the tiles. Gillian rushed forward to claim it, not realizing it was empty now and harmless. She was scooping it up from the floor when she heard shouts and the pounding of feet from the direction of the ramps.

Victor heard them, too, and knew what they meant. With a violent shove, he broke away from Cleve and scrambled to his feet. There were metal rungs attached to the patio wall, mounting to the catwalks from which the batteries of lamps were serviced. Victor reached the ladder and began to swarm up its length, intending to make his escape across the roofs.

Cleve, right behind him, caught him by an ankle and started to drag him down. There was another struggle. This time it was brief. Help arrived almost immediately, with uniformed officers streaming onto the patio. One of them joined Cleve, and together they hauled a howling Victor from the ladder.

What followed was swift and decisive. Victor, his face as wooden now as one of his marionettes, was handcuffed and taken away. Gillian, after comforting a shaken Sarah, turned her over to a paramedic, who promised to check the girl carefully for any negative effects from the drug Victor had administered.

Looking around for Cleve, Gillian found him on the other side of the patio. He was seated on the floor, his back propped against the wall as he answered questions for the officer standing over him.

She went and joined them, dropping beside Cleve on the tiles. She was worried about him. He looked drained. She waited until the officer finished and drifted away with his notebook, and then she asked solemnly, "How are you feeling?"

He turned his head and grinned at her. "Like I always do after I wake up from one of my blackouts, race up six flights of ramps, and go nine rounds with a lunatic. In other words, I'm rarin' to go."

"You have a souvenir from the fight. There's a lump on the side of your head."

He fingered the swelling gingerly. "It wasn't from the fight. I already had it when I staggered up here. I think that bastard must have kicked me after I passed out in the stands."

"Cleve, stop playing hard-boiled private eye and let the paramedic look at you after he's finished with Sarah."

"Only if you promise to hold my hand while he's treating me." He looked up in surprise as a new arrival appeared on the patio. "Hey, look who's joined the barbecue. About time, Costello. Where have you and your people been while we were playing tag here with Victor Lassiter?"

The homicide detective glowered at him. "Chasing phantoms down in Comiskey Park."

"Huh?"

"That's where the dispatcher sent us after the call came in."

Cleve looked baffled for a second. Then he slapped his forehead in understanding. "Moody!"

"I don't suppose," Gillian said dryly, "that one of you would care to explain what you're talking about."

Cleve turned to her, his arm sliding around her waist to draw her toward him. There was a gleam in his lion's eyes that could only be defined as wanton. "Maybe later," he growled. "Right now I have something more important to do."

Lieutenant Costello, realizing he was in the way, moved off to find the officer who had the notebook full of answers.

Gillian made a feeble protest as Cleve hauled her onto his lap in a fierce embrace. "You're not giving me a chance to thank you for rescuing us."

"But that's just what you're about to do, counselor."

And for the next minute and a half, he permitted her to express her gratitude in a deep, bone-melting kiss that had at least three of the officers on the patio issuing long, encouraging whistles.

Chapter Fifteen

Friday morning, and the day was like something out of a Walt Disney movie. The sky out over the lake was a clear blue, the air crisp and exhilarating after the long heat wave. Chicago at its best.

A clear forecast for the weather. A clear forecast for Gillian's future. No more nightmares involving Victor Lassiter. He would go back to prison, probably for life this time. Sarah was no longer at risk, either from Victor or the drug he had dosed her with. Even the senior partner at Gillian's firm had phoned her this morning, eager to welcome her back, hinting at a full partnership for her.

All she needed to complete the Disney image, Gillian thought wryly, was a chirping bluebird on her shoulder. Nothing to think about but being happy.

Except she was anything but happy as she sat behind the wheel of her Volvo and drove north toward Lake Forest. Life wasn't resolved like a Disney movie. Not hers. Not yet, anyway. Maybe never. Because there were still complications, serious ones, and she was deeply worried about them.

Last evening, coming away from Wrigley Field, Gillian had urged Sarah to spend the night with her and Cleve. It was the first time she'd been able to safely issue such an invitation. Sarah had declined, insisting she wanted to return to her school. She wouldn't discuss her refusal, but Gillian understood it.

She's confused and unhappy about Victor, she thought. Because even though she knows he isn't her father, she must be very upset with me for never telling her all these years that Victor had been married to her mother.

Gillian hadn't pressed the issue last night. Realizing finally that Sarah needed the comfort and security of familiar surroundings, she had let one of Lieutenant Costello's officers drive her back to Saint Bride's Academy.

Gillian owed the girl both an apology and an explanation, which was why she was on her way to Lake Forest. But she wondered if Sarah would ever forgive her.

And Cleve, she thought as she dealt with the traffic on the northbound expressway. She was even more concerned about Cleve.

He'd been his usual teasing self back at the apartment last night, playful even during their long, exciting session of lovemaking. But this morning, dressing for his appointment with the hypnotherapist, he had been sober and silent.

Gillian had understood his reluctance, just as she had empathized with Sarah's mood. Cleve was honoring his promise to her about the appointment, but he didn't want to meet with the therapist. Not because he had no faith in a cure and didn't want another disappointment.

He's afraid, she thought, remembering how she had figured that out before. Afraid to discover what might be buried down there in his subconscious. That he won't be able to deal with it. But he won't admit that, just like I wouldn't admit until now that I was afraid to confront Sarah with a terrible truth.

Cleve wouldn't let her accompany him to the therapist's office. He had made her go off alone to visit Sarah.

He's there right now with the therapist, she thought.

Maybe learning something at this very minute that could have profound consequences for both of us.

She tried not to fret about it, but that's exactly what she did all the way to Lake Forest.

SHE HAD PHONED Saint Bride's that she was coming. Sarah was waiting for her, looking morose as she sat on the front steps of the school, twisting a strand of her limp brown hair.

"Are you up for a walk on the grounds?" Gillian suggested.

"Okay," she agreed, but with no enthusiasm.

They strolled side by side under the trees.

"You're mad at me, huh?"

Sarah's thin shoulders lifted in a small shrug.

"I don't blame you. It was wrong of me not to tell you about your father. But I had some very good reasons for keeping the truth from you."

Choosing her words with care, Gillian explained about her pledge to Molly and how it had been necessary to protect Sarah from Victor. The hardest part was revealing that it had been Victor who had killed her mother. But she realized now that Cleve was right and that it had been a mistake withholding any part of the truth from the girl.

"I won't hide anything from you anymore," she promised. "You can ask me anything from now on, and I'll answer it."

They sat down on a sun-dappled bench, and Sarah thought about it. Gillian could see she was ready to forgive her, but there was something that still deeply troubled the girl.

"What?" she encouraged her.

"I know that sicko isn't my father. I believe that part of it. But you told me once when I asked that you didn't know who my real father is. Is that true, or was it just something else you kept from me?''

''That wasn't a lie, Sarah. Your mother never told me who he was. I realize that's hard to accept. Everyone deserves to know who his or her birth parents are, but in this case…''

''It's okay.''

''Look, whoever he was, he had to be a good person, a loving man, or she would never have had his child. Isn't that what counts in the end?''

''I guess so.''

Gillian squeezed her hand. ''Some kids never know anything about either of their parents, but you're lucky, Sarah. You do know about your mother and what a special person she was and how much she loved you. You have all those memories of her I've shared with you, and I'll try to think of even more now that there are no longer any secrets between us.''

''I'd like that.'' Sarah smiled for the first time, displaying the braces on her teeth.

Gillian left Saint Bride's with a promise to the girl that she could go on living at her school or, now that it was safe, she could live with her. It was Sarah's choice. But whatever she decided, Gillian loved her and would always be there for her.

Her mind was relieved about Sarah and her future. She had a feeling it wouldn't be that easy where Cleve was concerned. All the way home she kept thinking that he must have finished with the hypnotherapist by now. She was anxious to hear what he had learned. And at the same time, she was afraid.

The minute she got back inside the apartment, Gillian sensed something was very wrong. The place was too quiet. The kind of silence that indicates an emptiness. Then she realized the Lab wasn't there to greet her at the door.

With a mounting uneasiness, she went through all the rooms, looked into the backyard. The dog was missing. And, after checking the guest room closet, she discovered Cleve's suitcase and clothes had also disappeared. He had cleared out, taken Mike with him. There was a finality about his sudden departure that made her feel sick.

It wasn't until she wandered back into the kitchen that she saw the note taped to the refrigerator door. She took it down, her hand trembling as she read it.

"I'm headed back to my cottage up at the lake. Something I have to do. Don't worry. I'll call and explain everything."

That was it. Nothing more than a few scrawled words. Did he expect her to be satisfied with a message so casual and abrupt?

The room seemed to rock under her feet. She sat down at the kitchen table, convinced that the worst had happened. Cleve's session with the hypnotherapist must have failed. There could be no other explanation.

Her shoulders slumped as she thought about it. He must have learned something during the treatment that made him certain he could never be cured. That his only recourse was to resume his quiet life in the wilderness. Without her. Because he would have persuaded himself to believe he could never subject her to that kind of existence. Or burden her with what he perceived to be a man who was useless.

That's why he hadn't told her he loved her, and never would without hope of a cure. It's why he'd gone away, believing there could be no future for them together. She had lost him.

Gillian sat there for a long time, steeped in misery. Wondering how she could possibly go on without him. Unless Cleveland McBride shared it, what real meaning could there be to her life? She couldn't bear it.

Sometime later she became aware that she was still

clutching his note. She glanced down at it again. This time his words triggered another emotion. Anger. An anger that had her crumpling the paper and tossing it on the table. How dare he leave her with nothing more than a few brief words?

Well, it just wasn't good enough. If he no longer wanted her, then he could tell her so face-to-face.

Her anger was followed by a steely determination. Whatever was wrong, whatever the magnitude of the problem, she was prepared to deal with it. She refused to give him up. Not without a fight.

Squaring her shoulders, Gillian got to her feet and hurried off to her bedroom to change and pack a bag.

THE DRIVE TO Michigan's Upper Peninsula was a long one, the distance to the shores of Lake Superior on its north side making it even farther. She had no choice but to break the trip with an overnight stop at a motel. By sunup the next morning she was on the road again. Within a few hours she reached the entrance to Cleve's cottage.

There was no need to go on from here. His sporty red car was just emerging from the mouth of the long, wooded drive when she arrived. Blocking his vehicle with her own, she left the Volvo and went forward to confront him.

There was a look of astonishment on his face as he climbed out of his car. She stopped him before he could express his surprise.

"Don't you dare ask me what I'm doing here! Why wouldn't I be here after what you pulled!"

"Gillian, let me—"

"Running out on me like that with no explanation, no apology!"

"Uh, the note that I—"

"Oh, yes, the note! The note was supposed to cover everything, wasn't it? Twenty-two words! I counted them,

Cleve! Twenty-two measly words that said absolutely nothing! I think I deserve better than that!''

"But I tried to phone you last night, and—"

"Well, of course, I wasn't there! I was on my way up here! Though it suddenly strikes me now that I'm a fool for coming! And where's Mike? What have you done with poor Mike?"

"Left him at the cottage while I—"

"I suppose you're running out on him, too!"

Oh, hell, thought Cleve. He might as well just relax and let her get it out of her system. The gate was just behind him. He leaned against one of its posts and waited for her to finish.

She had her head tipped over to one side, like she did when she was squaring off with an opponent in court. She even wore that tight little smile between outbursts that said she meant business. He forgot how good she looked like this. And with the morning sun gleaming on her silky red-gold hair...

"Are you grinning?" she challenged him furiously. "Because if you think there's something amusing about all this—"

"Hey, no way."

He lifted his hands in a gesture of surrender, and she suddenly seemed to run out of steam. There was a long pause, and then she appealed to him plaintively, "Why, Cleve? Why did you leave like that without giving us a chance to work it out together? I know how hard it must have been when your session with the hynotherapist failed, but—"

"Whoa! Who said anything about its being a failure? It wasn't. It was a success."

"A success? That's wonderful! But why did you leave?"

"Had to. There's a demon I need to exorcise, and I could only do that here where it all began. Yeah, I know, I'm being mysterious again. Never mind, I'll explain everything on the way.''

"What are you talking about? Where are we going?''

Cleve refused to tell her anything until they were in his car and driving away from the lake on a winding back road. Maddening. But she could no longer be angry with him. He looked too wonderful for that, with his compact body so temptingly close to her own, and the chiseled, expressive face that she loved.

Gillian was struck by the change in him. Overnight he had shed years from his age, as if an old and terrible burden had suddenly been lifted from his shoulders. Whatever had emerged from that session with the hypnotherapist had made a vast difference, and she was deeply grateful for it. But impatient to hear the explanation he'd promised.

"She was good,'' he finally began. "Your therapist was every bit as good as you claimed. Turns out my seizures are completely psychosomatic, which I guess is no surprise. She explained how they're the result of a repressed memory. Seems that every time this unbearable memory threatened to surface, my defense system shut me down in the form of blackouts.''

"But why?''

"The attacks all happened at critical moments, Gillian.''

She gazed at him in wonder. "Guilt? Are you saying this is all related somehow to guilt?''

"Yeah, a major guilt that's been buried for years, along with the experience that caused it.''

"And she was able to unlock it?''

"It all came back under hypnosis, the whole tragic business.''

"What was it?''

"Something that happened when I was a kid, ten or so. I was vacationing with my family here in the Upper Peninsula. Staying at the cottage with my uncle. Remember, I told you I inherited the place from him.''

''Yes, go on.''

''Friends of my folks were with us. They had this little boy. He must have been about five years old. He insisted on tagging along with me everywhere I went, and I resented that. I was hanging out a lot with a local boy my own age, and we didn't want any part of a five-year-old.''

''And I suppose the adults looked at it differently.''

''Right. They made me responsible for the kid whenever we were out playing.''

Cleve paused to draw a steadying breath, and she realized how difficult the memory was for him still.

''Kids our age love to wander and explore,'' he continued. ''That's what we were doing that day out here in the countryside. There was this abandoned rail spur that came from one of the mines. It crossed a trestle over a deep ravine. The neighbor boy and I were fooling around on the tracks nearby, not paying attention. Next thing I knew...''

''The trestle,'' she guessed. ''The five-year-old went out on the trestle.''

''That's just what he did. Got out in the middle and then panicked and couldn't get back. He started to scream, and I went after him. I didn't reach him, Gillian. He fell to the bottom of the ravine. He died, and it was my fault.''

''You were only ten.''

''Doesn't matter. The guilt was still there. Only I couldn't deal with it, so I put it away along with the cause of it. Kept all of it hidden deep down inside me.''

''Where the memory has been dormant all these years. But the blackouts, Cleve. You never suffered from those until just within this past year. Why now?''

''Not sure. But it could be connected somehow with Harry Rosinki's death,'' he said, referring to the P.I. who had been his mentor. ''He meant a lot to me, and he passed away about the time I had my first blackout. Harry had a lot of pain at the end of his illness. I was pretty upset over that, with that helpless feeling of not being able to do anything for him.''

Gillian nodded. ''It sounds like it could be the explanation. So what happens now? Will you have any of those awful blackouts again, or are you free of them?''

''That's just what I'm about to find out.''

She suddenly understood their destination. ''We're on our way to that trestle where the boy died, aren't we?''

''Wrong,'' he said, pulling over to the side of the road and cutting the engine, ''because we're already there.''

She gazed at him anxiously. ''What are you planning to do?''

''Exorcise a demon, remember?''

She was afraid to wonder exactly what he meant by that. She stopped him as he started to get out of the car. ''And after you've exorcised your demon? What then?''

What about you and me? That's what she was really asking him, and Cleve must have realized that. It's why she looked so sober when he answered her with an evasive, ''Let's settle that afterward.''

She said no more, following him as he left the car. They struck off on a narrow footpath threading its way through a field thick with knapweed and Queen Anne's lace. The August sun beat down from a clear blue sky, hot and glaring.

Coming through a belt of trees, they reached the rail spur. The tracks were rusty from disuse, the bed between them rough and weedy. They followed the line in silence and came to the wooden trestle weathered with age.

Cleve stood on the edge of the ravine, gazing down into its stony depths. Gillian at his side could see that he was suffering from the memory of that long-ago tragedy. It worried her, because she suddenly knew what his intention was.

"You can't go out on that thing," she begged him. "It might not be safe any longer. The timbers could be rotten by now."

"I have to go out there," he said simply. "There's no other way to get rid of my demon."

"The therapist wouldn't have recommended this, not if she knew how dangerous it is."

"She didn't recommend it. This is strictly my idea."

"Then let me come with you."

She didn't say it, but they both knew what she was thinking. If he should experience one of his blackouts on the high trestle, and no one was there to catch him, he could fall to his death on the sharp rocks below.

He shook his head. "I have to do this on my own. It's the only way I can conquer it."

He refused to let her accompany him, and no amount of appeal or argument would change that. On another level, Gillian could relate to his need. Hadn't she felt a similar responsibility for Molly and a guilt over her death? Nothing as extreme as Cleve's, but it had existed just the same.

She felt helpless, knowing she loved him and knowing she had to let him go.

He caught her hand, squeezed it briefly with reassurance, released it, and then he was gone. Moving away from her out over the narrow trestle that had no guard rails. Nothing to hang on to, nothing to grab if dizziness overcame him.

He didn't pause until he reached the center of the structure at its highest point above the ravine. And this was where he halted. Gillian tensely watched him as he looked down between the timbers. He was a man frozen on a tightrope above a terrible chasm. A man who stood there coming to grips with an old, devastating memory.

She shared his struggle in the long, agonizing silence that followed. And she prayed. Prayed that something horrible wouldn't happen. Was it her imagination, or was he beginning to sway, his balance surrendering to a sudden bout of light-headedness?

Everything inside her clamored for her to go out on the bridge and rescue him. It was only with an enormous effort that she resisted the powerful urge. Cleve's future depended on her restraint.

No, it was all right! He wasn't weaving! He was simply turning around, slowly and carefully!

She was relieved when he faced her, when she could see his expression. His features were no longer wracked by the pain of guilt. He was smiling.

"It's over with," he said. "I should be able to put it behind me now. Everything is going to be all right."

Gillian hadn't realized she was holding her breath until she released it in a long shudder that left her limp.

"Hey," he said, chuckling, "I think you're the one who needs something to hang on to. And I figure it ought to be me."

"Yes, please."

With a quick, easy step he came back across the trestle. When he reached solid ground again, Gillian was there to meet him. His arms went around her in a tight embrace. She clung to him fiercely for a few seconds, face buried against his chest. Then she lifted her head, her gaze anxiously searching his face.

"Are you sure you're all right? You didn't experience any dizziness out there?"

"Not a sign of it," he assured her.

"Can it be that simple, that easy?"

He shook his head. "It wasn't a magical cure. The therapist warned me not to expect anything like that. It's going to take other sessions with her, but I've taken the hardest step on the road to a full recovery."

"You'll need to be in Chicago for those sessions," she said eagerly.

"I wasn't planning to be anywhere else."

"That's good, because when you left like that, I thought…"

"What? That I wasn't coming back?" His tawny eyes gleamed with humor. "Gillian, it wasn't for me that I had to come up here. It was for *us*."

"Really?"

"Really. I had to get rid of the past. I had to be free before I could come to you and tell you everything I've been feeling."

"And all these things you've been feeling…can you tell me about them now?"

"Let's see…" He thought it over for a minute. "There's my practice, for one. Looks like I can safely return to being a Chicago P.I. Lieutenant Costello ought to love that."

"He'll understand that's just where you belong."

"And there's your own law practice. You'll want to continue with that after we're married."

"We're going to be married?"

"Don't interrupt. Then a house for us. I thought maybe something out in the suburbs. You wouldn't mind commuting, would you?"

"We're going to buy a house, too?"

"Have to. That apartment's too small for the four of us."

"*Four?* What have I missed here?"

"Well, sure. You, me, Mike and Sarah. Think she'd like that?"

"We'll ask her. What else?"

"Isn't that enough?"

"Is it?"

He gazed down at her, his wide mouth forming a slow, wicked grin. "I guess not. I guess there's something I've omitted to mention…like how much I love you. On the other hand…"

"What?"

"Actions speak louder than words."

Which he proved when his mouth claimed hers in a long, searing kiss that convinced her without question exactly what Cleveland McBride felt about her.

There was an emotional huskiness in his voice when he finally surfaced. "Now, where were we, counselor?"

"I think you were saying something about loving me, and I was about to tell you that I love you. But it can wait. I want to hear more about this house."

"No," he insisted, "it can't wait. It's already waited for fourteen years."

He began to kiss her again, but Gillian didn't forget about that house in the suburbs. She hoped it would be a good-sized house. Large enough for the babies she wanted them to have. She'd have to get around to telling Cleve about those babies, but right now...she had more urgent matters to see to....

"Fascinating—you'll want to take
this home!"
—Marie Ferrarella

"Each page is filled with a brand-new
surprise."
—Suzanne Brockmann

"Makes reading a new and joyous
experience all over again."
—Tara Taylor Quinn

See what all your favorite authors
are talking about.

Coming October 1999 to a retail store near you.

 **HARLEQUIN®**
Makes any time special ™

WIN A DREAM

In celebration of Harlequin®'s golden anniversary

Enter to win a *dream!* You could win:

- A luxurious trip for two to
  The Renaissance Cottonwoods Resort
  in Scottsdale, Arizona, or
- A bouquet of flowers once a week for a year
  from **FTD**, or
- A \$500 shopping spree, or
- A fabulous bath & body gift basket, including
  K-tel's *Candlelight and Romance* 5-CD set.

Look for **WIN A DREAM** flash on
specially marked Harlequin® titles by
Penny Jordan, Dallas Schulze,
Anne Stuart and Kristine Rolofson
in October 1999*.

FTD

RENAISSANCE.
COTTONWOODS RESORT
SCOTTSDALE, ARIZONA

K·TEL

COMING NEXT MONTH

#525 AFTER DARK by Rebecca York and Caroline Burnes
43 Light Street and Fear Familiar—a special 2-in-1 Intrigue!
Two couples must hide from the day...and anything can happen after dark....
Counterfeit Wife by Rebecca York—When a madman comes after her, Marianne pretends to be Tony's wife—and can no longer deny the desire burning between them....
Familiar Stranger by Caroline Burnes—When Molly's son is kidnapped, she has no choice but to find her mystery lover—and tell him of their son's existence....

#526 HIS TO PROTECT by Patricia Werner
Captive Hearts
In twenty-four hours, three women's lives were forever changed in a hostage crisis. Now Tracy Meyer must put back the pieces and fight to keep her stepdaughter, while sexy cop Matt Forrest moves in to protect them from the hostage taker's revenge....

#527 ONE TEXAS NIGHT by Sylvie Kurtz
A Memory Away...
In the heat of a Texas night Melinda Amery found herself staring into the double-barreled blue eyes of Lieutenant Grady Sloan. And he wanted answers about the murder of her neighbor. Only, she didn't have them—didn't have any. She had amnesia. But Grady was the type of man who wouldn't let go until he got what he wanted. And that included Melinda....

#528 MY LOVER'S SECRET by Jean Barrett
Only one man could protect Gillian Randolph from the madman who stalked her: private investigator Cleveland McBride. Their sultry past aside, Gillian trusted Cleve with her heart, but could she trust him with her secret child...?

Look us up on-line at: http://www.romance.net

HARLEQUIN · CELEBRATES

FIVE DECADES OF ROMANCE

Starting in September 1999,
Harlequin Temptation®
will also be celebrating
an anniversary—15 years
of bringing you the
best in passion.

Look for these
Harlequin Temptation® titles
at your favorite retail stores
in September:

CLASS ACT
by Pamela Burford

BABY.COM
by Molly Liholm

NIGHT WHISPERS
by Leslie Kelly

THE SEDUCTION OF SYDNEY
by Jamie Denton